Concealed

Victoria R. Benson

Concealed

Book III: The Daughters of Boersen Series

Cover photo credit: blackdressbooks.com © 2021
Cover Model: Elyssa B.

Visit blackdressbooks.com
to preview these other books authored by Victoria R. Benson.

Daughters of Boersen Series:
Captured / Claimed / Concealed
Diamond Cliffs: Anthology
Indie Songs
Just for Now
Perfect Timing
Reversed Roles
Someone Else

ISBN: 978-1-7325443-9-0

Black Dress Books

Dedication

To my son, my daughter and my readers…

Break the mold. Step outside of the lines. Make your own mistakes, then learn from them. Be your own version of flawless. Lead, but be willing to step aside and let others pass when necessary. Always remember, it is your imperfections that make you perfect. Be courageous! Be strong! Be wise! Be you!

The advantage of hindsight is that the view is unobstructed.

The Daughters of Boersen who preceded Galeena tried to recreate straight paths from their own mistakes to ensure the successes of their future generations. However, as with all children, the advice and wisdom of elders is often blatantly ignored. Descendants will discover their own hardships, mishaps, and catastrophes to muddle through. In the end, no one can be protected from all the world has planned. Therefore, survival remains the only objective.

Chapter 1

Make no err in your judgement of me, for a lady I am not.

Proof of this ongoing, self-fulfilling prophesy is evidenced by my inability to even shudder at committing such acts as piercing the throat of a man nearly twice my size during any battle. Tis most unfortunate that many useful men have had to lose their lives for attempted offenses against me or my neighbors.

Further proof of my claim can be established by my possession and skill in usage of a personal collection of artisan crafted daggers, each designed by me, for me. Their purpose is a result of the reality that being caught off guard is not an option for a princess; although, I utilize the term *princess* with significant delicacy. My identity is more of a protector of the land to which I have been entrusted by birthright and by choice.

Often I wonder if my role as a protector would have come about whether I was abandoned in it or not. Had I been raised donning decorative silk dresses and fine jewels, would I have not rebelled and escaped such frivolity for a life outside of my parents' castle walls?

One may never know what could have been, what should have been, what might have been. For the only fact that is certain is that destiny is a strange beast. One could lose their sanity wondering if we find it or if it finds us.

With that said, before I delve into the depths of my story that is forthcoming, I'd like to offer this: I believe we are under the charge of a great and powerful being who places us in our paths so a will which we can never comprehend can be done. I believe... destiny finds us.

* * *

Terror, fright, screams, death, blood, violence, were all the events of a day that I never imagined would come and never thought possible. Beneath the eyes of my father's armies, my village was attacked. My village! My home! My land! My people! All were being ravaged by another band of Norsemen. What made this particular event so unimaginable was that it was happening within steps of my father's most securely guarded fortress, and he knew I was present among the chaos.

Ships delivering men and women from the Northlands had been arriving in Northanglia for nearly forty years. Every person in our country and our neighboring countries knew of their presence, their potential and their capabilities in destruction. The problem we all constantly faced was that these Norsemen were like slithering snakes. They appeared, they struck, and they took hold without provocation and usually without notice until it was too late to defend against them.

I had battled them on occasions, but in instances of preparedness. Never did I expect to have to fight them in my own village, and never did I feel victorious in any of our confrontations. I found our encounters to be most unfortunate, as these men and women were my own flesh and blood. Perhaps some of those I killed were even my relatives. Disclosure of such connections would never be made though, because my identity had been kept concealed by me and by my parents since I was of a very young age.

Hearing the screams of the women who were my friends triggered my instincts to defend. Arming myself with a number of daggers, I erected from my seated position within my small hut. Before reaching the door, a Viking charged in and stood between me and my exit. The sworded man smiled with pure pleasure, obviously contemplating his pending conquest. His eyes spoke volumes to mine of his intent to savor the time he would have in my company. A cowering female was his expected prey.

The man, I judged to be of nearly thirty years, stepped through the threshold of my humble home never removing his ravenous eyes from mine. I did not back away, nor tremble. I remained calm, ready, prepared. He was not the first, nor would he be the last enemy I would face during my lifetime.

There was no need to seek his weaknesses, for I already knew them all. My lifelong training had centered around knowing the precise location of each human being's bodily death targets. However, as he measured my potential vulnerabilities, I sought any signs of likeness to me. Since my defense skills were substantial, I had begun seeking connections each time I faced attackers from the Norse. That morning, the enemy who stood in my presence wore brown leather coverings from his waist to his feet, and his tunic was constructed of faded blue linen fabric. His complexion and hair were not fair. Therefore, I doubted he was of any relation to me. I flinched my eyebrow and unwittingly shrugged. The man would undoubtedly die in my house that morn.

The Viking detected my reaction to his entrance, and he spoke in his native tongue, "Does my appearance interest you, Miss?"

My fluent reply in his language shocked him. I said, "I sought relevance in you. I sought a reason to spare your life. Your appearance captivated me only long enough to determine we are not of the same blood. Tis ill-fated for you that we are not joined by the fluid that flows beneath our skin, for now you shall have to die."

Further surprise by my statement lured his concentration away from his initial plans to have his way with me. He slowly closed the door behind him, then asked, "You may interest me and be pardoned from a certain death if you are willing to speak the name of your bloodline. From whom do you descend and how do you know my language?" The man seemed to have reason to believe his quest in Northanglia was complete.

Standing prostrate with my feet planted like roots of a mighty tree and my hands at my sides, I responded clearly, "I am Princess Galeena Helene Stefania Styrkes, a daughter of the great King Boersen of Gudsfelt."

His eyes widened, a smile nearly appeared at one of the corners of his mouth. I allowed him the courtesy of believing he would somehow be able to claim victory that day. His back straightened. His hand tightened around the handle of his sword. Then, the very instant he lunged in my direction, I flung six small daggers at him, for three were hidden in each of my hands, piercing his neck, heart, thighs, and midsection.

The valuable Norseman looked down at his exquisite body in disbelief. His gaze returned to mine. I waited, though feeling impatient, for hearing the continued screams beyond my walls was disturbing.

When the man finally collapsed to his knees, I took small arrogant steps toward him. Mindful of his sword, I reached my hand to his face and held his chin. He lived long enough for me to bid him farewell in his birthed tongue, "I am sorry that I found no mutual identity in you, Icelander. I am certain the world will miss a man as strong as you. Speak your name."

He smiled again and softly choked out, "Arrik the Fortunate."

I smiled back, gifted a more than generous kiss to his lips, then tilted his head so his ear was within my reach. I whispered warmly into it, “Not today my friend, not today. Rest well.”

He closed his eyes.

When he sprawled in defeat, I became disappointed that I would be returning to a soiled floor and unnecessary chores later in the day. Attention to the matter would have to wait though as my assistance was needed in many directions.

I released the laces of my frock and stepped out of it wearing my leggings, boots and blouse. My tresses were freed. More daggers were collected and tucked into various openings in my clothing. Then, I barged through my doorway to join the fight in my streets.

Surveying the altercations, it was easily determined that the men were on their own for this fight. I would guard, then guide, as many of the women and children as possible to a safe retreat. Once they were escorted to the nearby tree line, the likelihood of their survival would be much more probable.

Carefully releasing knives into the scurrying crowds of villagers being assaulted by Vikings was disorienting. I feared not the violent men and women; I feared only harming one of my own Anglos. Had this event been conducted less the exorbitant numbers of women and children, I would have felt more confident. My job had to be done though. Therefore, I continued flinging blades into the throats, the hands, and the faces of our attackers. Aiming high would save the masses from amicable demise.

Each time a Norseman fell, a few villagers were freed to escape to the woods. Causing such massive breakdown of their plot drew attention, and one man ambushed me from behind. As his right arm swiftly raised his sword to decapitate me, I spun and managed to plant one of my daggers into the blood vein of his wrist. With the distraction of such an unexpected blow overtaking him, I was able to disarm and disembowel him.

Turning my attention once again to the battle, more Norsemen were arriving. I hoped my father's armies would assist. In that moment though, it seemed I had done what I could to save as many as possible from the fates of slavery, violation, or death.

Frantic, I pulled my hair back from my face. My eyes gathered images of only what was before me, and while contemplating my next move, a voice spoke, "Tis time for you to leave or die."

Though I did not understand, nor did I seek, from whence the instruction had come, I heeded its protective warning. Witnessing the end of this fight would not be my fate. I fled the blood-stained, howling center of Castleton.

Chapter 2

The preceding event was documented on the first scroll removed from a chest found deep in a hidden passageway beneath the ancestral home I inherited. I, a modern woman living in the nineteenth century, not yet aged to twenty became sole proprietor of something I could scarcely comprehend. A distant relative passed from this life to the one eternal leaving me in possession of a decaying home that once was the center of a region called Northanglia.

Excitement and determination led me toward a task I never imagined I would be pursuing. Somehow, cobwebs, creatures, and chilling spirits deterred me not from obsessive explorations. My reward, three treasure chests filled not with gold or silver or jewels, but filled with countless parchments each depicting events, both private and public, of three women.

Having discovered truths about these ancestors clarified my own identity. The women who meticulously recorded their histories live within me. Their spirits surround me, shape me, teach me. I am them!

Though I exist in a world where men have dominion, this manor and all of its contents have been bequeathed to me. I will not fail it. I will not fail my relatives who have passed. I will not fail my future generations. I shall continue and conclude the tales gifted by Olivia, Adelia and Galeena. One fought with wit, one with words, and one with weapons. Each longing to be remembered. Tis only documentation that keeps us alive in *this* world. They wanted their stories told. They shall have their wishes fulfilled.

Chapter 3

Much daylight remained, and without a horse, Galeena needed all of those hours to reach her first night's refuge before darkness blanketed the heavens. Her hope was that most, if not all, of the villagers who were led away from the town center had made their way to safe havens. In between the time the final mother and child were sent westward into the forest, and she took her own personal retreat eastward, no others had fled. Thus, the path through the underbrush was quiet, untrodden and seemingly unoccupied.

Forward placement of one foot, then the other, propelled her in a direction that led toward serenity. By nightfall, the young soldier would be warming beside a fire and sipping tea while a freshly speared supper roasted. Until then, Galeena would strategize a method for recovery of her village.

As she veered in the direction of Broodenshire, a most immediate need captivated her. Removal of the sticky, red fluid that was drying upon her hands became an absolute necessity. While a struggle commenced to cleanse her flesh of the Vikings' blood with the hem of her white shirt, Galeena's mind continued to brood over resolution and what will be instead of what had been as it pertained to the events of the morning.

When it was apparent that her efforts to erase the visible stains were as futile as the efforts to erase thoughts that would lead her into a dark and guilt ridden state of mind, she relented. Instead, Galeena inhaled a deep cleansing breath of the temperate air, and she reached her soiled palms to the fullness of the canopy above. The princess studied her swirling, dancing hands. So much damage they had caused. So much protection they had provided. So much life they had given and taken.

With her hands above her, Galeena pretended to grasp the low hanging limbs. The motions of extending her arms in such a manner felt freeing and necessary to her neck and backbone. The release of tensions enabled her to focus on the revival of a peaceful disposition. Slowly, allowances were made for resetting and rejoining the reality of the world in which she lived. Acceptance of her place in life was inevitable, for no other choice had ever been given. Avoidance of her appointed tasks would also be useless. Idleness and denial were never routes to victory. Therefore, Galeena pondered the implementation of well thought out plans and methods that would guide her to a satisfactory conclusion.

Recovery and removal were the two problems that needed resolutions. As a soldier in King Wilhelm's army, the heir to

Northanglia would soon be expected to provide a proposal for settlement of their newest troubles.

With no accompaniment to be had on her journey, the concealed daughter began to feel the need to be somewhat busy. Therefore, she reached out as she passed a low hanging branch, she grasped, then snapped. A spindly limb was collected, and Galeena began to swing it at all that appeared in her path. The swishing of the stick as it broke the stillness of the air combined with the constant crackling of her boots pressing on the ground below became repetitive beats that kept Galeena marching toward her shelter.

Intuition and experience were enlightening; twas apparent that the morning's brazen invasion on Castleton was purposeful. The Norsemen sought more than land or treasures; they sought residence. And, since the residence they targeted was in such close proximity to the king's fortress, Galeena surmised they also sought *someone*. Perhaps the Danes were once again in search of her mother, Queen Adelia.

"What need would she fulfill for them? Has Jaegar dispatched his band of hooligans or is this invasion at Vidar's command?" she muttered. "They know nothing. Their trespasses here are tiring."

As the stick swung to and fro before her, Galeena contemplated the demise of the long held peace treaty Northanglia held with the Norsemen. The breach of their contract by the Vikings was an unmistakable statement that the time had come for crowns to be exchanged and new rulers to be established in Gudsfelt.

She smiled. Her steps slowed and she spoke again with her attention to the Heavens, "I've grown weary of hiding from the world. I am ready to claim all that has been appointed for me, Mother. My sixteenth annual reaches for me with its arrival only an arm's length away." With pride and increased determination Adelia's daughter lifted her chin and her steps continued.

"Queen Adelia, daughter of King Boersen, daughter of King Alexar, wife of King Wilhelm, my beloved mum." Galeena delicately spoke her mother's name, titles, and endearments. She stopped, lowered her hands to her sides, and stared with such intensity in every direction that twinkling stars began to appear before her eyes. "Please, please let me see you. Mother, appear, touch, speak. Remind me that you are real, please," she begged in a soft, heart-wrenching, desperation filled whisper.

A deep longing for the arms of Adelia nearly paralyzed Galeena. Her mother was the only being who could make her forget her purpose or her tasks.

Galeena's fist tightened around the only object to which she had a connection in those moments, and she sliced it at a tree as if it were a sword. The impact snapped the limb and once it was diminished to the size of a small dagger, she studied it for possible utility. Though useless, the similarity to a blade the stick now had was interesting to her. Galeena's hand maintained its hold and she progressed.

Using childhood memories, Galeena pondered what she should be doing that morning, at least according to lineage and history. A version of what it would be like to be living peacefully in the north lands consumed her imagination. She sought solace in visions of frolicking merrily upon the green expanses and mountains of her Grandfather Boersen's nation. Images of hunting, farming, and tending animals filled her dreams. Visions of participating in daily activities that ensured the prosperity and security of both Northanglia and Gudsfelt pranced through her mind. For a moment, the lighthearted thoughts brought a smile to her lips.

Galeena then muttered, "I *should* be living a very different life. Instead, I find myself fleeing from one intrusion upon one very small village by one band of Ice-landers."

The reality of not having been able to protect her lands from all invaders and from possible ruin lured Galeena back to the present.

A subtle scoff escaped and turned into a chortle. She continued mumbling, "Dreams, visions, fantasies... All are a waste of time because my incurable assignment from my king and my father is to permanently eliminate my own people from Northanglia. How ludicrous my path! Mother, though I sense you not this morn, if you follow, I ask again, hover about and take heed. You must know, your plan is no longer the best course for me. You have concealed me, and for what purpose?

We do not share fears. I am to be Queen of Gudsfelt, Queen of Northanglia, and perhaps queen of another land. What cause do I have to continue hiding? Tis time for me to choose. Tis time for me to emerge." Frustration, confusion and of course despair weighed within her core.

Stride after stride increased the distance between Galeena and her first defeat. Mindlessly, she pushed away branches that aspired to claw at her cheeks or entangled themselves into her hair. Decorative blue and white blossoms were sprinkled throughout the surface below her. Soft breezes, like those created by the wings of fairies, fluttered about through the sparsely set trees. But the only sounds that filled her ears were the incessant thoughts of a troubled soul.

A single realization prefaced a subtle gasp. Galeena's eyes widened as she recalled one statement offered in a voice she would never forget. The warm sensation and the words, *Tis time for you to leave or die,* repeated in her ear.

Galeena stood as if turned into a pillar of salt and inquired of the spirit world, "Why would one man allow my escape when all of the others wanted to kill or collect me? And, how did an enemy gain such effortless access to me? I have been more thoroughly trained and am more experienced in warfare than any young woman of nearly ten and six years should be. I know to watch for and expect attacks from every direction. I never sensed him."

One boot lifted. She watched it rise and fall. His voice echoed. Her other foot raised. Cautiously, as all obstacles in her path were avoided, Galeena began constructing excuses for what could have been a mortal failure. The predator could have taken her.

She whispered, "Perhaps the distractions of the women and children led to such a mistake. Perhaps the fear of harming my own villagers during the chaos was to blame for my error. Perhaps I was not quick enough, or strong enough, or vigilant enough. Or, perhaps he was more skilled than I."

That final thought generated disappointment, then anger, then jealousy.

"It shall not happen again," she declared with irritation. "He shall not sidle to me unnoticed. I have been trained with superior intellect and keenness. I have defeated the mightiest of foes."

Done chiding herself, because it accomplished nothing, Galeena furiously tossed the pointed piece of the limb which no longer held her interest. She wiped the flecks of gray bark from her palms, and she truly awakened.

"How much time has passed? My defeat has kept me far too distracted."

Galeena quieted and listened attentively to all that surrounded her. Her ears no longer listened to the haunts within her mind. They tuned outward to collect the sounds of snaps, flutters, chirps, and rustlings. Although she was still feeling free from dangers, an instant decision was made that absolutely no more audible chatter nor internal diversions would be occurring that day.

Chapter 4

The fortune of traveling beneath the rarity of a clear sky was most appreciated. The ground was firm, the sun bright, and the air warm. Having spent her entire life traversing the path between Broodenshire and Castleton, without study, Galeena knew the expanse of open fields lay just ahead. She was nearing the outer edge of one of the forests that decorated the quilted landscape of Northanglia.

The aroma of the sweet grasses floated amongst the trees and Galeena inhaled. The tiniest bumps raised from beneath the surface of her skin and a quick shiver raced up her spine.

"You're here," she exhaled in an inaudible whisper. "I am awake."

As the wind shifted she closed her eyes. Spirits moved in circles, large, gentle circles. They lifted loose strands of her walnut colored hair while teasing her soul. She listened and learned the lesson they had arrived to teach.

Although her wish was to remain entranced and comforted by the ghostly guardians, it was not to be. For a warning accompanied the souls in her midst. Galeena opened her eyes and sought the nearest and most resilient tree to ascend. After securing a perch, she finely tuned her attention to every living creature.

Sitting astride a branch with her back pressed firmly to the tree's core, Galeena studied the vicinity. In those moments when her senses were heightened, she knew she was Norse.

"You have not vanished nor retreated. I will find you."

Galeena listened to her Viking instincts. She peered right, then left. She looked to the ground below. Every direction was thoroughly studied. When her eyes returned forward, she flung two small daggers, impaling them into a tree that stood fifty paces directly before her.

"Which of us made the first discovery?" he asked with laughter as he pulled the knives from the limb beside his face.

"I have no doubts that you may boast Ice-lander," Galeena replied resting her head back and allowing her shoulders to relax.

"Boast? I certainly shall not. For you have made my hunt too simple. You have shuffled and chattered for hours."

Galeena wanted to kill him. He was an invader, he approached her undetected for a second time that day, and he was not wrong. Alas, his death would not be by her hand in those moments. His distance was too great. At best, she could have punctured him and hoped the wound would have festered. Irate at his arrogance and insult she called, "Since you've had an easy target all morning, why have you not approached, or shot an arrow through my back, or knocked me unconscious?"

"Aw, have more faith in yourself than that. I would have never been able to get close enough to you to do any harm. I witnessed your might."

He was correct, and Galeena secretly appreciated the reminder. Having been caught off guard twice in one day by the same man had her feeling insecure. Twas not the time for weakness nor reflection.

She asked, "How shall we proceed then? If your mission is to kill or capture me, you must know you will fail. If your mission is simply to continue performing the duties of my shadow, you must know, that position has been filled. Your services in that capacity are not needed. God has supplied. My only other assessment of your presence is that you follow me, desperate to be of service. To that pursuit I must confess, I have thousands of men at my disposal. They are loyal, trustworthy Anglians. You are a Dane and not needed in my king's army. Speak your intention so we can both climb down from these watch towers. We are not birds. We belong on the earth."

More laughter filled the forested space between the two acquaintances. When he regained enough composure to respond, he said, "I followed you with hopes of learning a secret. I thought you were escaping to notify troops of our arrival."

"You attacked within sight of King Wilhelm's fortress. Troops are quite aware of your arrival! Was that the only reason you allowed me to flee? You thought I would lead you to a camp?"

"That is the second reason I allowed you to live."

"And the first?"

An extended silence fell and Galeena realized she had lost sight of the Dane.

Then, the crunch of heavy steps neared her vicinity. She swung her leg over the branch upon which she sat and began quickly descending from limb to limb like a primate until she dropped before him.

Determined to show his bravery, the man locked eyes with his prey.

Galeena raised one eyebrow, shook her head and orated to herself, "Oh why could my pursuer not have been a putrid beast of a man? Why did it have to be you?"

He smiled.

"State your reason for not removing my head when you had an unobstructed opportunity," she demanded.

"I decided I like your head right where it sits."

The thought, *Why does he bear such interesting attributes? Why could I not have hated him? I must hate him, for I must kill him,* lingered in her mind.

He continued, "You inquired about how we shall proceed?"

"Yes."

"Do you seek more soldiers?"

"Most certainly," she shared honestly.

"Do you wish to kill me?"

"Again, most certainly, Sir."

"Do you believe you are able?"

Galeena bit the inside of her lip and pondered his question. Her hands moved to her hips as she continued in thought. She then asked, "May I have my daggers?"

He opened his palm.

The small blades were within reach, but she made no attempt to collect them.

Galeena answered, "No. I am not able to kill you today."

"Share your reasoning," the Viking requested as he examined the young woman.

She confessed, "If I agitate you, you will have reason to overpower me. I am not armed heavily enough to weaken you. You will prevail, and I will most likely awaken in a cell or a bed and find I have been violated. I choose preservation this day."

After a moment of thought, she continued, "However, I could easily escape, and if you followed me from the cover of these woods, you would die. There are men, women and children who lurk about utilizing the tall swaying grasses for covering. An arrow would surely find its way to your flesh."

The intruder smiled again at Galeena, and she immediately knew why her mother and grandmother had found these Danes to be so alluring.

The robust, fair-haired man confidently handed the daggers to the woman who had openly confessed that she wished to kill him, and he said, "I believe you, Miss."

Without losing eye contact, Galeena cautiously took her property from his warm palm. She then tucked one blade into the belt behind her back, and the other she slid up her sleeve into its hidden sheath. She then replied, "Do not grow accustomed to that feeling."

The pursuer leaned forward.

"Disbelief!" she shouted, pressing her palm to his chest.

"What have I said or done that places you in a state of disbelief?"

"The very idea that you stand here attempting to woo me is unbelievable."

"What in your experience leads you to believe my innocent approach was meant to 'woo' you?"

"Sir, I am not naive and neither of us is innocent."

"So, I shall not be the recipient of your first kiss," he teased.

"Agh!" Galeena shoved him with both hands and informed him, "You shall not be the recipient of any embraces, nor would you be the recipient of my first kiss *this* day!"

The brazen stranger gaped and struggled to withhold another gleaming smile. "I find you utterly intriguing."

"Speak your first reason for allowing me to live, Sir?" She waited for his name.

"I am Torren. And, I decided you were free to depart Castleton because I feel an overwhelmingly strong need to maintain a connection with you, even though the reason escapes me..." he elongated his thought to invite her name.

"My name is Galeena, though it matters not to you. Please understand, there is no connection to be maintained, for there is no connection between us!"

"We cannot yet be certain as to whether we share common interests or not. This is our first conversation. I watched you from the moment you burst through your door and bound to the street. When I had witnessed enough death of my own kinsmen, I intervened. You are alive because from a distance I thought I might know you."

"Know me? Is that so? Do you know many women in Northanglia? Did you bring all of your dearest friends here to show them how very widespread your name is among the earth?"

Torren chuckled. "Not exactly. I am here seeking one person in particular. I thought you could be her. Your agility, aim, and brute skill are not common traits of Anglian women. I needed to be nearer to you, so I could discern if you are a woman of the North. Now that I stand less than an arm's length from you, I see you bear no resemblance to the one I have been sent to find."

Her intuition that the invasion was in pursuit of someone specific was verified. Galeena requested, "Name the one you seek."

"I shall not."

Offended that he did not reveal his mission, the woman pointed eastward and countered, "Well Torren, if it is a Norse woman you seek, there are many of them across the North Sea. Return to your prowling warship and sail back in the direction from whence you came. I promise you, you will find all the Norse women you can dream of in those lands."

"You certainly are amusing. Perhaps I'll spend my first hours here in Northanglia continuing to trail you, or shadow you, as you so descriptively put it."

"Follow me? Even greater distances from Castleton? Sir Torren, we are moving farther and farther away from the safety of your rabid wolf pack. That would not be a wise course of action for you. In this very moment, you stand guilty of many crimes and offenses. I am being kind by advising you to part from me and seek the safety your numbers."

"I harbor no guilt. I have done nothing wrong."

"You harbor all of the guilt because of your arrival and your attack!"

"I killed no man, woman, nor child. I even saved your life hours ago."

"Your guilt then is based on your association! Additionally, my life would not have needed saving if your absence from Northanglia remained a condition for us all."

"My presence is on behalf of a political assignment. When my task is complete, I shall sail from your shores never to return. I stand firm in my profession that I have done nothing wrong. ”

“Oh! Such an innocent claim you make on your own behalf! Do confess then, how *did* those villains arrive who now occupy my home? Did they appear without transport? Did they materialize by the will of your gods? Were you as surprised by their presence and violent antics as I and all of my neighbors were?”

“You cease not in your humoring of me, Miss?”

“Nothing humorous was spoken by me. My inquiries are genuine. Answer? What is your specific role in the misfortunes that occurred this morn?” She paused and glared scornfully.

He chuckled. Then loud laughter was released from the Norseman. “I lead that pack of wolves.”

Galeena retorted, “I disagree, for at this moment you are a follower. That band of rogues is most likely pillaging wildly like animals.”

“We did not arrive here to plunder and steal, nor violate and murder.”

“Yet that is the course of action that has been chosen.”

“As their leader, I will do my best to protect what I can. You, dear one, must understand, sometimes there are casualties in war. We needed a place to inhabit; we chose Castleton.”

Having heard enough, Galeena raised a dagger to strike, but her swing was thwarted by a tight grasp of her wrist. For precaution, her other wrist was simultaneously gripped as well.

Torren advised, "Perhaps, if you attempt an assault whilst I am unaware of your proximity, you may have some success. However, one as skilled as you certainly must know you will not find success in your pursuits by facing an alert adversary."

Both hands were wrenched from his hold and she defended her attack. "If I meant to do harm, harm would have been done. My strike was merely a warning that my anger is being inflamed by your jests and lack of conscience over my losses. If you wish to gloat, return to your fellow murderers and celebrate there. If you are their leader, you will soon be needed anyhow. My king's armies will be preparing a counter-siege as we speak. Go! Leave me in peace! I need these hours to progress to my sanctuary for this night's rest."

"Where might that be?"

"What sort of question is that? Return to Castleton, Torren. Concern not yourself with my habitations. Go."

He simply stared into her eyes. Though she knew it was impossible, she felt as if they had met before. Galeena wondered if he shared the feeling. The silence had to be broken. She obliged. "Norseman, you say you shall protect all you can. If you are standing here, you cannot be protecting my property from those thieves."

"I'll take care on your behalf. Do not worry," he assured her.

"A promise would be most appreciated. I ask you to return to my home and recover all of my ruthlessly plundered belongings upon your arrival. I shall reappear in two weeks to collect some necessities."

"Must I wait a fortnight for another opportunity to enjoy your company? I fear I shall crave your cheerful disposition. After all, you are the first and only native I know of this land, and I believe a bond is being forged between us."

"The only bond you feel forming is the one that we already have in common; that is distrust of the other. You find yourself miles and hours from the safety of your group because you were certain I was going to alert my guards. And, you were correct. The only reason you still breathe is because you have shown no aggression toward me. When I tell you that others are watching, I speak with honesty. If you step from the cover of the foliage that surrounds us to follow me across those fields, you may find yourself with piercings you never intended to have."

"I do prefer to choose the locations of my piercings just as I prefer to live. But, I also wish to see you again. Will it be so?"

Her eyes raised toward the heavens and she shook her head. "If you declare repentance and live a life worthy of the one God of all, you may see me again in the afterlife. Otherwise, I have no plans for any further encounters between us."

"If that is your final proclamation on the matter, then I suppose tis time for me to see about my business here in Northanglia. Although, I do find it difficult to comprehend that your king would not include someone as skilled as you in his plans for attempting to reclaim the nearest village to his stately fortress."

The arrogance of the intruder was infuriating, as was his full intention. Galeena stated, "My inclusion in the king's plan is complete. I have no doubts that he witnessed the events at the birth of this day. King Wilhelm was acutely aware of my location in Castleton. His lack of interference could only mean that he trusted me to do my part to protect as many lives as possible. That I accomplished. The soldiers housed within the garrison were needed at their posts to ensure its security. I am certain an undetected dispatch was sent to gather more troops. Rest well this night, Sir Torren. Strategies are being devised to rid our nation of you all. I will reappear before you only if called upon to do so by my king. The gathering of my belongings from my home will be completed without detection."

Teasing her and desperately aiming to lure her by any means possible he added, "I understand. Fear is a powerful guide. You wish never to face me or my formidable army again." He closed his eyes and nodded with great condescension.

"Very well, look for me in two weeks. I shall be the one leading the troop that will arrive to rid my country of you and your multitude of raiders."

Torren replied with a smile, "I will gladly greet you and your company. Guests are always welcome in my village."

A fire fumed inside of her at his pride and arrogance.

Torren laughed as he watched Galeena turn abruptly and stride away from his presence. His keen interest and attraction for her was sensed, perhaps because the feeling was mutual. The Princess of Northanglia knew he would be watching her until she could no longer be seen across the open moor. When she had vanished from sight, without ever looking back, she was confident he would return to secure her private home at the center of Castleton. Galeena was also confident that she had walked away from someone who perhaps sought to capture or kill *her*.

Chapter 5

"Torren, the Ice-lander, seeks a particular female who bears the features of those born of the North. He has seized my village with the intention of drawing my king from his castle. He refused to speak the name of his potential victim. Huh! My first inclination was that he arrived in search of my mother. I was incorrect. Though he knows it not, he seeks me! He is not so unique or clever or mysterious. However, his skills do present an interesting challenge."

Certain the man who had trailed her until noon had turned back, Galeena's suspicious disposition eased. Realizing the Danes had returned to collect King Boersen's granddaughter also settled her mind. There was no longer a need to brood over unknowns.

It wasn't often that Galeena gave time to pondering her identities as Princess of Northanglia and Princess of Gudsfelt. Those titles, though commonplace in her mind, were never openly discussed. She had been so securely disguised by her parents at a very young age, that Galeena truly thought of herself as a soldier. Her public facade, the person everyone knew, was a kind and protective villager with no family, a young woman who was not to be trifled with as she was also a commander of King Wilhelm's forces.

Being labeled a princess, a soldier, and an orphan created states of constant opposition in her heart and mind. Galeena was to fight, spy, and still hide at all times. The contradictions left her having to relate to the one person she was allowed to be, a protector. However, the years of training she had faced due to existing in each of those personas were soon to show advantages. Galeena, the princess, was nearing her time of utility.

The king's daughter wondered aloud, "What was his intention? I know he witnessed the attack this morn. How could Father withhold all support from Castleton?"

Nearing a small stream and needing refreshment, she veered her aimed direction more easterly toward it.

Thoughts circled around her father's purpose and her role in it. Galeena's heart and mind united as she admitted, "My father has always maintained a pure and absolute possession of me. He commanded dominion of my upbringing. Mother fully agreed and never attempted to retrieve control from him. Her father, King Alexar, had been deprived of decisions and regulations as they pertained to his only daughter. Having been raised by two very loving, though battling men, Adelia never wished to hinder her husband from an all encompassing authority in matters of my interests."

The small spring appeared and Galeena approached. Kneeling, splashing, drinking, and taking a moment of rest she replayed the explanations she had been told as to why she was to be reared outside of her parents' palace by guards and soldiers.

Galeena's grandmother and mother had appointed companions who taught them languages, religion, politics, geography, and navigation of all of the lands beyond the protection of their fathers' fortresses. Her companions taught the same necessary subjects with the addition of battle, wits, warfare, quickness, and cunning defense of self.

King Wilhelm always intended for his daughter be the only heir to his throne. Therefore, twas demanded that she fight for her claim and for true respect. Kill or be killed may have been instilled in her grandmother and mother. However, that phrase was never a motto Wilhelm repeated. Kill and kill more was to be the lesson of his offspring.

Post refreshment, Galeena tuned her ears to her world, then proceeded toward her night's lodgings.

Living beneath her father's watchful eye in anonymity was necessitated by not only the inheritance of Northanglia, but also by her potential claim to the throne of Gudsfelt. Wilhelm's intention was to keep his daughter hidden in plain sight even though the irony of her situation was that every eye was always on her every move. Galeena was called the nomadic orphan. Twas often said that she simply appeared one night in the soldiers' camp near three years of age. No one questioned. Orphans were not out of the ordinary in any nation.

As a secret orphan, she enjoyed the lifestyle of freedom from palisade walls. She played with fellow children and ate her meals amongst neighboring families and guards. Galeena slept in her very own hut with a private governess who had been appointed by her Grandfather Wymer. The woman, Dreisel, attempted to care for the rambunctious child until the petite princess reached an age of no longer needing an overseer.

For the first seven years of Galeena's military rearing, she longed for the private visits that were gifted with her mother and father. The child was never neglected by them. Their lessons and private education were the foundation of all skills she would eventually possess.

Galeena was taught to exit the village in utter silence and make her way to her awaiting parents. The family, unescorted, would travel south to their cottage and spend two or three weeks there. Wilhelm and Adelia would tell endless stories of their family histories, and the Viking woman would train her children in the language and rituals of her people.

Throughout those years of visitations, Galeena always wanted and needed much more knowledge, experience and of course time with her family. Then, at age ten, her heart broke upon learning she would have to be diligent in retaining all she had been taught when her mother fell ill. Their final ritual together, Adelia broke the sacred rule, and she had Wilhelm accompany them in the ceremonies. The husband, father and king was to learn all that was to be taught by his wife lest his daughter forget due to her young age.

Prior to her departure, Adelia informed Galeena that contact had been made with their relatives in the northlands. Having been raised a Viking, she assured them her daughter was as loyal to their ways as she had always been. Full disclosure was made that their conversations had only been held in the language of the Norse, though Galeena was instructed never to reveal that knowledge to anyone outside of her immediate family. The Boersen legacy mark had been stained beneath her hair at age three, and before Queen Adelia parted from their existence, Galeena had been well versed in all of the rituals that identified her as a Daughter of Boersen.

When the sun was nearing its time of rest, Galeena faced that she was not going to reach her resting place before night fell upon the lands. Desperately, she had hoped to reach the Broodenshire cave, her family's haven, at an hour that would allow her to hunt, cook and eat. However, judging from her location, it would be hours past the middle of the night before she arrived.

Fatigue and hunger seemed to be increasing with her new awareness. Frustration began to steal her remaining energy, "Torren, you menacing Dane, you have taken possession of my home, caused me to flee my own village with no food or drink, and are fully to blame for my horseless travels."

Walking down the center of the gravel road that leads north to her father's garrison and south toward Dornwold, Galeena debated her options. "Do I sit propped against a tree-trunk and wait for morn? Should I take a momentary rest, then forge onward? Or, do I turn in the exact opposite direction of my current aim, hasten my steps back toward the north, and spend most of the night in my chamber within my father's home?"

Her steps slowed, "All of my choices require that I hunt. I suppose I should be somewhat grateful that this morning's invasion did come post break-fast. My energy has been sustained thus far on one meal. Weakness will soon take charge of me. Oh, the complications of needing to eat. Oh, the intrusion of Norsemen. Oh, the inconvenience of having my escape interrupted. Oh, how I am filled with spite and hate." Galeena sighed. Constant survival was tiring.

A turn eastward into the forest was her immediate call.

While listening and searching for her soon to be meal, Galeena appreciated the truth that survival instincts are remarkable. Without noticing, she compartmentalized her talents. Parenting, hunting, fighting, cooking, learning: all of these various skills emerge when needed. Earlier that day, she had to kill humans to survive. During this early evening, she would have to use a completely different knowledge base to kill an animal to survive. Before receiving nourishment, Galeena would have to cook the animal. Then, prior to sleep she would have carry herself to a secure and comfortable place. Tomorrow, all survival tasks would begin anew. A thought repeated itself in an eternal tense, *Constant survival* is *tiring*.

A shuffle was heard. Without turning her head toward its direction, the hunter struck. Targeting a lone rabbit was as simple as swatting an unsuspecting insect. Twas done. The fattened animal was collected. Galeena and her supper were peacefully en route to her private abode... within King Wilhelm's fortress. Claremont would be where she rested this night.

Carrying the deceased hare in one hand and tossing pebbles with the other, a new irritation welled within her. One thought began to itch at her peace of mind, *Dearest brother, where were you this morn? Tending pigs, chickens and cows I presume. Tis my assessment that your seclusion is far more peaceful than mine.*

Chapter 6

The hammering and grinding of heavy metal pounding rock grew louder behind her. Progression halted, and she whispered, "Will I ever reach a place to rest?"

"Galeena? You travel in the dark?"

"Aye, Robert." Relief was felt as Galeena looked over her shoulder and watched the approaching rider until he and his horse were halted at her side.

"On your way with a report for King Wilhelm?" she asked.

"Yes."

"My gratitude to God for your arrival. Care to deliver a second package?"

The messenger chuckled. "I'd be honored to have you join me. Certainly your company will be informative and up-lifting."

Robert reached downward to help hoist his comrade onto the horse's back. She handed him the lifeless rabbit, then leapt up onto the mare's rump without assistance. Galeena swung her leg over whilst her escort tugged at her belt. A steady trot commenced.

"Robert, where is Lukah?"

"Simeon carries a notice of the invasion to Lukah at his farm. Our misfortunes of this day have come quite unexpectedly. I am pleased you are safe. Lukah will be on his way to you soon. I know he will be relieved when he learns that you escaped."

"I'm ashamed to say that your choice of the word 'escaped' is more accurate than I'd care to admit. We were outnumbered. The arrival of the Danes was incredibly shocking. I could hardly believe the chaos. We have seen battles, but I never imagined those people would invade Castleton. We were utterly unprepared."

"The casualties? Was there much loss?"

"No. We lost a few of our men, but most villagers evaded capture by fleeing into the western forest."

"I am certain they have you to thank," he complimented.

"While I appreciate your confidence, I believe it could have been far worse. The Norsemen may have been withholding the full force of their capabilities. Also, I do not fight for recognition. I fight because I have no other choice."

"You *protect* because it is in your nature, Galeena."

The exhausted soldier rested her head on her friend's back. She was very weary and very hungry.

As she quieted, Robert heard the gurgles of her empty core and instructed, "Reach into my pouch. I have cakes and apples. We shall trade, your hare for my meager stores?"

"Thank you."

Eating provisions and sipping water from Robert's pouch revived Galeena. There was no doubt that he had been dispatched from one of her guardian spirits.

When she was able to hold her head upright again, Robert asked, "When shall the bells ring for you, Galeena?"

The corner of her mouth tucked into her cheek. Tiring of that very question, the young woman of fifteen responded, "King Wilhelm holds all rights to me and the ringing of bells. He has mentioned his plans a time or two."

"Care to share? Will you be marrying Lukah?"

The very idea was nothing less than grotesque to her, and it was another question she was longing to never have to answer again. Staking her claim, their claims, to their identities was going to eliminate the constant questioning of their relationship. Galeena retorted, "Why do I repeatedly get asked that question?"

"We all know you could have your choice of thousands of men, but Lukah is dearest to you. He always has been. It makes perfect sense that you two should wed."

Continuing to be disgusted by the very thought and words, she was thankful he could not see her expressions.

"Lukah will find a meek, genteel, lovely bride. He truly is more like, like... a brother to me."

"I have stated, you have thousands to choose from all about you. Tis my opinion that you would be most jealous to see Lukah married to another."

"Your opinion could not be more wrong. Do recall, King Wilhelm has plans for me. I will be far too busy with my own nuptials to concern myself with Lukah's."

"Many of us have discussed,"

"You mean gossiped!"

"discussed, that we believe you were orphaned by a royal. Tis why you bear such beauty, grace, wisdom, and agility. We also have thought this because the king takes special care of you. The imperials do lack discretion too. We commoners are not the only ones who sometimes stray from our virtuous expectations. You could have been abandoned by royalty."

Galeena huffed a laugh and said, "I will not argue virtues, but I will defend our ruler. King Wilhelm cares for me because his father practically raised me. He also cares for me because his wife often visited me. I am certain she had a voice in ensuring he would see to an advantageous marriage for me. Growing without a mother and father in my house was often quite sad. Tis why I spent so much of my time with my beloved Wymer. Oh how I miss his scoldings."

Robert laughed. "Yes. Lord Wymer did maintain an obvious and deep affection for you. He's the one who made sure Lukah was always at your side. You'll have to forgive me for not thinking of him as *beloved.* The rest of us found him to be vicious and unforgiving."

Galeena smiled remembering time with her grandfather and brother. "He was stern because he was creating an army to defeat all armies. For me, many of the memories of my childhood replay with fondness because of his attentions."

"His role is understandable. We all were given to our king for service, and though it was frightening and lonesome, I treasure that we had each other."

"We still have each other, Robert."

"Aye."

No more conversation was exchanged between them. When they reached King Wilhelm's garrison near that mid hour of the night, Galeena thanked her escort and slid off the backend of his horse. She said, "Tell our king I shall visit him after I have eaten, bathed, and freshened my attire. I shall present myself like a lady in the morn."

"It shall be done."

Galeena vanished from the sight of all like the ghost she was raised to be.

Chapter 7

"Have you any final words to speak Torren, the Norseman? Your two guards had none. Although, that could have been my fault since my blades pierced their throats *before* I asked for their final contributions in this life." Kneeling beside the Viking with a small knife in each hand, both pressed to either side of his neck just below his jaw, Galeena glared, poised to kill.

Galeena's life had been spent in that single house, in that single village. Every creak, every obstacle, every beam of light were all known to her. Arriving at her own bedside undetected presented absolutely no challenge for her.

The decision to forsake a retreat to her quarters within the fortress was made the instant she had eaten. Revival gave her clarity. The confidence that Torren had chosen her home to occupy solidified her decision to complete a crucial task sooner rather than later. Without their leader, the entire group would be more easily conquered.

Torren's eyes opened. With a mild rasp to his deep voice he said, "Uh, yes. I do wonder, how long have I been asleep? I could vow that it was only today, when you bid me adieu, that you said you'd return in a fortnight. Has fourteen days passed so quickly? If so, I must express my disappointment in your waking me only to send me back into my eternal sleep. Such an action is far more cruel than if you would have just released my spirit from its mighty yet oblivious shell."

Her mouth shone a hint of amusement. Her eyes could not hide the enjoyment of his humor. The half smile that appeared, quickly disappeared when she felt a large, cold blade press to her own throat.

He offered, "Let us die together. Shall we, Galeena? My mission here will be completed by the next man who receives my father's trust and respect. I may not be easily replaced, but I certainly *can be* replaced."

The daggers she held were released, and they tumbled centimeters to either side of Torren's head. Galeena replied, "I am not as easily replaced in my army. You see, I am the only one of my kind here."

He smiled and lowered his own weapon. From his position on his back, with her looming over him, Torren shown his empty hands as a sign of truce between them. Galeena had captivated his full interest, and she knew he wanted to touch her, though he did not. He said, "I agree. You are the only one of your kind that I have ever encountered. Tell me, how did you get in here undetected?"

Before answering, Galeena sought the location of his knife and the ease he would have in collecting it once more. The dagger instantly stole her attention and breath. “Where did you get that?” she asked.

“It was a gift. Do you find it admirable?”

Sickness gnawed at her throat. Laying beside her enemy was the very knife she had been promised when her time of concealment ended. It had belonged to her mother. “Who gave you such a gift?” she demanded.

Galeena’s interest became his interest as he replied, “My father gave it to me with my grandmother’s blessing. It was her father’s, King Boersen of Gudsfelt.”

His explanation caused the flesh of her body and the lining of her throat to burn. She became confused. Intense effort was given to hiding her true reason for questioning him. “I saw my queen with that knife when I was child. How did your father gain possession of it? Who is your father? Are you not of Danemour?” Without noticing, she had retrieved her small blades. They were gripped with fury.

“Woman, we agreed to allow one another to live this night. Release your weapons.”

Galeena looked at her hands, then into his eyes. All she could do was stare. He remained expressionless with his palms facing upward.

“Perhaps I shall help you,” he gently informed her.

Torren sat up slowly, keeping his hands visible. He then pried the knives from Galeena's grip while she watched his every move. When they both were free of their defenses again, she sat back on her heels upon the floor.

"I'll answer all of your questions if you'll join me up here on *my* bed." He smiled as he lightly patted the open space next to him.

Though suspicious, no threat was sensed. She squinted and shook her head. When Torren saw her shoulders relax, he held out both of his hands, and Galeena accepted his invitation.

As she climbed atop her bed, she asked, "May I hold the heirloom?"

"You're not asking so you can use it on me are you?"

A smirk accompanied her reply, "Not at this moment."

"Then yes, you may hold it."

Torren handed it over, and without thought, the Daughter of Boersen lie back, shifted her pillow to a comfortable position and began studying her great-grandfather's knife.

Torren was quite pleased with her ease. He asked, "Am I allowed confidence that I selected the correct house?"

The woman's eyes left the treasure long enough to affirm his decision. A single nod was given before her attention returned to the object. Delicately, both the handle and the point were held as she slowly and carefully spun and twisted her mother's keepsake. The Boersen symbol, her symbol, was carved into the base of the handle. Quietly, Galeena recalled the story of that knife slicing her Grandfather Wymer as he attacked her Grandmother Olivia. This was the very blade that her father used to kill the guards who imprisoned him. This piece of her history was credited for protecting Adelia when she fled from Dornwold in the night mere hours before her execution. Almost thirteen years had passed since she was promised ownership of that family treasure, yet her enemy had possession of it.

"Tis beautiful isn't it?" Torren replied.

"Aye," she whispered.

Certain she already knew the answer, Galeena asked anyhow, "Tell me, who is your father?"

Torren reclined beside her watching her fascination with his dagger. Galeena had not held the weapon since the last time she saw her mother.

He spoke, "My father is Jaegar of Styrkeson."

Without forethought, she inserted, "That means my..." she hesitated, then continued, "my queen killed your mother."

"Yes. Tis why my grandmother approved of my possession of this. Her daughter, Adelia, demanded it be delivered to my father through a man named Fredrick when she fell ill years ago."

His words angered the princess. Her first thought was, *How dare she!* But no emotion was shown. The following thoughts were all questions, but there were too many to ask. Each became lost as another arose. Galeena managed to inquire,

"What reason did Queen Adelia have for bestowing this to your father, and why would your father give it to you?"

"Tis my understanding that Adelia meant for the knife to be presented to her heir when she returned to Gudsfelt to rule. Adelia wanted Jaegar to give the gift himself as evidence of his acceptance of the rightful, blood descendent of King Boersen. However, since I am the only heir to the throne of Gudsfelt who has come forward to take the place as their future ruler and king, Jaegar, and my Grandmother Olivia agreed that I have earned my great-grandfather's dagger."

First Galeena corrected his irreverence. "*Queen* Adelia," she stressed. Then she questioned, "Olivia agreed to the claim that you are the only heir to Gudsfelt? Adelia has a daughter. King Boersen has publicly declared that Princess Helene has all rights to his throne."

A forced concentration was all that kept Galeena from physically ejecting the man who occupied her bed, her house, her land, and *her* coveted blade!

Torren turned onto his side and propped his head in his hand. He said, "You've asked enough questions. Tis my turn. Tell me, how did you enter without waking me?"

He received her attention, and she replied, "This is my home, Sir. Twas not difficult. What you should be asking is, how was I able to eliminate both of your night guards without stirring up even a single speck of dust?"

"I witnessed your swift and accurate skills twice in one day." He lie back once more, then concluded, "I know how you were able to kill two capable men without drawing any attention to your actions. Please do know, some of the men you are piercing are decent men who are here because they are loyal to the Boersens. Many of them refused to attack this morn. Additionally, the more of my people you kill, the more Danes I will need to call upon from Dornwold to fill their places."

Processing his claim filled Galeena with concern. She had always been careful about the Norsemen she faced. This particular invasion forced her to proceed carelessly. She defended her actions, "No peaceful man, nor woman, should have arrived here uninvited and with aggression. My purpose is to protect Northanglia. If good people die by my hand, tis their own fault for arriving unannounced and uninvited."

"Perhaps, but the Norsemen who vacated these homes for us were all Danes. The men of Gudsfelt who linger among us arrived post clearing of the villagers." Torren paused and shrugged. He then added, "May I have my dagger now?"

Too much information had been received. Galeena's mind was disoriented. She needed sleep so she could rearrange her thoughts and ask only the most pertinent questions. In a state of bewilderment, she handed the weapon to him then asked, "What does your name mean?"

"Tis an odd thought, but the answer is, I do not know. My father heard the word on one of his bartering voyages to the green island west of this land. He knew not what it meant. He simply remembered it and called me the name upon my birth."

"And your mother, did she have no input?"

"My mother, Frigga, was a warring woman. She was not very nurturing. My Grandmother Olivia is most like a mother to me."

Galeena gasped. A sudden awareness struct her numb.

Torren inquired, "Have you forgotten something or remembered something?"

Too much had been shared. Before she could respond to him calling her own beloved and only grandmother by the same name she knows her, Galeena thought, *This man and I share a brother!* She was sickened yet again. Torren had said to her when their paths first crossed that he felt a connection. As fate would have it, he was absolutely correct! They were connected. The two not only had a mutual a brother, but the Norseman had been raised by the woman she had longed for and idolized her entire life.

"Are you going to state your epiphany?" he asked.

Lie!

Smoothly, Galeena covered her reaction, "There is something I remembered; my presence is needed in the morn. I am to speak before King Wilhelm and his advisors. I should part. My thoughts will scatter if I am not soon to sleep."

"I wish for you remain longer."

Galeena looked at him with a pinched brow and said, "Perhaps, but *I* wish to leave."

Torren replied, "We have much to learn about one another. Daylight will be unwelcome as I am certain you are aware that we only have the hours of darkness beneath which we may become acquainted. Once the sun brightens this world, our friendship must end."

"There is no friendship and there will be no more sharing between us. I have gained all of the knowledge I need from you. I have not hidden that my assignment is to kill you and as many of your countrymen as possible."

He coaxed, "I ask you to stay… a mite longer. Tell me, tell me of your parents. That is a story that shall pass time."

Torren and Galeena rested with their shoulders nearly touching. She watched him place the Boersen dagger beneath his pillow, and she asked, "Do you wish me to stay because you have sinister plans for me should I fall into a deep slumber?"

A chuckled preceded, "While the thought has entered my mind, I assure you the answer is no. You have my protection. You've had it since my first glance upon you."

Satisfied, Galeena smiled and rolled onto her side facing him. Torren did the same. He whispered, "We lie near enough to feel the other's breath. Tell me of your childhood."

A version of her childhood was offered. "I too was raised by someone other than my mother or father. I grew here in this village, in this very house. I was named by the soldiers who occupied this town for many years. An elder woman cared for me until the soldiers decided I was old enough, skilled enough, and vicious enough to be on my own. That was age ten. I have supported, protected, and survived since then. The constant tension exhausts me. In thirteen days I will reach six and ten years of age. However, I often feel thirty or forty or *fifty*. King Wilhelm has promised me release from battles soon, someday soon. And, I trust him."

"Am I to presume that your disclosure of a return in two weeks was scheduled because of your impending annual?"

"Yes. My king has made arrangements for a... humble celebration. I hope his gift to me will be the release of my status in his army."

"If tis release you desire, then I hope that for you as well. My father, Jaegar, expects that I shall fight and rule until my last breath."

"Does that disappoint you?"

"Not at all. He has full confidence in me. I was born of two warriors who are legendary in Danemour. I gladly accept my lot in life."

"Yes. Even I have heard of Frigga. She attempted, on several occasions, to kill Queen Adelia. Though our queen was kind and gentle, she was not to be trifled with nor threatened. When her husband's infidelity was intertwined into the strenuous circumstances, Queen Adelia showed no mercy."

Torren interrupted to defend his parents, "You sound pleased by my mother's death. My father chose Frigga first. The infidelity was between Adelia and Jaegar, not Frigga and Jaegar."

Galeena sat up in disgust, "Your misfortune is not what pleases me. My queen's fortitude does. And the final word on the infidelity is this, Jaegar and Adelia had been promised to one another as very young children! She was willing to forsake the entire nation of Northanglia for him. Relations with the woman, Frigga, was merely a drunken indiscretion. Besides, tis more likely that Jaegar betrayed them both! Is that not the truth?"

Torren raised as well and growled, "You dare attempt to reduce my existence to a meaningless, drunken encounter?! You! A woman with no family and no name?!" Growing suspicious, he asked, "I'd like to know why your queen felt the need to offer so many details about her past to a servant?"

"My knowledge of Queen Adelia's path to reign is history. She was a well educated woman. She saw value and longevity of service in me. Do keep in mind, many of the details were not fully shared until I was older, and I plan to continue gaining insight into her life until my last breath."

"Your fascination with a woman to whom you are not related leaves me curious."

"Adelia is the closest thing I've ever had to a mother. Her memory will live on through me."

"She was almost a mother to me as well. Huh, I shall save that secret though."

Another nerve had been plucked. Galeena wanted to pry further, but she knew it was best to shift their conversation away from mothers lest she share too much information. She made a note to revisit his allusion.

Calmly she replied, "Though I will not apologize, I do ask that you accept my request for another temporary peace between us. I have stated that I am tired. Speaking on sensitive topics such as battling women is ill advised for us both. I require refreshment and sleep. Few hours of darkness remain, and I have stores of food that I'd very much like to retrieve. Since you are going to be living in my home and I will be relocating, I'd like to take some of my provisions and necessities with me. I will pack some items and secure them to my horse. You will not see me again until my king sends me back for negotiations or confrontations."

Torren braced on his hand and stroked the silken blanket. "Where shall you go? It is very late, and I hear the rain falling. If you would like to stay here this night, I can promise you a safe exodus at your leisure when the sun rises."

His offer was most appealing. Galeena had walked far out of the way just to return to Castleton when she could have been in her bed chamber in Claremont. After meeting with her father, her next destination was Broodenshire. It would take a full day's ride to get there. Then, she would proceed to her cottage in the south woods of Northanglia. Twas there she hoped to rendezvous with Lukah.

So much traveling ahead.

The Dane's offer to stay in her own home for the night was contemplated. Galeena asked, "This night's slumber will be within the safety of the garrison. Then, my aim is to complete my trek to Broodenshire until I am needed or summoned again. However, should I choose to forgo a retreat in the castle, where shall I sleep? Will you force me to seek comfort upon my own floor?"

Torren assured her, "Certainly not! You are welcome to share this lovely, feathered bed covered with linen and silk. Which, by the way, I'd like to know why a humble servant to the king has such fine bed clothes."

"Although my possessions are none of your concern, I will say, trading is not for men only. I've been afforded many privileges that others in my station have been denied. My skills have earned me great respect and elevated status in my country."

"You need not justify. The women of Gudsfelt and Danemour are allowed elevated positions as well. I was just told that the women of this land are suppressed and lack appreciation and freedoms."

"The information you received is correct. I am an exception because of my upbringing. If you'll recall, I'm not easily replacced."

"Ah, yes," he agreed. Torren then asked, "So, you'll be staying? I shall have the pleasure of a guest this night?"

She raised her eyes upward and in jest said, "I have a guest, and I cannot say that it is a pleasure because he is an intruder."

“Let us sleep, Galeena. I shall impress you with my chivalry throughout the coming hours.”

“I was able to arrive with great secrecy. Are you not afraid of me? Do you not fear for your life?”

Torren smirked, then settled peacefully pulling the bed covers up to his chin. He closed his eyes and confessed, “I fear only one thing.”

A squint of curiosity accompanied, “I have only one fear as well, Sir.”

Galeena finally rested. She then turned face down and nuzzled her pillow. Torren’s foot slid until it touched hers. She shifted so there’d be no mistaking how she felt. Her leg was draped over his. He sighed. Though neither of them had any intentions of sharing their secret fear with the other, they did enjoy a most restful night’s sleep.

Chapter 8

Dreams of a rocking ship haunted Torren throughout the night. The seas were restless and the waves billowed. Yet, the haven of the long vessel repelled him. Repeatedly, he attempted to clamber overboard, but each time he braced a boot to the gunwale, his father pulled him back into the boat. Jaegar placed an oar in his hands and commanded him to continue rowing. "You will not abandon your duties my son! Your obligation, your security, and your glory are all here!"

In Torren's mind, twas not the raging sea he feared. He was purely disturbed by the inability to choose the water. The longship was too small; the choices there were too restricting. The sea was infinite. It could possibly provide instant death, but it could also possibly provide eternal life.

The sound of a desperate gasp awoke him. His eyes opened and he strained to understand his location and his surroundings. The dream he dreamed was so vivid he could hardly believe he was not still upon a ship sailing west from

White Crested Cove to Northanglia. Torren blinked. He listened. He moved his hands. Luxury encased him. The surface upon which his body lay was solid, though yielding. The room was dark. Only the faintest glow from a crescent moon shown through the crevice of a curtain a distance before him. An inhale, then a sigh stole his attention. He turned to fight, his dagger gripped. Safety was comforting. Rest came once more as he replaced his knife at his side.

The jolt of awakening from such a state of stress left Torren unable to close his eyes again. His body was damp with perspiration. His nearly white curls adhered to his neck and cheeks. He placed his hand on his forehead, then slid his hair back and away from his face.

Galeena shifted from her side facing away from him to her back. She then turned toward him. His agitation had awoken her, and she knew Torren now watched her every motion. He listened to the sound of her feet rubbing against one another beneath the blanket. The presumed state of complete unconsciousness in which she lie was intriguing to him. He whispered, "This woman lying here, with an angelic face near enough to touch, killed many yesterday. She wishes for relief, God."

As he stared at the woman beside him, he gathered only details the dimness of the room would allow. Gently, he lifted the coverings and muttered, "Your garments have changed. When you arrived you wore trousers and a stained tunic. Now, you wear a sleeping gown that is as white as untouched snow."

During the night, when Galeena was certain the man in her house had fallen asleep, she rose, collected her lace trimmed gown from a shelf and dropped it over her body. Before returning to Castleton, she had taken time to splash in a stream. With a new plan to spend the entire night in her own bed, there was not a possibility that she was going to sleep betwixt her clean bedding in grimy outer garments.

Torren's next words nearly caused her to cough with laughter. He whispered, "When did you remove your clothes? I do regret I slept through that." He then snickered silently at himself. "I must fight to evade the images of this fair Galeena disrobing in my midst."

Not fully awake, nor asleep, his gentility allowed her the opportunity to continue dreaming. Having just spent her first night with a man, loving and joyous thoughts of him filled her mind until a frustrated moan drew her eyes open. She requested, "Please speak your discomfort so I can have peace."

From the partially raised position he held, Torren lowered to his back and said, "I am revisiting what pulled me so violently out of rest."

"You have an attentive ear. Do share."

He smiled.

"The last vision I had before my eyes opened was of me diving into the frigid waters of the North Sea from the security of my father's ship. The icy sensation stole my breath, and to escape death, my mind brought me back to reality. Do you believe I've had a premonition? Shall I take leave from this world by choice?" The Viking turned his attention to the woman at his side and added, "You were absent, Galeena."

She replied in a whisper, "Why would I be there? We know not one another."

Rolling onto his side and scooting his body next to hers, Torren pinched a lock of her hair and pressed it to his nose. "Such a sweet scent. Tis burned into my senses forever. Tis the very reason I instructed you to flee from these streets. You killed my friend. I reached for you. A breeze carried your aroma through me. I could not harm you. In that moment, I knew I could never harm you. However, your return here leaves me facing one single fear; I may someday be to blame for your misfortune. Why did you come here alone? Facing you in a battle amongst a multitude of warriors would have been much easier had I not been gifted even these brief moments with you. Lying beside you, inhaling your breath, touching your hair, feeling your flesh against mine, how can I fight you now?" Torren boldly caressed her cheek with the backs of his fingers.

The throes of a sincere infatuation enveloped Galeena. She knew Torren was aware that he had gained her trust. Otherwise, the woman of war would not be so peaceful in his presence. Torren touched her feet with his to test his place; Galeena did not pull away.

"I believe we do know each other," he said just before he kissed her lips.

No retreat, no apprehension, not even a twitch was given in response. Galeena took equal part in his affection then asked, "May we have more time to sleep?"

"I beg you, take as much time as you desire. I'll be here with you." He pressed another kiss to her lips.

* * *

When Torren awoke for the second time that morning all around him was visible, all except Galeena. She had slipped away in the same manner that she had arrived, without detection. Torren raised his head to inspect where she had been and found that her nightdress was displayed atop the bed covering as if she were still within it.

Her playful and cunning antics amused him. He was glad to know her plans. He was confident that Galeena could lead him to Adelia's daughter.

"You were quite mistaken to think that she would be here when you awoke," Torren spoke to himself while his senses absorbed the lingering essence of his guest.

Galeena parted the moment his breathing regulated and the tension between his eyes subsided. Since the night guards had already been *relieved* of their duties, she faced no opposition walking from Castleton. She didn't even bother to collect her horse, because she knew the path to her father's home was clear.

Upon arrival to the fortress, Galeena entered through an undisclosed portal and strode to her small sleeping chamber.

The soft soles of her boots ensured her presence remained unnoticed. According to Robert, she arrived hours after the sun lowered. Galeena did not want her father to know that she returned to her cottage in the village without an official command from him, so she needed to be found in her own bed when the household began to stir.

As her head sank into her pillow, Galeena's final waking thought was of Torren saying, *"She was almost a mother to me as well. Huh, I shall save that secret though."*

"He has met my mother, and I shall learn of their encounter before the sun sets on another day."

Galeena dozed off once more.

* * *

Rapping knuckles on wood awakened her from a deep sleep. A state of confusion held her speechless. Galeena opened her eyes and immediately worked to place herself. Once she realized that she was in her small cell-like room within the walls of Claremont, she began trying to figure out how long she had slept.

The visitor knocked again.

"Yes," she called.

"Galeena, you've rested long enough. King Wilhelm demands you rise at once and report to his table. Tis time for the first meal of the day. He awaits and not with patience."

"Has he stated his expectations for my presentation?"

“The king’s instructions were to retrieve you and have you appear with haste.”

“Please tell him I’ll be seated within the hour.”

“Not acceptable!”

An inaudible groan preceded, “Minutes. I shall present myself in minutes.”

“Better!”

The sound of determined heels tapping on the stone floor diminished.

A pack of clothing was on the table at the foot of Galeena’s cot. She arose, livened her appearance with fresh water, dropped a gown over her head, pulled a thin woven rope from a pouch, and tied her hair into a loose, decorative roll at the base of her neck.

Within the promised time frame, the anonymous Princess of Northanglia was en route to her beloved father’s side.

The king and his advisors had not waited for her arrival to begin their meal. Galeena was certain to appear hurried yet reverent when she entered the dining hall.

“Approach Galeena!” the king called the very moment her foot crossed the entryway.

“Yes, Your Majesty,” she replied.

“I’m glad you’ve been able to join us before the first meal was fully consumed. Tis my guess that you should be quite famished.”

"I am King Wilhelm. My last meal was at this same hour a day past. Thank you for the invitation to eat amongst your political subordinates."

"Sit soldier. A place is set for you."

Galeena saw that only one place setting was unattended. She asked, "Will Lukah be joining us, Sire?"

"I've yet to receive correspondence from him. Simeon was sent, but a return message has not been received."

"Perhaps he hunts?" Galeena suggested.

Wilhelm shrugged and sipped from his cup. "You were nearing Broodenshire when Robert collected you?"

"In a manner, yes. I had actually turned northward. It was clear that reaching the monastery was not possible."

"And you rested well in the guards' quarters?"

Galeena's eyes locked with her father's. He knew. She was not sorry. Half of her mouth smiled as did the outer corners of her eyes. She replied, "I did not sleep well at all until just before the sun rose."

"Huh," he puffed with a hint of anger. His expression seemed to say, *We will discuss this at another time.*

"Speak all you know," Wilhelm requested.

Galeena informed her king of the attack. She shared the number of invaders, the list of casualties and that no one was being held against their will.

"Do I even need to ask from whence they come?"

"Gudsfelt *and* Danemour."

"And their purpose?" he asked.

"Tis my assessment that they have come for your daughter, and they have no intentions of leaving without the one they seek."

"Have you any confirmation on this?"

"No Your Majesty. This is merely what I have gleaned from their placement so near to your fortress."

"Have you experienced any other interactions with them?"

Galeena finished chewing the piece of ham she had in her mouth, then sipped her tea before responding.

"Yes. I have spoken to two of them. One of the two remains alive. The first was a bit more threatening than I thought was necessary. The second, well, he showed no aggression and he even saved my life from mass ambush by his countrymen. Therefore, I returned the cordiality by not killing him while he slept."

"Was that wise dear child?"

"I haven't been a child for many years. And, I do believe it was wise. If given another opportunity, I believe the man named Torren will find himself at ease in my company."

"I'll not hear of it! You'll free yourself of any obligations in matters concerning those people, and you'll leave the eliminations to Lukah," Wilhelm ordered. He then added, "Your nuptial contract announcement has been arranged, and you shall begin planning your relocation to Solsworth with Prince Henry. Until then, you have only two choices for how to spend your time. You may remain in my home accompanied by a guard at all times, or you can depart for the monastery with an escort. There you shall stay, with a guard, until you are brought back here for the celebration."

Wilhelm did not want to risk his daughter making any decisions that lacked discretion. Most young women her age were already married. He had honored her mother's wishes to preserve her independence until her sixteenth annual. They were thirteen days from Galeena being bound to a husband and settled in the far south where she would be able to retire to being a wife and mother. Wymer and Alexar were in Solsworth, and he was confident they would ensure nothing but the absolute best awaited her. Wilhelm also knew his daughter would be adored and honored there until the crown for Northanglia was passed to her.

"I'm nearly at a loss for words King Wilhelm. Am I truly understanding that you wish for me, one of your commanders, to pass the next two weeks guarded at every moment of the day and night? I am a guard, I do not need one following me. I have not been tended since I reached the age of ten years. You will be quite disappointed and, forgive me if I sound irreverent, but you will also be quite frustrated at having to monitor my whereabouts for the upcoming weeks. The thought of evading a nurse sounds entertaining."

Of the eight men present, six snickered, but two glared.

Galeena bit the inside corner of her mouth and waited for her father to scold or punish her.

As the king, he cared not what his fellow staff thought of their exchange. Their opinions in these particular matters were meaningless to him. Wilhelm raised one eyebrow and showed no amusement toward his daughter. He said, "Collect your plate and vanish from my sight. I'd like to eat without ailment. I'll hear only words of gratitude from you before you exit."

Galeena stood, lowered her eyes and her head, and she gathered her utensils, cup and platter and quietly walked toward the door. As she reached the archway, she turned and said to her father, "Your Majesty, I was not dishonoring you or your command. I am grateful. Please try to view the world from my eyes. I've been raised, trained, then placed, to lead all others. Being told I shall be under watch is distressing. Thank you for your concern. Discuss your sentencing with your advisors. If they feel I need a male lady's maid, then so it shall be. If, however, the men you trust most believe I am capable of surviving thirteen more sleeps without a protector, then I ask that we forget this conversation occurred. Shall we be in agreement?"

"Take your leave," he gently commanded.

A curtsy was offered and Galeena strode proudly toward her father's strategy room. When she was only a few paces from the dining hall she paused as she heard a man say, "My advice is this Sire, leave the girl to her own care. You've received news that your daughter could be in danger. That orphan is not your priority and soon she will no longer be your concern. You have been more than generous with her. Prepare yourself for a battle. The Danes could be calling upon their brothers and sisters to join them from Dornwold as we speak. That girl holds no value to us."

Accustomed to oversights as they pertained to Galeena, Wilhelm made no emotional reaction. He turned his head slowly and addressed the man seated three chairs to his left. Those in his line of view leaned back from the table.

"I have selected a woman as an equal commander because she has innate abilities that no man shall ever possess. No greater spies will ever be born than keen women. Galeena will gather every last piece of information I need, and she will then dispose of the enemy with no remorse. Commander Wymer has infused a very special skill set into her. She is graceful, beautiful, wise, quick, and very strong. She is not worthless to us."

Wilhelm motioned for his attendant to pull his chair. A young boy of near fifteen years hurried to their king's aide. As he stood he said, "Collect your assigned delegations and ensure they are prepared for expanded watch rotations. Let us all be vigilant to hinder any further invasions. Those who were able to make their way from the sea to Castleton did so from beyond our sights. I'll send a summons when I feel we need to reconvene. Blessings on you all this day."

Chapter 9

Galeena had no interest in what her father had to say to her upon his arrival. Her only concern was access to her mother's belongings. The Boersen women were excellent documenters, and there was no doubt in her mind that she would find some inscription that pertained to Torren. Wilhelm had never allowed her to plunder through Adelia's storage chests, but she had also never asked.

The iron knob turned and the door opened. King Wilhelm entered alone. When the door latched behind him, all thoughts of defiance faded and Galeena rushed to her father's open arms. After and extended and joy-filled embrace, he pulled her back by her shoulders to study her face. She smiled and relaxed in his hold.

Wilhelm placed a kiss to her forehead, and Galeena leaned into him once more pressing her cheek to his chest.

"Father, I'm growing weary of fighting. A Norseman was able to sidle to me twice yesterday without my noticing. No guarantee can be made that I will be of any use to you for much longer."

Holding his daughter tightly he assured her, "You have never been useful to me. You were not placed in your current situation because I, or your mother, felt you would be useful to us. Neither of us felt that you'd become who you are meant to be if you were hidden behind these walls."

"Instead you hid me out there." Galeena pulled slightly away and pointed behind herself with her thumb.

"You may not fully realize it, but you've accomplished more than many men will ever achieve. You've seen lands beyond Northanglia. You've learned languages. You've been educated. You know how to survive without being fed and watered like all other royal daughters who exist in your situation. You are beautiful."

Her eyes lowered, "I am not delicate, Father."

"Delicacies are unnecessary."

"Mother was delicate, very delicate."

"Perhaps, but only in certain ways." He smiled lovingly and added, "However, she was the only one allowed to be so enchanting. You share equally in her beauty. Having you raised strong and defensive should have never been at the result of having you feel inferior as a woman. You are magnificent, the very model of perfection. You are the rarest diamond and I'll not have you believing otherwise."

Galeena tilted her head and said, "Father, perceive me not to be disrespectful nor unappreciative, but yours is a biased opinion, and thus leaves me uncertain of its validity."

"Shall your melancholy disposition force me to confess to you my dearest child how many men have come to me asking for your hand over the past eight years?"

"They seek the hand of your daughter. Not my hand."

"You are incorrect, my love. They have asked for your hand."

One eyebrow lifted. Her interest was piqued, "Why would they come to you?"

"The men of this realm have always known that I am in your charge. Some attempted to hoodwink me by approaching your governess, but she would never have handed you over to anyone. She was most protective of you."

"Then why did she leave? She could have continued to care for me and fulfill other duties."

Wilhelm shifted and walked away from his daughter. With a distance placed between them, he responded, "You had to be reared strong. Further dependence on anyone would have hindered your capabilities in survival. You and Lukah are the only son and daughter I am ever going to have. Your mother and I have done our best to provide freedom to you both. Having a governess for you and a priest for Lukah was necessary. Twas only a matter of time before enemies came to collect you, Galeena. You and your brother needed to be invisible. No one would ever suspect that a girl child would have her own hut with no attendants. Lukah, a farm boy, possible, but not a girl. You had to be insignificant in every way."

"So it has been, Father, and I have thrived."

Wilhelm observed Galeena's manner of dress and grooming and smiled. He was pleased to see her well presented.

"Now my dear child, shall we discuss your evening?"

Galeena most certainly did not want to talk about sleeping in her bed with a strange man. She grasped her wrist behind her back and swayed apprehensively from side to side. She replied, "I'd rather talk about Mother's belongings. May I have the key to her chests?"

"What do you seek? I can tell you anything you need to know about her."

"My preference is to learn of her memories on my own. I do not wish to have an audience."

"The parchments will be useless to you. I've hired scholars to view the scrolls, but no one has been able to translate them."

"Father, I can translate them! The language and symbols mother scripts are for Boersen daughters only."

"Are you certain? Do you think Lukah could read them?"

"Lukah is not a Boersen. He's..."

Galeena did not complete her thought. Lukah's paternity was not to be discussed. Wilhelm claimed her brother as his own and there was never to be a mention of any difference between them.

Wilhelm felt a momentary sting, but he did not dwell on the reality of his son's conception and birth. "You have been concealed from this world for your protection just as Lukah has been concealed from Jaegar for his. A day will come where your identity is revealed, and you should know a plan has been set for Lukah to be announced as an heir as well."

Having to share her parentage with her brother could mean that he would receive the crown of Northanglia. "Father, Lukah may not want the responsibilities of your throne. Have you asked him how he feels about being named an heir to Eichman, Alexar, Adelia, and Wilhelm?"

"I have not."

"You may want to have this conversation with him before you have it with me. I have always been told that I am named the future Queen of Gudsfelt, Northanglia and soon Solsworth. I accept. Lukah prefers being a nameless farmer, a revered commander, and a silent royal."

"We shall see... as soon as I hear from him again, we shall see."

Exhausted by what-ifs and premature scenarios, Galeena reminded her father of her request, "The key, Father?"

"You haven't forgotten those scrolls?"

"I have not, nor do I intend to."

"Do you intend on telling me why they are suddenly so important to you?"

If Galeena told any form of the truth, her father would, for a second time during their conversation, be reminded of Jaegar's role in her mother's life. She decided to avoid offering a direct response. "My hope is that I will know what I am looking for when I find it."

"Respectable answer. Thus, if you feel you are prepared for all the truths Adelia may have recorded, then you have my blessing to retrieve her documents."

Wilhelm walked to his desk and selected two keys from a leather strap. "One is for the door to her private chamber and the other unlocks the standing cabinet containing her bound histories and rolled parchments. Though I am unable to read the language of the Norse, I know every story."

"Why are you allowing this, Father?"

"It will keep you in my house and away from your own!"

King Wilhelm did not want to accept what Galeena's father already knew; she had formed an infatuation with an enemy. After all, she was part Viking and that blood line was a strong one.

Chapter 10

Galeena rushed from her father's strategy room to her mother's standing closet. She unlocked the cabinet doors, placed several of the volumes on a table, and she began reading.

Thankfully, she quickly realized that Adelia had placed all of the parchments in an order. Galeena only needed to search the shelves until she found the documentation of their travels to Gudsfelt. When those stories appeared, she slowed her pace.

Reading Adelia's account of the thirty nights spent at her childhood home reminded Galeena of events both pleasant and otherwise that she had forgotten. Silently, she created a vision of their visit from her own memories as she read.

King Alexar, ordered and arranged our voyage to Gudsfelt. Twas my suspicion he sought an opportunity to visit Olivia. Wilhelm, our children, and I were all anxiously anticipating our travels each for a different reason.

Wilhelm longed to see the legendary Gudsfelt and meet the king who held tightly to his claim upon all of the women in his line. Galeena was just past nine years of life and she was ready to be away from Castleton, Driesel, and the army of men and boys who relentlessly followed, teased, and guarded her. Lukah would not admit to anyone what was held in his heart, but I knew he prayed incessantly for an opportunity to even have a glimpse of the man who fathered him.

As for me, I wanted everything! I wanted to see my mother, the father who raised me, the grandfather who adored me, the people I could possibly rule someday, the countryside, and of course my childhood home: my precious Styrke's farm.

Although going to Gudsfelt was going to be a relief from the constant charades Wilhelm and I had orchestrated, it was not going to be without its own challenges.

Galeena's existence had been disclosed, though the true year of her birth had been falsified. She was a sprite of a child, so sharing that she was younger than her actual age was simply another protection for her future.

Lukah did not exist at all according to my Norse family. He had always been told that a man named Jaegar of Styrkeson was his father, but I had yet to be strong enough to reveal to Jaegar or my family that Lukah was of their blood.

Alexar loved that secret. He loved my son, his grandson, and I believe he had made arrangements with the church for Lukah to have his share of entitlements. Alexar has a male blood descendant and he is quite proud of him. Wilhelm, he loves Lukah as his own.

Again, I believe there are strategies at play amongst the Northanglian men in my life as far as my son is concerned. Whether or not I shall ever be privy to their plots, only time will tell.

Galeena squinted at the implications written about her brother. No rumors had ever surfaced of his power or preference over her, but that did not mean that a path of rule was not being established for him. The pure love she felt for Lukah usurped even the slightest thought of jealousy. She was there to learn of Torren's interactions with her mother. Possible scenarios would not be allowed to distract her. Besides, she was enjoying the research and the sound of her mother's voice in her head.

Preparations for the visit began weeks prior to our departure. Lukah was forced to spend all of the daylight hours out of any and all shelters. He was even relieved of his clothing on most days. It was quite a sight and my modest little boy hated me for such an assignment. My joy was full though. I remained at Wilhelm's farm in Chatsworth with my Lukah, and I would close my eyes tightly at sunset each day so he could enter our humble home and replace his coverings. Lukah would yell and order me to turn my back as if I were one of his subordinates. Oh, those blessed days with him. No one existed in the world apart from him and me.

The result of his complexion darkening to a tone similar of the native Anglians was his hair becoming significantly lighter. It became the purest silvery white I'd ever seen. He glowed like the angel he is beneath the moon beams. I could find him at night because he shone like a spirit orb in the fields. I wanted to change nothing about him. Oh the despair of adding the dye from the blackened walnuts to my child's God given gift. My maternal instincts said every decision I made was the wrong one. However, I continued onward.

Looking upon Lukah made my heart ache for Jaegar. Our child was his graven image in every way. He should know this wonderful person we created. Each gaze upon our son caused a remembrance for my Jaegar. As we grew and aged together, he was a demanding, protective and exceptionally affectionate child. The boy I loved as a brother was gentle and discerning. The man I loved as a husband was cunning, ambitious and ruthless. I wondered if Lukah would grow to be like Wilhelm or like his father.

As for my Galeena, she was going to love not having to forsake being in trousers and laden with weaponry. However, she was taken from the village, delivered to the fortress and kept indoors so she would appear fair like me. She became a caged bird as we prepared her for our travels to Gudsfelt. Dreisel added spices and the juices of putrid fruits to Galeena's hair until it bore a soft golden hue like the warmth of a sunset. She hardly recognized herself and Dreisel said she spent countless daylight hours looking at her reflection.

Our aim was that our daughter look more like a Norse child and less like an Anglian. Twas not her identity that was being forged. All would know her as mine and Wilhelm's child. What we wanted was for her description to be that of a Viking. If enemies prowled, they would return to their leaders with false attributes.

The final challenge we all faced was training ourselves to never mention the name Galeena. Every Anglian in our midst would have to refer to Galeena as Helene at all times. This task was going to be difficult for us adults, and we all imagined it to be nearly impossible for the children. New habits were instated and each of us began our own training.

The resulting games of having been held captive and being mere moments from an execution are internally destructive. I long for Galeena's sixteenth annual when all will be revealed, she will be married and if my grandfather, King Boersen, has passed with no heirs, she may be Queen of Gudsfelt. Though I am in line, I contemplate if or when I shall bequeath my title to my daughter. Soon, all will settle soon.

"Encouraging, Mother," Galeena commented. She closed the leather covering over the portion she had read and began scanning more documents. She paused again when another anecdote caught her attention.

Lukah traveled with us as an orphan. His age was revealed truthfully to those who inquired as approximately ten years, which would have been an appropriate age to begin training for his future duties as a soldier for our king and nation.

Upon disembarking from King Alexar's ship, my Grandfather Boersen rushed past all present to collect his great-granddaughter. Despite understanding the ritual that daughters bear King Boersen's name only when the father is deemed unworthy, Wilhelm held his peace as Grandfather called, "My Helene, our third generation Daughter of Boersen, join your papa."

Galeena was less concerned with the greeting than she was with her dearest life-mate. She knew our family's secret was important, but seeing Lukah's hurt at being ignored by their patriarch forced her to cry uncontrollably. Twas not a state we often witnessed with our daughter.

"Dearest one, speak your troubles," Grandfather coaxed in an infantile tone.

Galeena pointed to Lukah, unable to speak.

Our grandfather hushed her with great gentility and said to her in Norse, "Have you bonded with your servant my little love?"

Tears soaked her cheeks as she nodded an inaudible affirmation.

Refusing to allow the pain of his newest daughter to continue, Grandfather Boersen returned to Lukah and took his hand. Lukah smiled at the inclusion. He dearly wanted to be loved by my family. My own spirit was comforted by my grandfather's actions toward my son.

Alexar, who was to appear to have dominion over Lukah, nodded respectfully to King Boersen showing his appreciation for acceptance of both children present. Olivia immediately felt a connection to Lukah and suspected his true identity. She slowly approached him as not to draw attention to her sudden infatuation with the little boy. She whispered something in Lukah's ear, and he affirmed her comment. Looking back, I believe she eased his heart by sharing her knowledge of who he is and that her undying love for him was equal to her love for Galeena. She took the other hand of the grandson she proudly shared with Styrke.

From that moment, for the remainder of our thirty days in Gudsfelt, Lukah enjoyed his anonymity. He was free. Styrke also found a natural attachment to him. Perhaps his ease with my son was due to his guardianship of Jaegar's son, Torren. Styrke took a personal interest in teaching Lukah many of his own secrets to being a good soldier and protector. I wanted to be with the men, but mother and I spent our time with the animals, on long walks around White Crested Cove, or gathering with women and children telling stories of our lifestyles in Northanglia.

Removing Galeena from the reach of all of the men was quite an adjustment for her as well. She was to perform her duties as the princess of two nations. Her posture was to be somewhat pretentious though always polite, and she was to be genteel though confident. Her true nature was deeply suppressed during our stay in Grandfather Boersen's garrison.

No one was to know that Wilhelm and I actually placed her in our soldiers' camp with a governess.

Five celebratory nights were spent in the Boersen home before trekking to our family's farm near the Danemour border. Small troops were dispatched ahead of us, and some trailed after us, to ensure our protection from any Danes who might have received notification of our arrival. Our group contained three Daughters of Boersen and two kings of the western lands. Prevention of attacks was not to be taken lightly.

"So, Mother, you have written that you know of Torren's resemblance to Jaegar. You would have met him at the time of writing this memory. Hopefully, that encounter will appear soon."

Galeena once again delicately closed one heavy volume and began another. This time she made a conscious effort to pass over all details of their seven day caravan to Styrke's and Olivia's home. Her eyes paused when she saw Jaegar's name on a page.

The ache within me as we approached my family's farm felt as if I were being choked. My children ran ahead of us adults while my own strides barely moved me forward. To hold the entire scene tightly against my breast was my soul's desire.

My father, Styrke, turned to collect the emotion hidden behind in my eyes. He knew my heart in a way that no one else could ever comprehend. He knew my craving was to rejoin my beloved Jaegar in the place of our innocence.

Hearing Lukah and Galeena's squeals returned me to my own childhood. I remembered with great clarity my life amongst that landscape, playing beside those peacefully flowing waters, running across those grassy fields. I stood surrounded by those heaven sent mountains with my throat being crushed because every single memory had Jaegar in it.

From his stance behind me, Wilhelm pressed the length of his body to mine. His inviting hands were placed on either side of my waist, and his accompanying whispers reset my heart. "Tis time to create new memories, Adelia. Lukah and Galeena need their mother's full presence. Soon enough we will be back on the shores of Northanglia, and they will be returned to their caregivers. You belong with us. This visit has a single purpose. Time. Time for us all. Time for you and me." A warm, loving, sensual kiss moved from my ear to my neck. I leaned into his lips and smiled.

I turned my attention to him and pulled him to me for another kiss. I pleaded with my eyes and my softly spoken words, "Please do not ever give up on me. I love you."

My husband knew my struggles waxed and waned like the moon and the tides. Wilhelm said to me, "I accepted you and your son being fully aware that he was going to be your constant reminder of the path you once walked. To hate Jaegar, would be to hate our beloved child. Before I ever met you, I knew your heart loved deeply. Twas not my expectation that receiving you as my wife would be free from all challenges. You must know though, I'll not share your body, and I'll not share your life; I will only share your past."

Every member of our party, Alexar, Wymer, Olivia, and Styrke, had continued their progression to our home. With the guilt of hindering their advance lifted, I was able to relax and reassure Wilhelm that he never needed to fear sharing my present or future with anyone other than our children. After an intensely intimate embrace, I pulled his hand and led him into the dense population of trees.

From the midst of our life giving audience, a tree with a wide girth was selected and my husband was pushed back against it. I had felt his readiness the moment his fingertips tightened about my waist and his lips brushed downward to where my neck and shoulder meet. He did not touch me as he left me in charge of releasing all that bound him from my access. We shared smiles that lured the other with unmistakeable passion. And when he could withhold himself no longer from grasping me, he lowered me to the floor of the forest and encompassed us both with elation and pleasure.

No interlude with my beloved Wilhelm was ever insignificant or routine. Never in all of our days together were our intimate exchanges treated as a way to pass the time or gratify only oneself. We were both fully committed and fully satisfied during every meaningful act as husband and wife.

Chapter 11

“Tis time for our next meal. Have you found what you seek, Galeena?”

Startled and a bit uncomfortable with her father’s sudden appearance as she concluded reading about such a private interlude, Galeena gasped, turned and attempted to hide what lay before her. She stammered, “Oh, uh, not yet. However, I have learned and been reminded of many other events of the past years. I would like to take some of these parchments to my room and continue my study there.”

Wilhelm knew she was going to be encountering revelations of her mother’s deepest thoughts. “Have you discovered anything I should know about in those rolls and bindings?”

“No, Father, but may I take this one with me?”

“I am afraid not. Your mother would never hear of you separating her documents. They stay here, locked and secure. You may visit them at will, but you will not remove them.”

“Father, they will be secure. I’ll care for them.”

"Tis not an issue that we shall negotiate. Perhaps if you tell me exactly what it is that you hunt, I will be able to expedite your search."

"I am reviewing the histories of our journey to Gudsfelt. I want to know of Mother's encounters while there."

Her interest in that particular month caused an uneasiness to rise and Wilhelm questioned, "Why? What reason do you have for needing any remembrance of that time?"

"I want to know if Adelia met a Viking child while in Gudsfelt."

"I can tell you, she did. I believe she had at least two encounters with a young boy. If there were more, that was withheld or forgotten by her."

"Will you share what you know?" Galeena was excited by her father's honesty.

"I will share... but we shall eat now. Tidy your mother's documents and come."

Galeena set to replacing the books she had withdrawn from the shelves.

As she worked, Wilhelm offered, "You met the boy to whom I refer. He was with his father at the docks in Danemour. He held tightly to your mother. When I saw them all together I approached and led her to our ship."

The memory was very vague. Galeena halted her chore and searched her mind's eye. Awareness came. She had watched from afar. She recalled Lukah running to a strange man and wrapping his arms about his waist. When Adelia rushed after her son, a boy held to her. "I do have faded images of those moments. Why would the boy cling to Mother? Who was he?"

"You know who he was. He formed an attachment because he had spied and followed her around Styrke's lands. While the men hunted, she spent a night coddling him so he would not be alone in the woodlands."

"Where was his father?"

"Not a care that I have. Come."

"Wait. At the docks..."

"Come, Galeena. You need not question me any longer. You know who the boy was."

"Yes, I do know of him. His name is Torren and he is Jaegar's son."

"Now that you know the boy was left defenseless and unattended in the wilderness by his father, you also know why Lukah was withheld from that life. Jaegar left Olivia and Styrke to raise his only child while he sailed about the seas attacking villages and earning his ranking in Vidar's army."

Even though she did not know him, Galeena didn't care for the accusations against Jaegar. She said, "Jaegar saved my mother's life, correct?"

"Stefan, saved your mother's life, meaning I saved your mother's life. Tis why you carry the name."

"Yes, but *Stefan* was able to free himself and Adelia only with Jaegar's guidance and assistance."

Wilhelm was not going to warm to her defense of the man.

Galeena added, “Your other grievance against him is due to his abandonment of his son? Father, you and mother are not so different than him.”

“Dare you compare us to that man? You have been within my reach every moment of your life. Lukah has been given freedoms and provisions and luxuries of which no child could dream.”

“I believe Torren has shared a very similar existence.”

“You force my core to grow ill with this discussion. We are to eat and you will return to your room. You’ve had enough reminiscing for one day.”

Wilhelm held out is hand and awaited the placement of the keys upon his palm.

“Father, I’ll return the keys, but please, do not forbid me from further knowledge contained within these scrolls.”

“You shall be allowed access again, but not today. We shall first enjoy our evening’s feast.”

“Thank you. I’ll not argue with you again. You have my promise.” Galeena kissed Wilhelm on his cheek and he kissed her back. “I do want to tell you though, I will be going to my cavern at Broodenshire before first light. You’ll not see me again until our guests have arrived. I believe I shall collect twelve peaceful sleeps. Is that permitted?”

“You may part unescorted. However, I insist you return here on the fourth sunrise after tomorrow. I have decided to expedite your wedding announcement. The banquet in honor of your binding ceremony will be held a week earlier than we planned. You must arrive before the gathering for your gown fitting. We will have strategies prepared for removal of the Norsemen as well. Your input is crucial as is your participation."

"Before I rest this night, I shall deliver to you a sealed notice containing my thoughts. You may discuss them with your advisors and with Lukah. Tis my assumption he will arrive very soon."

Galeena placed her hand in the bend of her father's arm and he escorted his daughter to the dining hall.

* * *

Their meal lasted into the night and when they had their fill, Wilhelm returned to his suite. Galeena bypassed the offer of a night spent in her elegant room for a return to the soldiers' quarters below the main grounds. Once there, she traded her shimmering gray silk gown for her black tunic, leggings and boots. As she stooped to exit the stone walled garrison through a hidden opening, she donned a sly smile. "What expression shall I collect in the moonlight dear Torren when I arrive at your side this night? But first, I have one task to complete." Galeena reentered the passageway.

Dressed in her dark clothing, Galeena entered her father's office and retrieved the chamber and cabinet keys from his bureau. She proceeded to her mother's private suite.

Her steps made absolutely no sounds, and her fitted clothing did not have the swishes and drags of her gowns. The stone walls and floors were without echoes.

Accustomed to self-entry into various properties, Galeena's heart beat remained steady as she arrived to Adelia's chamber. Carefully, she slipped the first key into its custom slot and slowly turned until the latch released. The knob was twisted and she eased into the room.

At the cabinet, Galeena worried less about the minor sounds that resulted from its opening. She had carefully placed the volume she wanted atop the others instead of in its rightful order. Her shoulders lifted with glee at collecting the folder, re-locking the storage door and being able to exit without detection.

"Stealing from my house you thieving child?"

"Huh!" She gasped and spun.

Wilhelm snuffed a small laugh. Galeena could see him sitting in a chair beside her mother's velvet settee. A small fire glowed beside him. She had not thought to check for anyone in the lounge area of the room because a fire was always kept burning for her mother. Twas a benefit to her because it gave just enough glow to keep her from stumbling.

Galeena defended, "I am neither a thief nor a child, and I am not stealing. These parchments belong to me. They are written in a language that only I can translate; that makes them mine."

"Ah, a very wise retort my child." Wilhelm released another soft chuckle. He raised and began a threatening saunter toward her. As he approached, he pointed to what she held and where she stood, and he said, "I'll offer a counter argument; they are in my home, in my wife's room, and being held secure by my key. All of which, make them mine. What shall your next argument be?"

"No offense shall be taken, Father? If I speak my mind?"

"I'll allow you to speak openly, for I am most curious to hear your negotiations."

"Very well... this entire castle technically belongs to me. I am the heir of Eichman, Alexar, and Adelia through her only legal and God honored marriage. You are here as a result of marrying the Queen of Northanglia." She smiled a sly and defiant smile and said, "I allow you to inhabit *my* home."

"That was exactly what I thought you would say." Wilhelm stopped, leaving a space between them, then teased, "You are mostly correct. However, I am king and also a rightful heir by my own bloodline. Therefore, this," he waved his arms, "and all property contained herein actually belongs to me. It only becomes yours upon my death."

Her head shook back and forth and she tucked her lip into one side of her cheek, "Father, I've no energy left to play games with you. May I take this with me or not?"

"Hmm... I suppose you did go to a lot of trouble for it so it must hold your deepest interest... you may take it. Please return it though. Your mother's heart placed a great deal of value on those words. That is her entire life."

"You should also know that Grandmother Olivia's scrolls are in here as well."

Wilhelm's head tilted, his eyebrows raised, and he said, "That pleases me. I did not know that. Have you begun your own histories?"

"They are to begin upon marriage. Apparently marriage is the beginning of a very boring existence. The women in my family find they have nothing better to do with their time than put quill to ink to paper once they leave the altar. I thought fighting to be tiring. Documenting may be even more of a curse than slinging blades at enemies."

A roaring laughter was released from her father. "Oh the life of a wife. You'll grow accustomed to your new role. Henry will arrive soon. I'm anxious for you to meet him. Tis quite possible, you will be able to fulfill your duties as a wife, a mother, a scribe, a hunter, and a soldier. The Prince of Solsworth is quite congenial. Surely you will be in charge of your roles in his homeland."

"Ugh... a husband... speak not of it any more this night. Knowing that you have expedited my nuptials is strain enough on my bones. I wish to return to my chamber."

"Then go. Blessings to you this night my love. Send your prayers to the heavens and sleep well."

"Bon soir, mon père."

"Bon soir."

Chapter 12

"I know these parchments will contain all I need to know. Thankfully, even if another's eyes gaze upon them, they shall not be comprehensible. Norsemen are illiterate with the exception of the few related to King Boersen. And even of that group, only Annika, Olivia and I have been taught this language."

Galeena returned to her quarters to retrieve a leather pouch. She placed the protected pages inside and parted once again for her cottage in Castleton.

Wanting to arrive in silence meant she would have to walk. This mattered not because her aim was to leave before light on her very own horse.

The approach to the village was a cautious one. With her elimination of the Viking guards the night before, she surmised the group would have increased their number of watchmen while also expanding the surveyed area.

Her expectations were not incorrect. There were men and women scattered throughout the fields on the north side of the road.

She muttered, "The challenge has been increased, but I've traversed these moors and woods since I could walk. It will be interesting to see if I am capable of evading such highly trained and keen Norsemen."

Galeena stepped lightly in a crouched stance. Every few meters, she paused to listen for breathing or shuffling. Each time a watchman was detected, she used their location to create a new path. This continued until she reached the northern edge of her little town. Her final task was to reach her own house on the south side of the center road.

There was no desire within her to follow the outer edge and cross beneath the cover of the trees to the west, so she had to simply hope she could hide in the shadows. Wearing all black and having hair the color of the richest soil would all aid in her ability to succeed.

Galeena slid from shadow to shadow and at the open road, she crossed slowly and upright. If she would have been attacked, she wanted to react with alertness and accuracy.

When she stepped to the side of her home, she heard voices. Two men were walking from the western woods. She crouched once again and held very still until they passed. And with that, she was free to enter her cottage.

Beneath her chicken coop was a cellar door that also opened into her great-room near the hearth. She crept to it, lifted, lowered down one ladder, then ascended another to complete her entry.

Once again, she stood next to her fireplace peering at the Icelander sleeping peacefully in her bed. Galeėna stepped to his side, pointed a knife at him, and said, "You really should have your own guard."

Torren opened his eyes and rasped, "I have one hundred of them. Did you slaughter them all this time?"

She snickered, "Perhaps in my dreams. This night, I harmed none."

"How do you do that?"

"Tis none of your concern."

"It is my concern if I am going to continually awaken to a mercenary with a dagger at my throat."

"I am not a mercenary. I am a simple soldier." Galeena shrugged with humility.

Torren raised up onto his elbows. "What purpose do you serve by visiting me again? Well, other than practicing your training."

"I have no purpose and I need no further training. However, I do intend on collecting my horse and vanishing before sunrise."

"Appearing unnoticed is a skill you have perfected." He yawned, then asked, "Have you truly no reason for arriving here?"

Galeena suddenly realized that her only purpose was to see him, but she was certainly not going to disclose that information. She responded, “Would you like for me to leave?”

“No. I would not.” Torren pointed to his left, “Look, I kept your sleeping dress next to me where you left it. Join me again.”

“Shall you judge my next statement?” she asked.

“Never. Speak your mind, Galeena.”

She smiled, lowered her blade and said, “I’m quite happy to have the invitation.” She leaned over the man who lie, at least half undressed, beneath her silk and linen coverings, and she pinched the collar. With a flirtatious and excruciating tease, she pulled, allowing her gown to slide across Torren’s bare chest.

He enjoyed the scent, the softness and the taunt.

“Shall I be allowed the vision of you changing from your battle garments to your sleeping dress?”

“Not *yet*,” she replied as she walked away from his sight.

Her tone and words filled him with a hope he should not be experiencing. Jaegar had given him one assignment, and falling in love with an enemy soldier was not it.

Galeena moved to a shadowed corner, and for added insurance of there being as little revelation as possible to the man who would most likely spy, she turned her back as she removed that which covered the top of her body. The gown was then raised and lowered. Once she was covered, the removal of her boots and leg coverings was completed.

A lift of her softly curled hair allowed it to drape like a cape about her back and shoulders. She then turned and stepped into a moonbeam.

He had been watching her every move.

"You could not gift me even a moment of privacy as I changed into my sleeping garment?"

No verbal reply was given. Galeena received only a smile and one turn of his head to indicate a negative response.

"The anticipation of your presence between these sheets is nearly murderous," Torren confessed. "Every drop of my blood rushes through me and I fight utter confusion."

"Tis lust that you experience, Norseman."

"No. I think not, Anglian. Join me... with haste. I must envelop you with my entire being."

"No. I think not." Galeena fed his words back to him. "I'm not your prisoner who must follow your commands. I stand here perfectly capable of controlling my... hmm... my *desires*."

By this time, Torren was sitting up in her bed. After she refused his invitation, he tossed the cloth that rested over his lap. Her curiosity was secretly satisfied.

"Cover yourself at once!" Galeena shouted whilst turning her back.

A reply was not offered, and she could only listen.

He stood and moved closer until he could reach her. His breath tickled the nervous hairs on her neck.

"You may face me once again. And, try not to shout this time. The village sleeps. Unless you wish for us both to face an inquiry, you should keep your location a secret. Please, turn."

With intention, Galeena kept her eyes lowered. If Torren remained exposed, he would continue to have only her back to view. Her chin pressed to the front of her shoulder. Her eyes were closed. She slowly eased around peering toward the floor until she saw that he held a drape for modesty about his waist. She smiled.

Her apprehension revealed her innocence and her single fear: breach of her purity.

"I am not as men of the north are rumored to be. I'll not harm you."

Torren's gentle assurance comforted Galeena. He took her hand and pulled her toward him as he moved slowly backward toward her bed. His lure was so strong she could not even formulate thoughts nor arguments. He guided her with hardly a connection to her fingertips. At the edge of her haven, he lifted his chin inviting her to sit. Without question she did as requested. Still holding the blanket for covering, Torren knelt placing himself between her knees.

She smiled.

He raised his hand, held her head, and leaned forward.

"Tea?" Galeena asked, just before his lips reached hers.

The slightest hint of disappointment was revealed when Torren raised from his position, and the corner of his mouth tucked into his cheek. He had moved close enough to experience that coveted first passionate kiss, but alas, Galeena was not quite ready to permit it.

She wanted to grin, but a tight lipped, wide smile shown her amusement adequately enough. When her soon to be bunk mate did not immediately move to fulfill her request, she firmly nudged his thigh with her foot.

Torren said with jest, "Tis apparent I am not moving quickly enough for you, Your Royal Highness. Do forgive me. I'm afraid I've never worked in service. My lack of experience is to blame for my lack of enthusiasm. I fear my next words will severely disappoint. I have no tea prepared."

"Be not afraid Sir, warming and fetching a cup of tea for your hostess will not be the death of you. However, *not* fetching my tea might."

Torren laughed. He then asked, "If the precious woman before me is accustomed to having tea brought to her whilst she rests abed, do confess, who generally performs this task for you?"

"You are mistaken, tis not my habit to partake of my libation from bed. However, in this moment, I believe the distraction will be to our benefit. If you would proceed to prepare, then the preparer can also provide?"

"Such magic with words!"

Torren's laughter was like music to her.

Upon realization of something, he immediately shared his thought, "By fetching you tea, you will remain right where I am wanting you. Perhaps your plan to evade my interest will not work for much longer." He leaned close to her and said in a sultry tone, "You need not stir. Recline Miss, your tea will be in your hands and to your lips in moments."

Torren stood and teased a drop of the blanket. When Galeena quickly covered her eyes, he laughed and said, "It would be wise for you to grow accustomed to the male form. You appear to be beyond age for matrimony."

"I'm not a stranger to visions of male nudity. I have just never been in this situation with a man who has forsaken all clothing. Refraining from mocking will be to your benefit."

"You speak the truth. My apologies. Shall we be patient with one another?"

The situation in which she found herself may have been new, but Galeena was not naive. The thoughts of the man in her house were not mysteries, nor did she find them offensive. An accepting smile and an alluring glint in her eyes was received by Torren. The appearance of anticipation glazed with apprehension could not be mistaken. He moved to retrieve two cups of tea. Torren placed a kettle over the dying fire. He stirred the embers and waited.

Upon his return, he sat quietly at her side and while sipping politely, Galeena mentioned, "The night is escaping us."

"That is because you refuse to allow the *day* to end."

A small snuff of a laugh showed her agreement with this claim. Galeena said, "I feel I can rest now. I will soon need to rise, gather more of my belongings and part for Broodenshire.

Tis my guess that I will not be able to return to this home until you and your cohorts sail from our shores. All present will continue to grow more watchful day by day, night by night."

"At last, we can lay ourselves and this busy day to rest." Torren smiled as he took the empty porcelain cup from Galeena and placed both dishes on the planked floor. After shifting closer to her he said, "You are the first woman who has ever held my interest."

Even though Galeena was clearly more inexperienced than Torren, she was not immune to thoughts and wonderings of the opposite sex. Additionally, *neither* had ever encountered someone who impressed themselves into their hearts so quickly. Galeena needed a little more from him though. "Torren?"

"Yes?"

"What is your age?"

"I am nearing twenty."

As expected, he wasted no time implementing his pursuit. When his lips moved closer, she whispered, "Why me?"

The distance between them was not increased. He said, "I have suppressed all desires. I have not felt the almost uncontrollable urge to fully pursue a woman until I saw you run from this home and debilitate men twice your size." He then asked, "Why me? You have now returned to me twice. Why?"

Galeena giggled. "Last night, my purpose truly was to kill you. This night, I returned to look upon you. I thought of arriving and leaving without waking you, and I could have. But, seeing you in my bed, I had no choice but to hear your voice. My actions are very reckless, but you hold my interest. I simply cannot help myself."

"If you are a soldier—"

"I am," she inserted.

Torren rephrased his thought, "As a young woman who is also a soldier, why are you not married or even promised?"

An honest reply was given, "I have been reared amongst thousands of men. I have found them all to be repulsive... until you placed your family's heirloom to my throat last night. Your smile during that single action seemed to have opened my eyes. Suddenly, I felt I should know you."

"A connection," he proudly reminded her.

She laughed and agreed, "A connection."

Torren was done waiting to touch her. He could no longer refrain from satisfying his one single need, a kiss.

Galeena kept her eyes on his as he pressed her onto her back with his upper body. He then extended himself at her side. His fingers slipped between hers, and he pulled her hand to his lips.

Not yearning for control in that moment, Galeena eased closer to him and waited. Lying face to face, Torren buried his hand in her hair and with great love, he gave her no choice in their embrace. They shared their first meaningful kiss.

Full participation from Galeena was all she had to give him. His eagerness was genuinely shared, and she wanted him to feel her acceptance of him. Comforted by the absence of inhibitions, he moved his lips to her ear, and his hot breath exhaled the words, “You are every dream I’ve ever had. Do you object to my hands performing their own exploration?”

A gentle, though audible giggle, joined by a soft tug upon his waist invited Torren to satisfy his curiosities. Lying on his side, facing her, he attempted to slide even closer. Galeena placed her leg over his thigh, hooked her heel at the back of his knee, and she intimately positioned him. Torren whispered, “Shall I die from the torture of restraint?”

She replied softly, “I’ll not allow it. All you have is welcome to search or wander about. Liberty is yours to receive your fill as you wish. I only ask—”

“You need not ask,” he assured her.

His heartbeat increased. Heat emanated from his flesh. Though he tried to hide it, she heard his struggle to regulate the strengthening of each breath.

Torren’s left hand held her at the blade of her shoulder. It then slipped down to her ribs, then to the furrow of her waist. Carefully, his fingertips circled and pressed as his hand moved lower to the roundness of her hip.

“May I?” he asked.

Galeena nodded.

Grateful, Torren smiled as he gripped her gown and pulled it measure by measure until nothing prevented the full contact of his palm upon her.

When his eyes lowered, she placed a finger beneath his chin and lifted. He reached upward and kissed her deeply.

"Trust," he coaxed.

The closing of her eyes, the relaxing of her shoulders, and the tightening of her calf, were the only replies he needed.

Before Torren eased himself fully onto her, he reached downward from her thigh to the top of her foot. The repetitive caressing told her of his amazement. "Your skin is as smooth as the silken blanket that lay bundled at our feet. You have not a single flaw."

His compliment was absorbed. Galeena did not tense. She followed his natural lead when he eased himself to her center and pushed against her. The night dress was raised even more to expose her stomach. Torren tasted just below Galeena's birth scar. He then kept his bottom lip in contact as he moved his lips to her heart. There, he pressed another firm and loving kiss.

The thin fingers that held knives to his throat entangled into his hair. Gently, she pulled and massaged while Torren immersed himself in the passion of their mutual enjoyment.

Torren's affection breached her coarse surface and descended to a depth within her that had never been touched. The man Galeena was supposed to hate was not a monster. He was gentle, loving, and keenly affectionate. How many men had she killed over the years had wives waiting for their return? How many women were left longing for this very experience just once more from their husband?

Torren felt her core tighten. Each of her ribs were secure in his warm hands. First he pressed his forehead to her center. Then, he raised his eyes to observe her face, not daring to remove his lips from their placement over Galeena's heart. Her brow was slightly pinched. One barely noticeable wrinkle exposed the sadness she felt as she stared at images generated in her mind. He watched one tear crawl from the corner of her eye, then another slid down her temple into her hair.

In a deep, yet soft tone, Torren attempted to soothe the woman he was loving. "Each tear released represents a single pain, but each one also heals the same pain. How many recoveries do you desire this night, Galeena? I shall find comfort in remaining with you until your strength returns."

A small jolt and one deep inhale preceded a silent cry. She did not want to show weakness. Galeena had not expressed complete sorrow in all of her independent years. The only memory she had of allowing more than a tear or two to be seen was when she and her brother sat in their father's arms and privately mourned the passing of their precious mother. But, this was the moment that six years of aching would be released.

Torren repositioned so he could hold Galeena against his chest.

Guilt, lies, hatred, love, loneliness, anger, exhaustion: every emotion was a response to knowing that she was days away from being asked by her father and brother to deceive, then murder the man who held her in his arms.

Chapter 13

The summer season was soon to end, and the rain had chilled the cottage. Elated by the exchange between himself and Galeena during the night, Torren was unable to remain still; he needed a task. He arose and rebuilt the fire that had faded while they slept. That did not require much energy, so he then set to rummaging for food.

Galeena listened to the rustling as he searched her shelves. “I have a pen of chickens behind my house,” she rasped.

Slowly the latch was lifted as if he were suddenly afraid of waking her. She scoffed, listened to the muted thumps of his heavy steps upon the wooden planks of the porch, then the crunches of his boots as he walked along the side wall to the rear of her home.

The disturbed hens clucked, squawked and complained. Galeena knew how they must have felt when the stranger shuffled them about in search of their eggs. She too had been jostled by the Viking.

After placing eggs into the leather pouch he had found hanging by the door, Torren returned. He entered, then placed the sack that contained their morning meal on the table.

An unexpected stillness caused Galeena to watch him. Torren stared at the back wall of her cottage. He spoke in a hushed tone, “Hmm, I continue to wonder, how did you enter while I slept last night?” Shaking his head, he stood, rested his hands on his hips, and noticing she was looking at him, he said, “You are very entertaining. Everything about you holds my attention.”

“May I please sleep?”

“It appears you no longer plan to part before the sun reveals all that grows and works upon the lands. Therefore, I see no reason for you not to gather as much energy as you feel you’ll need for this day.”

“Yes, tis apparent I’ll not win a race with the sunrise.”

“Then you may prolong your slumber, for now. You have my vow of silence. I have no intentions of cooking until you’ve had your fill of rest.”

Torren placed the kettle he had refilled over the flames. While he waited by the fire for the water to boil, he stared. Galeena tried closing her eyes but both were feeling hypnotized by the flickering flames.

“Shall I rise, Torren?”

“No, not yet. I am considering a return to bed. I am not certain I have the will to wait patiently for the beautiful young woman who lies across this room to join me.”

Galeena closed her eyes and turned her back to him. His decision to sit at her hearth or rest at her side mattered not. A deep breath was inhaled, and before she had fully expelled the intake of air, her door abruptly opened and a Dane stood in their midst.

From his knelt position by the fire, Torren bound to his feet. Galeena turned and sat upright. She held her blanket to her heart with one hand while she sought a weapon with the other. Utter disappointment and fury filled her when she realized Torren had removed all methods of defense from her reach. This was the first time in her memory that she would have to rely solely upon a man for protection.

Though his initial expression was one of alarm, the man quickly shared a sinister smile. Torren eased himself between the doorway and the bed. Though the uninvited visitor leaned attempting another inspection, Torren commanded his attention. In Norse he said, "State your purpose Gunnar, then leave."

"That woman is not the reason we have come here."

Galeena feigned ignorance with a hint of fear.

"I am perfectly aware," Torren replied.

"You have one assignment," Gunnar chided as he leaned for another glance.

She glared.

The Viking studied her with a more discerning interest. He then added, "I am confident your father would allow you to keep her as a servant though. Have her sent to Gudsfelt on a slave ship. Enjoy her there." A sly smile appeared.

Torren replied, "The business between this woman and myself is none of your concern, nor my father's. Again, why have you come?"

Gunnar focused and frowned, "I came to request another meeting about our plans. Imagine my shock at the sight of this woman in your bed."

"How did you obtain such a sight?"

"There was no invasion of privacy for me to peer through the window. I shall not ignore that I know she was the one who slain our guards two nights past. They were killed with the same small blades she threw at many of our men the morning we arrived to this village." He looked to Galeena, pointed, and said, "She works off the debt for each life. When the others learn of her presence here, they will expect nothing less. Tis possible that only the arrival and intervention of the gods themselves will save her from a fate of slavery or public retribution."

"Tell me what he says Torren, and never remove my blades from my reach again."

Torren turned only the slightest bit toward Galeena so he would not take his concentration from Gunnar. He replied, "We shall discuss this exchange without an audience. I ask that you remain motionless and unarmed."

He then said to Gunnar, "She does not need an appearance from the gods. She has me."

"If you are not willing to hold her accountable for her offenses, then perhaps she can be traded." Gunnar studied Galeena once more despite Torren's protection. "Her king may find value in her. She has proven to our people that she could earn respect."

"The woman will be leaving today. No one else need fear her."

"Fear her? Is that what you believe? I don't fear her, nor will anyone else. She cannot kill us all."

"Torren, I hear the aggression in his tone. Speak to me."

Again Torren did not look at Galeena as he spoke. "This man's name is Gunnar. He demands your service, your torture or your death. I have assured him of your immediate departure with no more losses of the lives of our people."

Galeena roared with laughter. "You can make no such assurance on my behalf. I do as I please. And, this is *my* village! If opportunity arises to rid it of even one intruder as I leave, you be assured I will do just that."

Torren fully turned toward her and shouted, "Galeena! You stand no chance of surviving even until the sun reaches its peak in the sky if you do not accept my assistance and part peacefully."

Finalizing the discussion with Gunnar, Torren firmly stated to his partner, "She will go from us today. She will not return. I will join you post morning preparations. Do not come here seeking this Anglian again. Take your leave."

Gunnar backed out of the entry and stood stoic. Clearly he was not going to leave.

Torren stepped close to him and whispered in Norse, "She will lead us to the last Daughter of Boersen. She shall not be harmed, and you will not question my strategies." He then closed the door.

After securing the latch to prevent any further interruptions, Torren once again looked to Galeena. She lie in her bed. Feeling amused, one eyebrow raised as if mischievous plots entertained her thoughts.

He asked, "Why do you rest there with the appearance of a wolf who has spotted unprotected prey? You will be allowed freedom and safe exodus this day. I advise you not to stray from that single plan. Make no alterations to graciously mounting your horse and riding away. Do not circle back here again tonight. All are expecting such a visitation from you. I cannot withhold an army from pursuing punishment if you breach my agreement with them. Now, tell me why you smile at this situation."

"I smile because it has been a very long time since a man has disarmed me, ordered my plans, and stood between me and a potential target. Not many place themselves in protection of me. Generally, I am the protector, I am the one disarming others and standing in between the innocent and the attacker. I never anticipated that all of these actions would occur by an enemy. You should not have done that."

"Yes, I should have. Gunnar is not a Dane; he is of Gudsfelt. His purpose is to hold all accountable for their transgressions and ensure safe retrieval. I feel my purpose has become to keep you alive. Allow me to do that as I deem necessary. I may not know you, yet, but I do know them." He pointed toward the outside.

Galeena smiled again. She truly had never met a man with the ability to embed himself into her dreams and desires the way Torren had. Their eyes could find nothing else but the other's gaze. Torren finally returned her smile.

"You'll not place yourself in harm's way, at least not in my presence," he instructed.

"You'll not weaken me with your interferences. I must be able to defend myself at all times, Sir."

The man to whom Galeena was forming a quick attachment strode across the great-room moving slowly toward her. She gripped her blanket. He enjoyed seeing her tense. Even after their intimate exchange during the night, he still had not relieved her of her one and only fear.

When Torren reached the bedside, he knelt. Having only seen him at night, she was enraptured with the lure of his eyes. The most handsome and appealing man she had ever beheld wanted her. His eyes were almost devoid of any shade at all as they were nearly gray. Since he had not yet fully dressed, Galeena was able to admire how the sun had bronzed his skin. Torren's broad shoulders rounded down creating distinct shadows where the muscles blended at his upper arms. His unkempt hair fell just below his jawline.

Her eyes lowered for a moment as she wondered what his mother must have looked like. Was she beautiful or hardened by choices and battles? Then, the very instant Galeena began to worry if her choices could defile her own complexion, Torren exhaled a sigh of restraint. She looked to him again.

Without touching, nor attempting to touch her, he spoke softly and lovingly, "Please, I will beg only this once, ever, in this lifetime. Please, please resist recklessness. I ask that you allow me as much time with you as possible. Never deny me the joy and the right to be the only person you allow this close to you. Never deny me the joy and the right to be the only man who shares this bed or any bed with you. And, never deny me the joy and the right to feel the unique and deep connection with you that is only shared by two people who are bound solely to one another."

The solid ground upon which Galeena had always stood softened. She was bewitched. She wanted his words to be true. Though her heart was touched, she felt compelled to inquire, "Dare you play tricks on me with your affectionate words? I heard you whisper something to your countryman. Is your only aim to lure me and gain my trust?"

Taken aback and surprised, Torren protested, "No! I am sincere. My final message to Gunnar was an order to not return here nor scheme against you."

His expression and the sound of his voice were contemplated. She studied his eyes seeking changes to their black cores. He needed to know he had her confidence.

Galeena's hands relaxed and rested onto her lap. The deep rounded neckline of her gown allowed the chilled air to settle on her skin. She asked yet another question, "Before I make any such vows or promises, you must speak honestly to me, how many times have you made similar requests to other women?"

"I shall repeat myself if it will comfort you. You need not fear my sincerity. I have never spoken with such emotion to anyone. There is far too much pain to be received if one knows your true feelings. With you, however, I have no doubts that you share, to some extent, my sentiment."

Whether he was aware of it or not, his single fear had been released. Torren did not want to suffer the pain of unrequited love as his father had.

The knowledge of his deepest dread compelled Galeena to one confession before the furthering of his fondness toward her could be allowed. "Torren, I have been promised to the Prince of Solsworth. I am expected to marry him during my sixteenth annual celebrations. King Wilhelm will make our nuptials public knowledge soon."

Torren's brow pinched with confusion. He raised only enough to sit beside her on the bed. He gently slipped his right hand beneath hers, and he began shifting her fingers with his own. Her words made him question his ability to complete his assignment. He genuinely felt that his heart would lose someone it was growing to value. He asked, "Is that what you want?"

Galeena shrugged and said, "The decision was made without my input. There is a kind man who is a relative of my king. His name is Henry. Upon the advice of his own king, he visited and asked for a wife from our land. I am not unknown in this nation. King Wilhelm created a contract on my behalf. I am to be married in less than two weeks."

She thought about how much she had been looking forward to the ceremony, because it was also to be the end of her concealment amongst the citizens of Northanglia. Galeena was to be acknowledged as their next queen, and her time as a soldier was also to end.

Torren mentioned, "I know of Solsworth. Is that not where your former king, King Alexar, went during an unrest amongst the people?"

"It is. King Alexar vacated the crown here so Adelia and Wilhelm could rule. He stepped in as regent there, then was appointed monarch."

"How is this Henry a relative of Wilhelm?"

"Henry is the son of Christiahn and Khara. Christiahn is King Alexar's brother. The relations branch in many directions, but Henry is a distant cousin to my king. Truthfully though, who can possibly keep record?" Galeena rolled her eyes.

Seeming confused, Torren asked, "Other than the obvious reasons any man would want you for a wife, what does a prince of his own nation want with a wife of no standing in your courts? What does he have to gain by accepting you?"

At first, she appreciated his insinuation that she was physically a good mate for any man. Then, offense was taken. And finally, she accepted that in the Norse nations, marriages are more often based on choice rather than rank. In the North, all are allowed to earn their stations of respect and governing. Torren's question was valid based on his knowledge of the culture of Northanglia and its neighboring nations.

Galeena replied, "Henry gladly accepts and awaits a union with me, because even though I have no ties to any families, I do share the highest ranking office in King Wilhelm's army. My betrothed is interested in a wife he feels he can depend on to be loyal and strong."

Acceptance of Henry meant that Galeena would someday be queen of Northanglia, Gudsfelt, and Solsworth. That information was not to be shared yet though.

Torren tightened his hold on her hands. He learned of her rank. He fought the deception. His eyes lowered to their hands which continued to dance with the other. He could not fight his emotions. Torren said, "I want you to consider other options Galeena. You need not be assigned to anyone who is not of your choosing."

"Have you any idea how marriage works in Northanglia?" She asked him with implication that his question was ludicrous.

"I ask you to make no decisions about marriage today."

Galeena smiled and assured him, "*That,* I can promise you."

He softly asked, "For today, may I have your full attention?"

"You may have it until I am upon my horse."

"And the exclusive nearness I requested?"

"Tis yours until I part."

A sizzle at the hearth distracted them both. Torren hurried to the fire and removed the kettle from over the flames. Since he had already prepared cups, he poured the water, then hastened back to Galeena empty handed.

Taking his place once more at her side, he leaned toward her. She flipped the linen cover away from her. This pleased him.

"I have already missed my pre-dawn departure. I see no harm in warming one another while our tea cools."

Torren seductively extended his body the full length of hers and said, "I believe we are supposed to hate one another."

"Aye, we are. Perhaps our discord can commence when I am beyond reach of you and your army."

Holding her head in both of his hands he pulled her mouth open with his thumb that was placed delicately on her chin. He then entered her soul, and within moments all barriers were removed.

Betrayal may have been their intended course, but an affectionate allegiance was forming an unbreakable bond.

Chapter 14

"Despite the unexpected arrival of a few hundred Norsemen to Castleton and the rising of the sun, I shall not alter my plan to proceed south."

"With the company of your horse, much distance should be gained depending on your animal's ability to perform its duties. Tell me, how many hours do you need to arrive at Broodenshire before travel is unmanageable due to the lack of light?"

"I should have parted while the sky was still gray. By leaving this late into the morning, I will arrive in darkness. I have no intentions of cantering my horse because I have delayed my departure. My tardiness is not his fault."

"If all is true, and there is no hope of you arriving at your next location before dark, then I see no reason for you to scurry about in an attempt to race time. Enjoy your tea. Let us share our relief meal from the night's fast. Join me. Sit and tell me, what does your king believe of your location?"

"King Wilhelm believes me to have left pre-dawn."

"Ah, since you have no appointment and your king will not be in search of you, I ask that you do ease your mind about tardiness. It is my understanding that Broodenshire is merely a resting place en route to your next destination. Is this correct?"

"Broodenshire is my retreat. Tis where I go to be alone, to contemplate, to rest."

"How long will you be there?"

"Four nights. I hoped for twelve, but the king insists I report back for duties sooner than planned."

"Duties that include our seizure of Castleton?"

"Of course, Torren. Regardless of the lovely moments we have shared these past two nights, my job remains to be removal of you from our country."

He smiled and said, "Since you honor me with your assignment, shall I honor you with mine?"

"I presume you are here from Gudsfelt and Danemour to abduct the Princess of Northanglia. Enemy nations do not become allies unless they have a common interest. Although I have not received official documentation of the matter, I also presume Jaegar has finally taken control and title of King of Danemour from Vidar. He now sends his only son to collect Adelia's daughter so he can have Gudsfelt as well. Your possession of Adelia's knife spoke volumes without actually speaking a word."

"Clever and discerning you are, Galeena. You know all this, yet you have no remorse sharing intimate moments with me?

You know I've come to take Princess Helene to Gudsfelt and deliver her to my father, and you still allowed our mutual gratification to occur?"

His suspicious tone worried her. Galeena had to comfort him. She did what any woman would do. She stood, stepped to his side, placed her leg over his lap, and she sat upon his thighs. She kissed his neck, cheek and lips, then asked, "Did our time together not satisfy you? Neither of us is ignorant of our relationship. We are opponents in this battle, Torren. That will not change. Nothing can change it, not embraces, not soft kisses, not breakfast or tea, not even sharing a bed regardless of what we do there. I will not trust you and you should not trust me."

"I'm going to Broodenshire with you. This camp will last four days without me."

"Do you follow me this time because you fear I'm going to retrieve more troops, or do you go because you fear a night alone in my bed will be sleepless?"

"The second option. The first matter has already been settled. We no longer have the element of surprise. Our presence is well known."

"Then let us part soon. That man, Gunnar, will have the masses calling for my public atonement if I am not absent from my very own home soon."

Torren reminded Galeena, "Tis I who gives the orders here. I assured him of your plans, and I assured you of your safety. I shall escort you to Broodenshire myself."

"I believe tis I who will be escorting you, Sir. I've warned you of the scouting soldiers throughout the woods, moors, coasts, and roads. You shall be under my protection."

Torren pressed his hips upward and replied, "Tis not my fear. I shall enjoy today's adventure as much as I enjoyed last night's."

Galeena closed her eyes and shook her head. "Our time, though enjoyable, will remain free from immoralities. No lines shall be crossed. My groom awaits."

"My need to possess your exclusiveness strengthens, Galeena. You are not married to another, yet."

"Time for the deliverance of my hand is near."

"Not if I refuse to allow it," he countered.

"Refuse? To allow me to marry the man my king has selected for me? Dear Torren, you have no say in matters of my life, nor shall you ever have a voice in matters that concern me. Enjoy the access I share with you. And in four nights, think of me as nothing more than your enemy."

Chapter 15

Without incident, argument, or ambush, Galeena and Torren rode from Castleton.

After their meal, Galeena gathered a few articles of clothing and packed them around the book she held so dear. She then collected a supply of blades and placed them with her belongings as well. Torren did not have much. He had a bedroll and one tunic in addition to the one he wore. Together, a day's ration of food was wrapped and placed with Torren's supplies. Finally, the pair walked boldly to the stables. Galeena saddled her own horse and suggested a mare for Torren. They were soon en route to Broodenshire.

It was no surprise that Galeena's aim was to keep them out of public view. Their travel was to be through the forest then over the moorland until they reached as far as they could go without having to utilize the king's road. They would then have to travel a portion of the journey in full view of anyone, whether citizen or soldier, who would be on the same path.

Dearest Brother, have you received your summons yet? Galeena wondered as the sight of Castleton was lost behind them.

* * *

"Torren, I thought you rode away with the Anglian woman?"

The door to Galeena's village cottage abruptly opened and a Norseman stood perplexed. He drew his sword and continuing to speak in his native language he asked, "Who are you?"

A young man of medium stature turned and spied the one who had entered uninvited. His demeanor spoke for him. Any weapon drawn upon him would be useless. The glare that emanated from his eyes caused the Dane to shift, and his unsettled stance was one Lukah had witnessed during other encounters.

"Where is the woman who occupied this home?" Lukah asked in the foreigner's tongue whilst placing the cup he had been inspecting on the table.

"Who are you? Have you arrived from Dornwold?"

"The woman? Where is she?" he repeated.

The man answered believing he was speaking to one of his own countrymen or one of his commander's relatives. He replied, "She was allowed to leave this morning. Do you not know our commander? He escorted her to a place she called Broodenshire." The man studied Lukah unable to fathom the resemblance between him and Torren.

"I do not know your commander, Sir. I am a native of Northanglia. I heard of your raid upon this village, so I immediately abandoned my home to seek the inhabitant of this house."

"Why do you speak our language with such ease?" The sword rose to a more combative position.

Calmly, because his words were the truth, Lukah replied, "I live on a farm near the Dornwold border. In order to trade with the Danes of that land, I needed to learn the language. I've been able to communicate with the Danes for many years. The constant arrivals of your people leave many of us no choice but to accept your presence and learn to negotiate."

"Wise man," the Dane added.

"Yes, thank you. As for the woman, was she forced to guide the man you've mentioned multiple times, named Torren, to Broodenshire? To your knowledge, was she harmed?"

"She was not harmed nor forced. She left under our commander's protection."

Lukah was unsure if they were speaking of the same woman. He asked, "You say she needed the protection of your commander?"

"Aye. Our unit desired either her life or her service as compensation for the many she killed. Torren refused us access to her. Not trusting that we would respect his orders, or not trusting that she wouldn't return for additional retaliation, he left with her saying he'd return in three or four days."

Lukah was satisfied that his sister would have taken quite a few lives, and his sister was definitely not one to be trusted when faced with injustice. They were definitely both referring to Galeena. He stood relieved that she was in fact alive and most likely soon to be on her way to their shared home south of Broodenshire. He asked, “Who stands in lead position?”

“A man by the name of Gunnar. The woman, Galeena, she killed Arik. With Torren absent and Arik in Valhalla, Gunnar leads.” He added, “You certainly have an abundance of questions for a simple farmer.”

Lukah snuffed, then chuckled. “I never said I was only a farmer. I am leaving now. Please deliver a message to Gunnar. Tell him his violent seizure of this village will not be ignored. He has stepped into a den of lurking, ravenous lions. Tis my recommendation that none of you sleep until you have returned to your ships and set sail for Danemour.”

Undaunted, the guard replied, “We sleep soundly, aware that plots for our demise are being strategized. You’ll find no fear in our people. We will set sail for *Gudsfelt* only when our mission is complete.”

Suddenly desperate for all information pertaining to the invasion, Lukah said, “Our blessed queen was of Gudsfelt, and her mother still lives. Gudsfelt is not to attack our shores. The people of that nation are not to slaughter our citizens.”

“Tis the Danes who did the attacking. Those here who are of Gudsfelt arrived post occupation of this village.”

Disgusted, Lukah stepped toward his visitor with aggression. He demanded, "State your mission!"

"Tis not time to share our mission. You need only know that Jaegar of Styrkeson initiated this voyage so he can secure his own placement as Overlord of Gudsfelt."

His father's name was spoken. Lukah had not heard words as they pertained to Jaegar's existence since his mother spoke them before she passed. Galeena had no issue reminding him that a meeting with Jaegar would someday come to fruition for him. But, hearing his father's name as part of a conversation made the distant man real, more alive in his mind.

Pondering the news that Jaegar was seeking rule of Gudsfelt, Lukah immediately surmised that his anonymous father must have sent his band in pursuit of Adelia's daughter. For Princess Helene was the only one who could name anyone other than a Boersen as a successor.

"Have you finally emptied your mind of all questions?" the Dane asked.

Lukah responded, "I have. I repeat, leave Northanglia. King Wilhelm's properties and daughter are guarded by an army far mightier than this one that has arrived from the north. You'll never have what or who you seek. Jaegar need not pursue possession of the last daughter any longer. Gudsfelt belongs to the rightful heir of King Boersen."

With their mission revealed, the Dane threatened, "You'll not be leaving here peacefully Anglian."

"Yes, I will. You have no need of me. I came only for Galeena."

"How did you get in here? You never revealed that to me."

"I walked right through all gathered. I ascended the steps to this home. I opened the door, and I entered. Not one person questioned me."

"Tis your likeness to Torren that made fools of everyone I suppose."

Unsure and uninterested in the man's comment, Lukah said, "Sir," then waited for the man's name.

"Orem."

A bow preceded his farewell. "Orem, I shall exit Castleton in the very same manner I arrived. I wish not to battle anyone this evening. Will you be observing my departure?"

Orem smiled. He was truly amused that a stranger entered their midst unnoticed. "Since you have caused no harm, I shall witness your departure with glee no matter the outcome."

Lukah offered a subtle smile and bid his new acquaintance adieu, "Until we meet again, Orem."

"Fare thee well, Anglian."

Lukah did just as he spoke. He walked from Galeena's cottage and directly through the gatherings of men and women. He kept his head slightly down until he was beyond the village streets where he collected his horse, mounted, and rode toward his father's castle.

When his freedom from any potential harm was certain, Lukah muttered to himself, "I believe tomorrow I shall begin watching for a lone Dane traveling from Broodenshire. If Galeena does not kill him, I certainly will."

* * *

Within minutes, the garrison gates opened for Lukah's arrival. A stable boy was already running to escort the soldier's horse to the stalls. A quick and friendly tussle to the boy's hair was followed by, "Name the most formidable soldier to the king?"

"Galeena!" the boy yelled just as he yanked the reins and scrambled from Lukah's reach. Then, as he escaped the grasp of his elder, the boy said, "But someday it will be me who is the most formidable and feared of all the soldiers!"

Lukah cupped his hands around his mouth and called to the servant, "Your second response was the correct one all along!"

The boy called back, "You, Sir Lukah, are the most tenacious."

"You have saved yourself from a lashing, boy!"

Both laughed and waved.

No escort, nor announcement was needed for Lukah's appearance in his father's strategy chamber. The sound of his boots, like mallets hitting wood, and the clank of his sword rattling in its sheath echoed as he hurried through the hollow corridors to deliver his news to King Wilhelm. Without knocking he turned the ornate, metal knob and entered.

King Wilhelm was pacing and expectant.

"Speak son," he nearly pleaded.

"She is well father. You may rest your soul. Galeena disappears so she can torture the invaders with her silent hunts, and teases. She has lured their leader far away from the protection of his army. I shall be watching for his return to Castleton."

"That child of mine! Her untimely departures cause ailments to my core. I knew she was going to Broodenshire, but she was to stay here for the night. Her disappearance should not worry me so, but it does. Tell me, who is this man she has baited?"

"His name is Torren," Lukah paused. His disturbance at having to disclose the more exact identification was apparent.

Wilhelm nodded and spoke first, "So, your sister *has* stolen the attention of Jaegar's son? She came here wanting information about his childhood. I told her all I know and allowed her to take one of your mother's bound parchments with her. Is there any possibility that you can read the daughters' script?"

"I actually cannot. Father, I'm not a Boersen."

"Ah yes, you are of Alexar and someday will be introduced as Son of Wilhelm, if that is what you choose."

"Thank you Father. For now, shall we trust Galeena? She is not yet sixteen, and her heart could be very impressionable."

"Jaegar, Torren and all other Norsemen seek Princess Helene. Galeena will not reveal herself to anyone. I fear she would actually choose death over exposure. Your mother instilled obedience in her. I trust that."

"Obedience or stubbornness?"

Wilhelm laughed, "Both!"

"Galeena will play unnecessary games, she may even grow attached, but if you say she will withhold her position, then I believe you." Lukah conceded to his Father's wisdom and confidence.

Wilhelm stepped to his son and embraced him. Exhausted, he said, "I thank our beloved God that I need not worry about my son, and I shall only pace with agitation for a few days. I've asked your sister to return here sooner than her usual fourteen nights. I have made an amendment to her wedding announcement. Instead of holding the celebrations on her birthday, I have changed the presentation ball to five days from yesterday."

"The ceremony, it will be in four days?" Lukah repeated with inquiry.

"No, just the announcement and introduction of Henry to our people."

"Will Alexar be joining Henry?" Lukah asked.

"Not to my knowledge. Wymer sent a message indicating Alexar's departure from Solsworth. Wymer stands in as regent until your grandfather returns."

"Does grandfather know of this most recent invasion? Seems odd that he would vacate these lands in the wake of an attack."

"To my knowledge, I do not believe Alexar could know. I am sure he sailed from the southern shores before the events of two mornings ago."

"So we are to defend ourselves then?"

"Tis the way it should be. Tis the way it has always been. We are not weak. You and Galeena are not weak. I fear not these men and women who have arrived. All order will be reestablished very soon my son."

"Aye Father. Tis my expectation that Galeena will devise some sinister plan to rid us of the Norsemen. She will then immediately carry a guilt over the plot. Though my sister is necessary, and her antics keep us challenged and sharp witted, she is rapidly changing into a soft version of a warrior."

King Wilhelm smiled whilst shaking his head at Lukah's perspective and truth. "From what I've received from King Alexar and Adelia, your sister is quite similar in disposition to your mother and grandmother. Though she has been immersed in warfare and defense like all Viking children, she is still a daughter. As for her antics, I've heard tales of Olivia's precariousness as a young woman. Your mother was not as impish as the matriarch and Galeena."

Lukah nodded. Having nothing more to offer the anecdote, he thought momentarily of his own temperament. He felt he was far more serious and prudent than Galeena. She had a recklessness that often over-powered her ability to reason. On many occasions, she made rash decisions without thought for the outcome or consequences. Though Galeena was a trusted protector, Lukah was far more dependable and serious about his duties and responsibilities as a leader of the army.

"Is there any other news, Son?"

Hesitant, Lukah offered, "The man with whom I spoke informed me that the group is compiled of men and women from Gudsfelt and Danemour. They have banded together under Jaegar's command. Though he did not confirm their mission, I am certain they have come for King Boersen's granddaughter. The laws state that Princess Helene be honored as their queen unless she denies the role or perishes."

"My dearest son, your absence leaves you behind in reporting of new information. All you've spoken was confirmed. The only addition is the thought that Galeena's death is the only other route Jaegar could take to claiming the kingdom of Gudsfelt. You don't think he would kill her do you?"

Not wanting to implicate his father nor imply that he is truly a tyrant motivated only by greed, Lukah replied cautiously, "Sir, my heart refuses to accept that the man who gave me life, the man who grew at my mother's side, could possibly eliminate my sister. I choose to believe that a diplomatic compromise can be reached."

Wilhelm was jealous of Jaegar's hold on his son. Jaegar knew nothing of Lukah's existence, yet Lukah still held deep hidden affections for the man. King Wilhelm approached his son and stroked his yellow hair. He smiled proudly at the honorable man he had raised, who despite being a formidable opponent, was still a kind and optimistic man of God. He was his mother's son.

Wilhelm said, "Princess Helene is the only rightful heir because she is the only child who has been revealed to the governors and the citizens. Your mother was adamant that Jaegar know nothing of your existence until *you* felt it was time. Please think upon that."

"I have and I will continue to consider this, Father."

"You must keep in mind, if Jaegar learns of your existence, he would hunt you and anyone in his path would die. Adelia wanted you for herself. She grew with two fathers tugging at her heart. Adelia chose me for you Lukah, and more importantly, I chose you."

Lukah sensed that Wilhelm was beginning to worry less about his safety and more about losing him to Jaegar. He attempted to comfort him, "I know father. Grandfather Wymer, Grandfather Alexar, you, Mother, and Galeena are my family. I am aware that Jaegar would have taught me of plundering, pagan gods, and cruelty without conscience. My life here with you has been all I could have ever wanted."

Lukah spoke what he thought his father wanted to hear. He did not speak what was truly in his heart. In all of his years, he knew his mother loved Jaegar. She had confessed it. She stained Styrke's symbol upon his shoulder to declare his identity. Lukah was never considered a Boersen because his father, Jaegar, was a worthy man of the north. Adelia never allowed Lukah to believe he was a child of a monster. Jaegar sacrificed his freedom and his own happiness for Adelia's survival and comfort. Ambition for titles was a side effect of his lot in life. Lukah knew beyond any doubts that Jaegar would have treasured the child he shared with the only woman he ever loved.

Though in his heart he knew all of this to be true, he also knew that Wilhelm was correct. There was no doubt that two men lived inside of Jaegar. He was a full-blooded Dane who was loved by a mother and grandfather of Gudsfelt. Jaegar was loving and protective. He also was vicious, so Lukah knew to be cautious with his identity. He knew to protect himself not only physically, but emotionally as well, from the man who sought the throne of three nations.

Wilhelm knew from the distant gaze in Lukah's eyes that he was imagining his first encounter with his blood-father. He would not make any attempts to stop him. Though Wilhelm's concern was for both of his children, it was time to make Galeena his immediate concern. The Norsemen would stop at nothing to retrieve Princess Helene, and if she refused to relinquish her claim, he now knew Jaegar, or Torren, would kill her.

Chapter 16

"My horse wishes to canter across this field. She is restless."

Galeena laughed and said, "You are incorrect, Icelander. Your horse suffers beneath your excessive substance."

"What are you saying? Doth you declare that my physique is offensive?"

"Certainly not! I am trying to tell you that your horse is feeble. She is the horse we use to teach our youngest children to ride."

Torren was shocked and offended. "Why would you point me in the direction of this old mare? We should trade!"

"Oh no! What if we are attacked by a band of rogue Vikings? How shall I escape?" Galeena teased.

"I shall protect you. I now ask you, if we are attacked by King Wilhelm's army, how shall I escape?

"You shall not! Tis why I'll not be giving you my horse!" Galeena continued her hearty laugh until she could scarcely catch a breath.

Torren merely shook his head and rolled his eyes at her self-serving humor. He then asked, "Since there will be no hurrying to our night's abode, and I may or may not be arriving with you thanks to my feeble mule, tell me of your nearest partner in ranking?"

"Withdraw your insult of Queen Olivia's personal mare!"

Torren was stunned. "Are you deceiving me?"

"No. Tis no deception. That horse is very old, but very loved. I chose her for you as a gesture of endearment."

"Now I feel as if I should dismount and walk the poor old woman the remainder of the distance."

"Carry no guilt. She is well. So, are you still curious about my partner?"

"I am," Torren affirmed.

"Do you ask so you may hunt him, or do you ask to fill the silence?"

"Hmm... I suppose both. Tis never a bad thing to know your enemies weaknesses. If your nearest comrade has a vulnerability, I would attack there first."

"I confess, you ride beside Lukah's only weakness. Does owning that information encourage you to attack me?"

"Ah, Lukah? I have a name."

"Knowledge of one's name gives you no power."

"It does if he is to be hunted lest he hinder me from completing my mission."

Mildly agitated, she scoffed, "You could hunt Lukah, but be assured it would be a very short pursuit. He would gladly seek you in return and meet you for battle. Hunting a formidable man is not like hunting a fearful animal."

"I agree with you, though it does stir a bit of jealousy within me. You speak of him with a suppressed affection. Do not try to deny it."

Since Galeena was several paces ahead of Torren, she looked back over her left shoulder, pulled her reins and waited for him to arrive at her side.

As he approached he merely stared with one eyebrow raised. She asked, "Jealous? You envy another man on my behalf?"

"I meant what I said in the darkness whilst at your side. I want no other man to ever have the nearness to you that I have experienced."

Galeena smiled, "You must release your infatuation with me. And, you must not concern yourself with Lukah." A tap with her heels set her horse to progressing once more.

"How long have you known Lukah, and how will he feel about my presence here with you? Will I awaken with more daggers pressed to my throat? Shall I have to fight him not because of my presence in your country but because of my presence at your side?"

"You need not bear any concern about a fight, because there would be none. Lukah strikes like lightning. You may be larger and perhaps stronger, but he is intuitive. He would know your moves before you even plan them. He would enrapture you with his calm stare. You might even believe him to be weak or a man of peace, but he is not."

"Again, I hear affection. You are not hiding it."

"Tis not my aim to hide it," she owned her emotions.

"*That* we will discuss further, but I must know, you wish for me to believe a soldier of Northanglia can defeat me before I even realize I've been killed?"

"If I am not present to defend you, I have no doubt. Torren, I could have killed you two nights ago. You slept falsely comforted by your guards and neighbors. Lukah would have done the deed I could not perform."

Caring more about why there would be an altercation, Torren asked, "Now answer me, will this man's ire emerge from jealousy or from the natural need to defend his homeland?"

Galeena laughed at the thought of Lukah being envious. The idea also disgusted her.

Torren surmised, "Your amusement tells me my question makes you uncomfortable."

Her brow lifted and she looked outward at the sun setting on the rolling hills that formed their horizon. His question did make her uncomfortable but for reasons she could not disclose.

Galeena replied, "Lukah has been a lifelong friend. He has no interest in me outside of family and occupation, and the sentiment is mutual."

"So he has chosen another woman to pursue?"

"Not yet. He is waiting to pass certain milestones in his life before seeking a wife. Do be assured though, *I* will not be that wife." She closed her eyes, shook her head and giggled again at how repulsive the topic was to her soul.

"I care not about his endeavors as long as they do not include you in any manner."

Torren's deepening interest was perplexing but also intriguing to Galeena. He was forming a rapid attachment that was inflaming his need to possess her. Perhaps she was to blame. After all, she had allowed him very intimate access to her, twice. And, he did volunteer to accompany her for an extended retreat to Broodenshire.

Revisiting Torren's inquiry she said, "Lukah will defend me and Northanglia against any adversary. You are a foreigner. If he found you without proper escort, you would certainly face the challenge of your lifetime."

"Will you tell me how fate led to you two becoming King Wilhelm's most trusted pair?"

She shrugged, nodded in agreement and began, "The day I met Lukah was the closest I had ever been to feeling as if I was in a state of loss. I was not yet ten and tis possible I was not yet nine."

"A wee child, huh? Fill my ears with all of the particulars. Leave nothing for me to wonder," Torren encouraged with genuine intrigue.

She smiled at him prying for anecdotes about her past as she continued, "The soldiers of Northanglia had acquired a new group of youngsters. The boys were all near my age. I knew the army's commander was an elder man named Wymer, but a different man came to my home and demanded that my governess release her custody of me. He stated that by order of King Wilhelm she was to deliver me into the care of the guardsmen. Though my nurse was protective and desperate to see me become a lady who could be traded in marriage, she knew she had no power to deny the request of the king or anyone who could produce identification as a king's representative. Reluctantly, she packed a shoulder bag for me and sent me out the door into the possession of the stern man."

"Was the safety of your innocence never questioned?"

"I knew nothing of innocence at that time. Being violated was not a fear I had, so that concern would have possibly been discussed in my absence."

Torren nodded.

"Once I was released to the man, before I had even left the threshold of my door, a sack was slipped over my head and my hands and feet were bound. My guardian attempted to scold the soldier, but he told her I was none of her concern. He scooped me into his arms and placed me in the back of a cart. At first, I was a little afraid, but soon I had no doubt that it was a test of some sort. Our own soldiers certainly would have nothing to gain by nabbing innocent children and killing them. All citizens know that military training begins near age seven or eight. I was unique because I was a girl. Some of the children in the wagon were whimpering. The sounds irritated me as we were transported to an unknown locale."

"You were not afraid? Is that the truth?" Torren asked.

"I was not. I was happy to be out of the sight of my governess. I had lived amongst the military in Castleton. I had no fear of them."

He laughed.

"It didn't take long to realize that I had been the last child tossed into the load of trainees. No one else joined us after me. We all rode along, waiting, wondering. Most of the tears ceased but a few boys continued sniffling. After much time had passed, I growled at them saying, 'Desist your tears! Thou art to become a man. Raise your chin, or I shall discover your identity and kill you myself. Cowards cause more deaths than enemies.' Nearby soldiers roared with laughter and said, 'You boys have been subjugated by a little girl!' I turned my ear and voice in their direction and yelled, 'I am not a little girl! I am soon to be a soldier!' They replied, 'Yes child, I believe you are.'"

Torren showed humor while envisioning her tale.

"The band of guardsmen took us far, far from the reach of our king's fortress and periodically, they would throw a pair of us over their shoulders and carry us into the woods. Every hour, another pair was tossed or carried away. We were separated so no one set could locate another. We were instructed to return by sundown the next day or we would be hunted. None of us cared to know what it meant to be the hunted prey of an army.

"I had listened attentively to the numbers removed and the numbers that remained. In addition, I had set my focus on the directions we traveled. When I and my partner were thrown to the ground, only two boys remained. The boy with me began to whine right away. I felt so displeased to have a partner who had probably cried the duration of the day. My guess was that he was afraid of the darkened state created by his covering. Twas my opinion, the entire exercise was a game that I immediately began preparing to win."

"Sounds like entertainment to me. I believe I would have enjoyed the experience as well," Torren added.

"Yes. I had found no reason to fear. We had been dropped just before nightfall, and there was still enough light to search for the correct direction. But first we needed to free ourselves. Having the advantage of flexibility, I had brought my hands from my back to my front, removed the hood, used my teeth to loosen my wrists, and was working on unknotting the ropes about my legs. Mikah or Markah or Matty? I've no recollection of his name, began fussing for me to unbind him. I scolded him. The thought occurred to me to leave him there, but that would have been cruel. An animal could have taken him. Clearly, the boy was helpless. Therefore, once I was free, I graciously freed him as well."

"Very chivalrous of you, though disappointing. He should have been left as feed for the wolves."

Galeena added a note to Toreen's point of view, "You have no idea how familiar your words are. Be patient." She then continued, "Twas not in my nature I suppose. Though his reaction to seeing that a girl had set him free was typical. He made excuses about me being a servant to him, and he was testing me; he demanded I follow him. Then, the boy darted southward. I called out, 'You idiot! You run the wrong direction! You will receive the strap upon your backside if you have to be hunted.' Alas, he refused to heed my warning."

"Where is that boy now?" Torren asked.

"He's not a messenger!" Galeena said with a gratuitous tone and a shrug.

Her guest laughed.

She then said, "As he was adamant to be wrong, I quickly closed my mouth and let him go. I did not want such an imbecile benefiting from my skills, so I ran north as quickly as I could hoping he would not be able to find me. Once I was confident the little fool was gone, I began seeking anything edible in the direct path that I traveled."

"So when do I get to hear of Lukah's arrival in your life?"

"This very moment: when I stopped at a spring to refresh, I heard a rustle. I did not hide, for I wished to see who or what was stalking me. A strong boy was behind me. He said, 'I was last. My mate was unable to free himself. Thus, I left him. If he is unable to even complete the first test, then, in my opinion, he deserves not to be in my presence, nor does he deserve to live. I hope I'm allowed to show my gratitude someday to the animal that consumes him.' I laughed with such hysteria I was almost unable to speak. I said, 'I wish I had thought of that!' After determining he did not care if I suffered from insanity or not, the boy, named Lukah, joined me in the amusement."

"And thus a relationship with *Lukah* began?" Torren asked.

Though her story was true, Galeena could not reveal the entire truth. She said, "Yes, a working relationship began. However, shall I finish? There is only a bit more to be shared."

"Please do."

"Lukah is one year my elder. He and I hunted and prepared our meal for that night. We rested only in short spells, because neither of us wanted to cease our trek back to camp. He was equally skilled in the navigation of our return. Then, because we had only been taken a day's distance away, we arrived back to Commander Wymer before the sun reached its peak the following day."

"Who won?"

"Every child who arrived before sundown won, if that is how we think about it. Lukah and I were not first, but we were one of the first pairs. Do recall, twas a great feat since we were both parties of the last two groups abandoned in the forest."

Galeena and Torren arrived at a stream and he mentioned with amazement, "We've crossed the moors, traveled a distance of the king's road and now have come to a spring in the forest. I dislike that you've kept me so preoccupied that I had almost no awareness of my surroundings."

"You've been safe. You have me."

"I'm not yet sure if being with you equates to being safe. I've yet to decide if I can trust you."

"You cannot," she mentioned casually. "Let us pause for a few moments. I'd like to eat and utilize my own legs. Perhaps we can walk our horses for a measure after our meal."

Torren swung his leg over the hind end of his horse and dropped to the ground. Galeena did the same. She then released the reins, pulled her leather satchel from her saddle and took out a water horn. Torren took the food bag they had packed and joined her on a rock beside the stream. Both horses drank and nibbled on the grass blades.

He asked, "Did you not worry that day that you could have been going in the wrong direction? You never feared being lost?"

Galeena situated her food and said, "I did not know where I was. The area of the country was somewhat unknown to me. If it is your perception that those conditions are the same as being lost, then yes, perhaps I was lost. However, with basic skills, an understanding of direction, and knowledge of where home sits, I believe one can always find their way. The state of being lost insinuates distress. Many times I have not known my exact location, but I have always found my desired path."

"Tis true," he agreed. He then furthered his questioning of her, "As for this Lukah, be not evasive in your response to my next query about his present role in your life. Have you never, not at any moment, even considered that he would be the man you would marry? It sounds as if the military chiefs and king have found you to be a successful pairing."

"I've already answered that question. I'll not revisit it."

The two shared their meal and Galeena concluded her childhood memoire. "The next morning, Lukah and I entered the midst of the soldiers proudly, confidently. Commander Wymer marched to us and before all others angrily asked us both, 'Why have you arrived with a comrade who was not your assigned partner?'

"I smartly responded, 'How was I to know the boy whom was tossed next to me? There was a blinding cloth over my head.'"

"Having no patience for deception, he said, 'Do you wish to convince me that you are unsure of the boy who landed at your side onto the earth?' I again feigned ignorance saying, 'No sir. I am telling you, this *is* the boy at my side, and this *is* the boy who has been at my side since I removed my covering.'

"He bellowed, 'Child! Confess your sin!'"

"Lukah stood silent, waiting. Unwavering, I stated, 'There is nothing to confess.' Of course I was lying, but I was never going to admit it."

Torren smirked.

"Commander Wymer held his sword to Lukah's throat and said, 'You confess or he dies for your sin.'"

"I stepped in front of the point and carefully placed it at my own heart. 'I have committed no sin Commander.' He was irate. He directed the same line of questioning to Lukah. Fury consumed him when Lukah's story was identical to mine, and he too was willing to die for his documentary. Our commander smiled and removed the threat from us both. Then, he pointed his sword and demanded of us, 'My tent soldiers.'

"We advanced in the direction of his tent, and before I had taken five paces, he swatted us both on our backsides with a stick. I spun, grabbed the stick, broke it, and threw it. He gritted at me, 'You would not be so arrogant child if you were not a girl.'"

Torren was enjoying her record.

Galeena said, "I gritted back, 'Tis lucky I am a girl then, Sir!'"

"'Tent!' he commanded. Once inside, Wymer lowered his voice, 'Tell me how and why you traded partners.'"

"I defended, 'The other boy was an idiot. He insulted me, then wandered away in the wrong direction. I hope something ate him. Lukah was on the correct path, so we joined together. Lukah is much more suited to my disposition.'"

"Wymer replied looking at us both, 'Aye, tis not a surprise. I ask, are you willing to die for one another?'"

"'Always,' was our unison response, and that is the end of the story."

"Why did you feel the need to share that conclusion with me?" Torren sounded suspicious.

"I shared that because it is still true. You'll not harm me, my king, his daughter, or Lukah without losing your life. I heard you tell Gunnar that I could be useful to you. You are wrong. I am of no use. I am not a naive soldier you can manipulate or deceive. I am half of a pair that is truly one. Lukah will never let me get too far from him. We will die for our king, for each other, or together for our nation. Do you understand that?"

She confessed her knowledge of Norse. Torren was pleased and curious. He stared as he spoke. Leaning toward Galeena never losing her eyes and her attention, he whispered in his native language, "I've never had any intentions of harming you. My plan is to keep you... forever. Lukah will have to find a way to command King Wilhelm's army without his partner."

"Your plan matters not to me, Norseman."

Her fluent reply was intriguing, and it stimulated a tingle in him. He did not want to alarm her with the depth of his curiosity. He moved closer and asked, "Tell me, how do you know the language of the Norse?"

Galeena smiled, brushed her bottom lip against his, then teased his top lip with the tip of her tongue. She whispered back, "I know everything."

Chapter 17

Night had fallen upon them and there was absolutely no usable light for guidance. The skies darkened with clouds prior to the fading of the day. Galeena had led Torren on foot for the remaining hours of their trek. A downpour blanketed them, and he was quite impressed with her abilities in navigation under those conditions.

The distance that remained was unknown to Torren and just before misery was to be his silent complaint, flickers of light appeared to be dancing skyward. He assumed they had nearly reached their destination.

Torren asked, "Shall we be residing within the church's walls this night?"

"Heavens no!" Galeena replied loudly. "I sleep in those quarters as rarely as possible. I prefer sleeping in the surrounding fields over sleeping within the cramped spaces they provide. The only occurrences which require my presence overnight in the fortress are when I have been assigned a night watch, or day to night meditations, or guard duties for extended periods of time. Otherwise, I visit our monks, I share meals, I tend the stables, then I retreat to my cavern for solace."

"We will staying in a cave? Not a domicile?"

"The cave is my private domicile."

"Any respite from this deluge will be satisfying. Do you realize the rain has almost been incessant since we landed upon the sands of Northanglia?"

"Tis a sign, no doubt."

Torren laughed.

"We've had moments of sun, Ice-lander. Those moments become more treasured, don't you agree?"

"I suppose I have barely noticed them since the rain has saturated my memories. I shall try harder to note the few hours of sunlight."

"We're nearly there. It would be a falsity for me to say I do not mind the cold, dark, wetness of this night. Head down, follow. We have only steps before us."

The cave entrance would have been more than difficult to find without her guidance under the circumstances of that evening. However, it was quite apparent that during daylight, the shelter would have been obvious and intriguing for exploration. He wondered why she referred to this area as her private lands. Surely any passerby or visitor who accessed the area from the coast would find this location with very little effort, and attempt to make it their own.

With Galeena as his guide, they tied their horses, gathered their belongings, and they entered the blackened tunnel. “Wait here Torren lest you injure the lovely features of your face against the stone.”

He chuckled and obeyed. Her feet stepped lightly and barely made a sound on the sandy surface below them. He then listened to the tapping sound of wood and the music of a strike. A timid glow emanated from around a bend. It invited him to follow. As he entered the opening, Torren saw Galeena kneeling next to a pallet that was adjacent to a cozy fire.

“So this is also your home?” Torren asked. He allowed his eyes and senses to take in all that surrounded him. Provisions, supplies, food storage, were all placed neatly throughout the cave.

Torren’s attention to the shelter was entertaining. Her eyes parted from him to all that he beheld. She replied, “No, I do not live here. I simply camp here on frequent occasions. This is where I stay when I am on my way to my preferred home.”

He turned to her and with curiosity asked, “The village is not the home of your preference?”

“Mmm... As somewhat of a nomad, I have a few shelters that I consider to be homes. For isolation, I tarry from one cottage to the other. They sit a distance of two days apart. The village affords me human connections. My woodland cottage affords me complete peace and solitude. In addition to my lovely little houses, I have this cave, a small cell in Claremont, and an even smaller cell above us at the monastery. All one truly needs in life are shelter and food. I make my way quite sufficiently. Being a common nomad has many benefits. My comings and goings are not heavily scrutinized. I am at liberty to make most of my own decisions. Well, as long as I report via messenger or personal appearance before King Wilhelm each fortnight. He and Lukah keep record. Their interference does not offend. Regardless of my capabilities, I am still a woman without a husband, and therefore, I'm tracked more often than the men who have families."

Each story she had shared with him was utterly intriguing. Galeena held his attention with every word. Torren found that he definitely wanted a woman like her in his life. Perhaps he could disappear with her. No, his father, his troops and the Danes would never allow him to vanish. They would even search for his dead body if rumors circulated of his demise. They would demand evidence. *Perhaps she and I are not so different*, he thought.

Torren's curiosity continued, "How is this place so well stocked with supplies? Did you bring all of this here during your travels?"

"Not all. Tis part of the priests' occupation to provide and care for others. Also, they themselves come here for prayer or as retreat from storms on their walks. They supply my campsite."

"Monks huh?" Torren recalled stories his grandfather Styrke had told of priests and churches in Northanglia.

Though he was not yet aware of their personal and familial connection, Galeena sensed the Vikings thoughts. He would have been taught of the histories of that location. She begged, “Please do not go killing our monks and our priests. They mean you no harm.”

Torren laughed. “I shall not kill your priests... unless they attempt to interfere with my assignment.”

“I am not amused,” Galeena scolded.

“I have only one task and it does not involve material treasures. I am beginning to realize that finding Princess Helene will take a length of time that my father and I did not anticipate.”

“With absolution it will take longer than expected if you continue to leave your post to be my shadow. I assure you Torren, I will not be leading you to King Boersen’s daughter. She is perfectly safe where she resides. You, nor your men, will collect her. You do not have the numbers to murder an entire army that hides her. You all face a militia that has benefitted from having two Viking queens on the throne.”

“My Grandmother Olivia never sat on that throne.”

“No, but it was hers and she aimed to protect this nation with equal fervor as Gudsfelt. Olivia, Adelia and Helene are all part of this country’s greater plan for protection from and ceasing of the Viking raids.”

“This topic ends,” Torren declared with no more energy for argument. “We shall eat.”

Galeena did not mind moving their interactions in another direction. She conceded, “Yes. We shall. You are welcome to share all that I have.”

Torren smiled and complimented her, “Your generosity under the unconventional circumstances through which we have become acquainted is appreciated. It is second only to your captivating beauty, charms and subtle invitations for shared affectionate encounters.”

Appalled, Galeena gaped. “You will find yourself curled up to a tree trunk if you dare insinuate that I have in any way invited you into my bed and lured you into my arms. Both occasions of closeness between us were merely results of a lack of sleep and weakness of mind.”

“Yet here I stand, beside you. This entire day was spent with you having full control of your thoughts and your emotions.” He neared her and said, “There is no need for you to feel as if a treason has occurred, nor shall you bear embarrassment. We are once again alone in a private chamber. You must grow accustomed to my advances. You may have a lifetime of them.”

“I do not foresee a lifetime with you, unless my lifetime shall be a short one. I am to be married, very soon. Upon completion of the ceremony, I will immediately relocate to Solsworth.”

“You believe that to be true, but you would have to cross Dornwold to get to your intended destination. My reach is beyond Danemour, Gudsfelt and now Castleton. A word, a single command from me, and you could find yourself residing in the land between Northanglia and Solsworth."

"Stop!" Galeena shouted whilst glaring at Torren with slitted eyes. "Do not drape a threat upon me as if it is a cloak of triumphant conquest. I am not to be stolen, then paraded, then held captive."

"You shall never be my captive. My hope is that our bond will tighten. My vision was of freeing you from an unwanted marriage. Twas not my desire to raise alarm through intimidation. Please, accept my apology and allow me to show you what has been buried beneath my surface waiting for you, and only you, to arrive in my life."

His magic with words and their accompanying gazes did cause Galeena to believe that she too had found the man she never knew existed, but hoped would someday appear at her side. If Torren was like Jaegar, it was a wonder that Wilhelm was able to steal Adelia's heart from him no matter the circumstance. Galeena felt as if she could forgive Torren for nearly any offense. She offered, "If you can promise that the remainder of this night shall only be about silence, then I shall accept your apology with gladness."

A seductive glint sparkled in his eyes. "Silence? No. However, I can promise that no more speech of invasions or abductions or intrusions or missions will be allowed between us. We have three nights and it is my hope that before we return to our posts, we shall be unconditionally bound to one another."

"Please do not rest your happiness on such hopes. Our relationship has a barrier that can only be removed by you. I'll not forget all you've done and said. Before we lower our suspicions, I wish you to know, your intrusion here was unnecessary. Had you arrived with a much smaller band of cohorts, you quite possibly would have been offered housing within the territory. Advancing violently into a population of peaceful people was most barbaric, and the act will have consequences. Do consider your actions more carefully prior to strategizing the completion of your mission. Perhaps gather information politically before setting such a demonic and destructive plan into action. Now, sit. I shall present a meal, and we shall then rest. I would very much like to collect a full measure of sleep this night, a sleep that is only concluded by my own contented spirit."

Torren tuned his ear to her every word. Skepticism itched his thoughts like spices tickled his nose, no damage is done, but irritation is present. He was not sure of her motives, but one as clever and tenacious as her would have to be watched. His hope was that he could win her whole heart before she was to follow through with any mounting plans for resolution. That night, he was comforted by the belief that he would awaken at her side. Therefore, he sat, watched, and awaited his supper.

Chapter 18

Only pleasant exchanges had occurred as they ate. Post meal, Galeena placed their plates and cups away from the fire and she began her routine for sleep. Torren reclined against the slant of a boulder collecting memories of her every motion.

Galeena's hair had dried and it flowed once again about her back and shoulders. The curves of her perfect shape were revealed by her fitted clothing, and they left him not having to imagine what could someday belong to him. She was not unwise to his thoughts. A keen awareness of and personal experiences with men had filled her with the knowledge of their silent thoughts.

Even though her next action was certain to pique his interest beyond an ability to control himself, Galeena performed the deed.

She walked to her sleeping pallet and shook any settled dust from her blankets. Then, perfectly aware of her proximity to Torren, which was very near and standing over him, she brazenly, though very slowly, removed her boots, her silk tunic, and her leather leggings. After she was disrobed for her night's slumber, she sat upon her bed, covered herself with a single linen sheet, fluffed her dark tresses, and she lay her head on her pillow. "Bon nuit," she said sweetly.

Torren remained in awe of her and spoke only when he was finally capable of forming a complete inquiry. He asked, "Do you have any plans to apply more adequate covering to your person before daylight arrives, Miss?"

Draped only by her bedsheet, Galeena turned her head in his direction and responded, "Why do you ask such a question? Does my exposed *person* offend thee?"

"Most certainly it does not! I inquire on behalf of my depraved self. I feel I should fully disclose that if you choose to remain in this," he pointed at her from feet, to her head, to feet again, "current state of comfort, I shall make no effort to withhold my stares. You also must know, I shall most likely make no effort to withhold any part of me from you!"

With a snicker, Galeena raised her eyes upward, then shook her head. She suggested, "If you will rise, prepare your own sleeping mat on the other side of this fire ring, lie upon it, and close your eyes, you'll not be able to stare. With the vision of me removed, I am confident you will no longer have to hold yourself back from pawing at me."

He laughed heartily and said, "We've shared a bed for the past two nights. This one shall be no different. However, if you will apply your nightdress, you will at the very least have a barrier that will keep me from performing the immoral acts you hold so dear."

"First, we slept in my bed because there was nowhere else for the other to find comfort. Second, my nightshift is in Castleton. You are more than welcome to retrieve it if you intend to sleep in it because you feel it is the only protection I shall have this night from your advances."

"It was to be your only saving grace," he teased while still laughing at her suggestion that he wear her dress.

"You could be a gentleman and not remove your own trousers!"

"Not to be considered!" he retorted.

"Then Torren, find your way to your own bed. Leave me in peace. I wish to close my eyes and greet a new day with joy."

"As do I."

"Stop that. Go." Galeena held her covering about her chest, lifted her head and shoulders and pointed. "Go over there and make yourself comfortable," she commanded.

Suddenly, Torren had an urgent question to ask. "Galeena, do you sleep in this state amongst other men, or Lukah?"

"Tis not your concern, but to save my own reputation, I'll answer; of course not. I am either fully dressed when I rest amongst the troops, or I have a private tent. Satisfied?"

"Yes! I am!"

She closed her eyes and suppressed her amusement at his worries. After only a few breaths, cool air brushed her back and his heated flesh pressed against her.

"I'll be here with you, right where a shadow belongs."

Galeena did not push him away or react in an offended manner. She had fully expected such a response from him. She said, "Tis night. We have no shadows."

"You are very wrong. Those flames created a perfect map of where your shadow resides. I merely filled in the empty space."

Her giggles were followed by the turning of her face to his. A gentle pull of her shoulder was not resisted. Torren slid his body over hers and only gave her brief moments to collect breaths. Intimacy with Torren was simple and natural, and because they had previously shared this experience, neither felt any apprehension.

She pressed upward.

Before accepting her invitation, he smiled and asked, "Which of my impure thoughts will you allow me to perform?"

Galeena giggled, "Any that do not produce children. My betrothed would certainly take offense and my king would reach a level of anger that I dare say would frighten any deity."

He took all he wanted and needed from her, honoring her single request to abstain from her ruin. Galeena in no way made him believe that she was not enjoying all he offered, because she absolutely was.

Another gratifying interlude was stolen from Galeena's list of forbidden interactions with men who are not her husband.

Before he dozed off for the night, he whispered into her ear, “I’ll not be able to exist on this earth without you, Galeena, goddess of the seas.”

“You know my name?” she asked.

“I do.”

* * *

Parched, Galeena slipped from Torren’s arms. She wrapped herself in a bath drape that was folded and shelved nearby, and she opened her travel satchel to retrieve her water horn. As she withdrew the drinking container, she saw her mother’s volume. Her attention returned to Torren. He slept. She realized she had fallen in love with him.

Admitting her true feelings to only herself, Galeena’s curiosity about his encounter with Adelia left her unable to share in his peaceful state. She pulled the book out, unwrapped it, and began reading.

Before the sun had revealed itself above the jagged peaks in the eastern distance, I had risen, fed the livestock, collected eggs, thrown my axe at the target stump, and filled the basins with fresh water from the river. Returning to life on our farm revived my need for simplicity and silence. The work reminded me of the very few months I lived independently in my woodland cottage prior to meeting Stefan and being held prisoner by the Danes. A longing for solace caused an ache within me, and fantasies of rearing Lukah and Galeena far away from watchful eyes filled my thoughts.

With the morning chores complete, I decided to refresh my body in the hot pools north of the pastures.

"I shall return soon, Mother. I wish to bathe."

"Yes, my love. The children are well occupied here with me."

I gathered the hem of my skirt, tucked it in the front of my belt, and I walked leisurely to the bathing pools.

At the edge, I knelt and pulled a cloth that was stored in my pocket. Soaking, wringing, wiping, and repeating the actions led me to want full submersion. Thus, I sat and lifted my foot to remove a boot. In the instant prior to my first pull, a small, soft voice spoke from the forest, "Dette er mitt hjem." (This is my home.)

Without looking, I replied, "Ja. Min også," (Yes. Mine also.) That was immediately followed by, "Do you speak Anglian?"

The hidden visitor said, "Yes, though I prefer the language of my home. Anglian is foreign."

"Perhaps, but you could also choose the perspective that no knowledge gained is foreign. The Anglian words are now part of you." I turned and strained to catch a glimpse of my young guest, but he was very well concealed.

I requested, "Will you show yourself, or do you intend to remain beneath the cover of the foliage? Will you gift me the pleasure of your company?"

The boy stated again, though in Anglian this time, "This is my home." A small sniffle followed.

I felt as if the hand of my invisible guest reached inside my breast and squeezed my heart. I stood and released the fabric of my skirt from the belt I wore. Then, with a voice as smooth and sweet as honey, I said, "Young Sir, I shall join you now. Please allow me the privilege and honor of seeing the face that accompanies the voice that is like music to my ears."

Peering into the edge of the forest, a milky hand with dirt beneath its fingernails reach outward from behind a tree. I smiled, then stretched my own hand toward the little palm that was speckled with crumbs of bark. Slowly, the distance between the two of us closed. The draw to that little boy was as strong as the ropes that secure the ships to the docksides. Slightly hunched, I stepped. The hand that was my destination remained steady reaching outward for me. Closer I eased until our fingertips touched. I gripped, pulled, and my visitor was revealed.

Other than my own son, I beheld the most precious boy I have ever seen. A child with glowing white curls and gray eyes emerged. One drying path of a recent tear shimmered on his cheek. I wiped it with the backs of my fingers while smiling at him.

"What is your name? Uh, I mean to say, hvad hedder du?" I asked.

"Torren," he replied.

"Hello Torren. I am Adelia. My mother is Olivia. My father is Styrke."

"Hello Adelia. I know your name. Olivia is my grandmother, Styrke is my grandfather, and Jaegar of Stenbjerg and Styrkeson is my father."

The family connections were not needed. Torren was unmistakably Jaegar's son. His resemblance to Lukah almost caused me to enclose him with my arms and kiss him relentlessly. His resemblance to Jaegar kept me following my instincts but only because I was so desperate to study him from head to foot.

I replied, "It seems that we have much in common."

He nodded and looked at his grand home set across the green field nestled into the hillside. Torren then said with disappointment, "I shall be punished for my disobedience. I was not to return here without my father. He was to bring me home after thirty nights. Only eight have passed."

"You shall not be punished my sweet. Your father will have to cross me to collect you."

"What are you doing over there, Galeena. Come, come back to my side." Torren extended his hand.

She loved him.

Galeena closed the bound parchments and wrapped them securely with a cloth. Holding the towel about her body, she returned the precious possession to her leather satchel.

When she again loomed over her match, she collected his attention, released her covering, and rejoined him in their bed. Torren scooted against her.

Galeena drifted to sleep wondering what happened next.

Chapter 19

The glow of daylight beaming through the tunnel's entry shone through Torren's eyelids arousing him from a depth of sleep he had not experienced since childhood. The surroundings puzzled him for but a moment. His arm searched for Galeena prior to his head lifting from the comfort of its resting place. Discovering she was not present, he sat upright and peered in every direction seeking her.

Galeena's absence and nature's calling forced him to a stance. After gathering his clothing and footwear, Torren exited the now seemingly dreary cave in search of fresh air and answers.

The world beyond their shelter was celebrating the risen sun. It was brimming with life, though perfectly serene. The sounds of the forest held his attention until he heard a familiar hissing in the distance. Waves. Galeena had informed him that if the gurgle of the creek or the chatter of the raindrops were silenced, he'd hear the sounds of the sea.

Their arrival had been from his right. The ocean was to his left. Galeena's footprints were not in the direction of the fresh water supply. Torren followed them only for entertainment purposes, for one need not be a genius to find an ocean that was within earshot.

After tracking each footprint, he reached the tree-line where the forest ends and the expanse of coastline begins. A deep inhale prefaced a quick scan of the sands and the sea for his new companion. As a wave crashed, then rolled to its demise, Galeena was spotted. Facing the infinite horizon, she waded shoulder deep a fair distance directly before him.

Though his focus was forward as he walked toward a pile of cloth, a periodic glance to his right, then left transpired. The Viking sought ships in the far distance. He scanned the vastness of the open shore in search of allies, enemies or priests. The only appearance of human life he perceived was Galeena.

When Torren reached her belongings, he examined them. She had left her bath sheet and a tunic piled together atop a brown satchel. His attention turned back to Galeena, still wading, now swimming. Unsure whether she was aware of his presence or not, he disrobed and proceeded into the frigid water. The waves were gentle but invading as they splashed each part of him that had not yet been submerged and acclimated to the extremely chilled temperature. His muscles tensed and shivered.

The sound of Torren's suction for air broke her dreamlike state. Modestly, she peeked over her shoulder at the man who drew nearer and nearer to her. "Does the water frighten you?" she called to him.

She was completely soaked, and her hair floated atop the minute crests around her. The woman before him surely had to be from a dream. He offered only half of a smile to show his amusement. "There is no pleasure for me in drawing from the warmth of a soft, linen and fur encasement, to a wet, cold, no *icy*, bath in the sea." He continued his lumbering forward motion.

Galeena enjoyed watching him approach. She had her arms crossed in front of her with her hands gripped to opposite shoulders, and her chin pressed to her wrist.

Without asking permission, Torren lifted her the instant she was within his reach. Cradling her in his arms, he pressed his forehead to hers and asked, "Is this to be our usual morn? Uninhibited bodies tranquilly intertwined."

"It bothers me not. You?"

"This state of dress and intimate contact with you has my full approval. However, I would prefer to eliminate the gathering in the sea. Do you submerge every morning when you awaken?"

Galeena's tone was calming, accepting, comforting. She spoke to him as if they had been together for many years. "No Torren. I know the salinity to have healing powers. Since my night was filled with rest, I wanted to strengthen my limbs with a soak and a swim. My next tasks are to bathe in the stream, then hunt and eat. After our morning nourishment, I'll be strong, gallant, and invincible. You may want to watch yourself around me. My fighting spirit returns."

"You and I have no cause to battle, and I thought you were days away from retiring as a soldier." Torren swayed her mostly floating body in the water.

With her arm now around his shoulder and her hands holding onto one another at the back of his neck, she replied, "Much can happen in one day. Therefore, I am to remain alert and ready until I am secured within King Alexar's fortress in Solsworth."

"You speak as if that is going to be your future."

"It has already been decided, Torren. We've had this discussion."

Apart from Galeena was not where he wished to be.

She requested, "Release me love. I am cold. I wish to begin our day."

He boldly asked, "Will you be allowing me more moments with you?"

His wishes needed no translation. Galeena raised one eyebrow and said, "Upon the shore, you shall have more of me."

Feeling they would be over-exposed on the shore, he inquired, "Do you not concern yourself with the local priests?"

"Not today. This is their day of worship. They are in the chapels. Also, for fear of receiving accusations of loitering, they keep their distance. If I should arrive at the gates of the monastery's fortress in need of prayer, I am welcomed. Otherwise, they know when I am here; they leave me in peace."

"So no one will interrupt us?"

"Do you see anyone? Do you fear that one of your own men would have left my village and followed us here? Do they lurk?"

"No. Certainly not. They will all remain together in Castleton. Dividing into smaller bands makes us vulnerable until we have a keen knowledge of the land. For many days, they will only extend out short distances from the village. Soon, small scouting groups will venture farther to gain familiarity with our surroundings."

So they will divide into smaller groups soon, she thought.

"Out of the water dear one. This conversation can wait," Galeena insisted.

Torren released her and swam at her side to the shallows. Reaching shore, he stood and continued his exit. The waves were rolling upon the tops of his feet when he searched for his newest interest. Galeena remained behind.

He returned to her and peering downward, confused, he asked, "Are you able to walk?"

She covered her face with both hands and nodded.

He smiled believing he knew the reason for her hesitation. "Speak your challenge. I must hear it."

Galeena dropped her hands and punched the water as another wave pushed against her. "Ugh! Will you turn your back to me please?"

"That is most likely not going to happen. I've become quite familiar with all that makes you a woman." He laughed saying, "You shall stand on your own, or I shall carry you. The choice is yours to make. Please recall my dear Galeena, you have promised me another encounter as soon as we are removed from these icy waters. Collecting on that promise is my priority. Now, I can watch you shuffle and shiver your way up there," he pointed to their pile of clothing, "I can carry you, or you can fulfill your covenant in this very locale. What shall be your decision?"

Another wave rushed over her shoulders. Galeena gathered and squeezed the water from her hair. Looking up to him she finally said, "Torren, will you not allow me the pleasure of your vision as it parts from me? If you turn your back and advance slowly to our belongings, I will receive my own view of you. Should you be the only one who benefits from this exchange between us?"

"Such a clever ploy you suggest. However, dearest Galeena, you need not feel pride in this moment. At some point between here and there, you will have to risk my gaze upon all of you. Be logical. Your modesty is not necessary."

She confessed, "We've collected unobstructed views of one another in the dark during intimate interludes. Walking exposed like a harlot in the light of day is another matter. I must maintain some sense of decency."

Exasperated, Torren sighed, he then bent and scooped Galeena from the water. "Giving you no choice is symbolic. I have literally stolen the goddess of the seas from her true home. You now belong to me for all time."

Galeena laughed and pressed her forehead to his chin. She said, "Gratitude for your chivalry is all I have to offer you, Sir."

He replied, "Gratitude is not all you have for me." They laughed as he carried her briskly away from their morning soak.

When they reached their clothes, Torren placed Galeena on the large sheet atop the sand. She reached for her tunic saying, "I shall wear my covering. I must be warmed, for I tremble violently."

"Yes. That will be acceptable. You wear only your tunic, and I will wear only my boots."

Shocked, Galeena screamed, "Ah! No! You shall not seek a private moment with me dressed in only your boots. The very image disturbs my craving."

"Likewise, your small gown disturbs mine. Be not concerned about your chill. Have confidence that I shall warm you soon enough." He moved his body over hers, forcing her onto her back. She laughed and could not remove her gaze from his.

"Toren?"

"Yes love?"

"How will we know when the time has come for us to..." Galeena paused and lowered her eyes from his.

"That time has passed. I await only your invitation."

"If I were your betrothed, would you not be irate and disappointed that another man had ruined me?"

"Tis not the way I think, Galeena. You became mine three days ago. Any decisions you made before the first moment I beheld you matter not to me. A man of honor will love the woman God gives him as she is. You do not receive a beautiful gift and insult it or despise it. Think of the gowns that your king gives you, the fabric has been through very harsh processes to achieve its final transformation into colorful silk. You do not hate the garments because of their past. A man, a true man, sees the woman he loves for who she is, not who she once was. You have not even met the Prince of Solsworth. You may not like him. And Galeena, although your king has not promised you to me, I believe you are the only one with authority over yourself. You decide what and *who* you want."

Would anyone ever know? She wondered as she stared into his loving soul.

Torren scrunched his brow straining to read her heart. A guilt welled within him, "My dear, if you must think this deeply to fully accept me, then I shall stop. I've never been in love with any other, but I know I want my emotions and my desires to be matched. Something holds you back from me."

"Yes. I am still unsure. Tis probably a number of things. You have only been in my life for three days. You are still an enemy. You fully intend to steal my king's daughter and deliver her to your father. That delivery means your absence from Northanglia. All of these concerns lead me to one conclusion. That is, I care not to bring forth a son who has no father. Nor do I wish to bear a son hidden beneath another man's name. I have been raised out of the reach of my parents. My children will have all of me and all of their father."

A tear fell from the outer corner of each of her eyes. Galeena was forthcoming, "It is best if you return to your countrymen sooner than we planned. My suggestion is that we leave immediately upon completion of this day's first meal. This attachment we are forming must end. My life will go on without you."

Time with Torren was beginning to make her believe she did have free-will. However, she was the daughter of King Wilhelm, the Princess of Northanglia. Her husband had been chosen, the date of her wedding was set, and Galeena had no intentions of raising the child of the man she loves as the son of a man she does not want.

Torren spoke the final words of their embrace that morning. "I feel my current position with you affords me the right to speak my mind freely. First, having different beliefs does not make us enemies. We do not have to hate one another simply because we are from different lands. Next, whether we leave today or in three or four days, we'll not be out of each other's lives. Tis far too late for that. I'm here. I am your present and I intend on being your future... somehow. And the last thing you need to know is that I am not my father or my grandfather. Styrke and Jaegar both brought sons into this world with women they did not love. That is not a path I will take."

Her heart pounded for him.

Chapter 20

Careful to ensure his eyes caught no sight of her below her face, Torren reached and gripped Galeena's tunic. He placed it between them as he raised from her warmed body. Neither breached the other's privacy as they covered themselves.

Torren completed his robing and held his hand out to Galeena. She took his offer for assistance politely and stood with her sheet and satchel bundled under one arm.

"We'll bathe separately. I'll go prepare our breakfast," he mentioned.

"If you'll wait for me, I'll help," she replied.

A demure smile appeared and Torren acknowledged her kindness with a nod.

They walked toward the tree-line and into the sparse forest together in silence. When they reached half of the distance to the cave, Galeena flung a blade across his path.

Shocked, Torren complained, "I could have walked into that." He then looked to his right and saw a bleeding rabbit. He added, "Where did you get the dagger?"

Laughing, Galeena replied, "I am always armed. I have many blades in my bag. One must always be prepared for all that could arise. I heard the shuffle. My weapon flew. Tis not an action I give much thought to anymore. You were never in danger. I would not have hit you."

Torren picked up the hare by its hind legs. "I'll clean it. You can enjoy the spring first."

"Together. Let us complete our chores together. These are our final moments of solitude. We shall talk, learn, laugh, then load our horses again and return to our stations in life."

"No, Galeena. You tend to your needs and I'll supply our food."

Her direction veered to their left and his to their right. Galeena arrived at the flowing creek, removed her tunic and lowered into one of the pools. After the sea water was rinsed from her skin and hair, she reversed the order of the bath preparations and rested beside the gurgling waters before returning to the cave.

Disappointment and hunger were beginning to reveal themselves as irritation. Torren had retrieved a pot, butchered the animal, built a fire outside of their abode, and had the meat boiling all before Galeena's return. He grew impatient waiting, so he set off to find her.

Downstream, he spotted her bent over searching the underbrush.

"Galeena, what are you doing?"

"Another hare pounced by me so I decided to kill it too."

"It shouldn't be difficult to find."

"I missed." She stood, placed her fists on her hips and scrunched her nose in anger.

"Come."

"I want my knife. What if I step on it one day?"

"Wear boots! You'll not need to worry about stepping on anything!"

"I just want my knife. Will you help me?"

A snuff was released as Torren shook his head at her complaint and reaction. "Come eat! Forget the dagger! If we are returning to the civilized world, we need to part soon."

"Help me," she demanded.

Wanting to expedite the search, Torren joined her. He shuffled and looked, though not with much effort. All he did was more to appease the woman at his side.

Frustration finally took control and he said, "This task can wait, or what would be even more preferable is to abolish this chore all together. Your obsession can be eased simply by not running bare-footed in the forest, any forest, ever. Tis a miracle your bare sole has not found a serpent, or a hive of poisonous, flying demons."

She knew he had spoken truthfully, thus she succumbed to his instruction. "Daylight is being wasted. Very well, let us eat. I will return this way someday and seek the blasted blade myself. For now, tis no longer my concern."

An extended hand led her away from the leaves, fallen limbs, and saplings, and right onto the dagger.

"Agh!" Galeena screamed.

Torren's reaction was swift. She was cradled in his arms before she had taken another breath.

"I told you it was a danger for me," Galeena said wincing and holding her bloodied foot.

"Wear boots!" he ordered.

At the edge of the stream, Torren placed Galeena upon a rock and inspected her wound.

"Tis not too deep. It shall heal in time. My advice is to refrain from running or dancing."

"You tease me?"

"Yes. However, I speak the truth. Good fortune is yours that you have your horse, and me of course." Without asking, Torren picked Galeena up once more and carried her back to their waiting breakfast.

The warmth of her silent giggles comforted him though he fought to ignore the feelings.

Upon their arrival back to the shelter, both noticed a visitor had been in the vicinity. Galeena dropped her legs from his hold, scrambled from his arms, and made her way to the opening. Torren attempted to halt Galeena's entrance to the cave, but she limped undaunted past him. Inside, all was as it had been left, except a loaf of bread had been placed on a cooking pan beside the fire ring.

"Monks?" Torren asked.

"Mmm... perhaps not. They should all still be in prayer."

He appeared concerned that some other passerby could be present. "Is the offering from someone you know? Or, has someone else arrived here for rest?"

She pointed. "I believe this is an offering. You need not worry."

"And the giver?"

"On his way to the king's home," she replied, though clearly withholding information. "The loaf will be a perfect compliment to our eggs and rabbit. I have berry preserves here as well. This is a welcome treat from an ally. Worry not."

"Who has been able to come here without my notice and depart so quickly?"

"He was probably here for hours without either of us noticing."

"Do you speak of the man Lukah? Your equal in King Wilhelm's army?"

"I do." Galeena smiled with great joy.

"Should that man's arrival concern me?"

"It should concern you if you are seen by him on your return to Castleton without me at your side. He will be hiding along the road. There is no doubt that he is aware you accompany me. Your footprints surround this area. Surely he already sees you as a threat if you are near me."

"A threat on your life?"

"Possibly."

Torren's anger was increasing rapidly.

Galeena hobbled to the bread, picked it up and sniffed it. "Ooo... it's still warm."

The chemicals that race through any man's veins surged within Torren. To keep from exhibiting too much jealousy, he demanded, "Sit. Let me wrap your foot. Your blood will draw wolves or vermin to this place."

Galeena sat on their bed and lifted her injured foot into the air. Her elation was infuriating. Her words were sharper than the dagger that had impaled her foot. "I am anxious to see him. It has been quite a while. The amount of time we've been apart escapes me, it has been so long. I am only half of a person when I am not with him."

Anger over his thoughtless decision to leave Castleton for a woman who was clearly infatuated with another man caused him to chide her, "Did you lure me here, Galeena?"

She sat up, fumbled for a moment adjusting her gown for cover, and with a raised voice she said, "You trailed me Torren. You have had every opportunity to leave and return to your army. Get up. Walk directly west. You will come to a road. Follow it north. I recommend you use caution and remain out of sight. A lone Dane will be pierced with no opportunity for questioning offered. I am not holding you prisoner. Go. Do not place your weakness upon me."

Torren clambered over her, grasped her shoulders and forced her down. He glared at her. She was exceedingly calm. "Why are you not afraid of me?" he asked.

The knife that was protruding from the bread loaf was pressed to his throat. "I have no need to fear any man. I fed you, sheltered you, directed you, and..." Galeena mustered, "and... I will kill you." Those were not the words she wanted to speak, but they were the only ones she could produce.

Torren took the knife from her grip. "Nothing in this world has ever challenged me, apart from you. I have no plans to give you reason to kill me. I must ask the same of you. Go back to Claremont, marry the Prince of Solsworth, and leave Northanglia. I would very much like to complete my father's assignment and sail for Gudsfelt. Our plan was to take Princess Helene back to our country and give her the choice to relinquish her claim, marry me or die. This distraction that is you, is the reason Jaegar told me to speak to no one outside of my own party."

The combination of his confession and insult infuriated her. She yelled, "I should have killed you when I had the chance. Be warned Ice-lander, you will die very soon."

Galeena attempted to shove the man who held her to the ground, but his mass was too great. With speed and strength, he raised both of her hands above her head. His sinister smile did not frighten her as he said, "You have nowhere to go, soldier."

"I'm not ignorant, Torren. Removing you may not be possible for me, but you cannot stay in this position forever."

She struggled to free her wrists from his hold.

"Have you had enough of this man yet, Galeena?"

Torren didn't remove his eyes from the woman beneath him. He said, "Lukah?"

Galeena smiled and nodded to affirm his query.

The Viking smiled back. "I'm glad he's here. No better circumstance could have arisen for our first meeting. It was going to happen any day now."

"He doesn't leave me, Torren."

"Nor would I if you were mine."

Chapter 21

Every muscle in her body relaxed.

"Lukah, you must leave us," Galeena requested.

"Your current state indicates otherwise," her brother replied. He then spoke calmly to Torren, "Norseman, the only reason you are not dead is because she has not given the command. My sword will separate you from this world the instant Galeena shows even the slightest sign of discomfort or surrender."

Torren straddled her midsection, thus kicking would have only exposed her to her waiting sibling. Galeena's legs remained together and tightly tucked to the side.

"Torren, Lukah will leave us if you will remove yourself from my body." She then whispered, "But please do it very slowly."

"Perhaps I choose not to surrender," he replied whilst his grip on her wrists tightened.

"Please don't provoke a battle with him," she begged for fear of losing them both.

"You've spent the past three nights with me, and I believe you did lure me here. In your mind, having me here alone makes my defeat easier. I was blinded by you."

"I did not bring you here to kill you, nor did I call upon Lukah to assist in killing you. Do not falsely accuse me."

"You will be the recipient of many accusations should we remain in each other's company, for I have decided that I do not trust you."

"Tis a wise and fair statement," she assured him.

"In this moment though, my only option is to do my job, and that is remove one more Northanglian soldier from his duties."

"No!" Galeena yelled as she was rolled on top of the Viking for a moment of protection. Torren then released her hands, grabbed the knife from his side, aimed, and threw the dagger toward Lukah. The intent was not to pierce, but to distract long enough to get to his feet for an equitable fight.

"Get your weapon, Norseman," Lukah coaxed smoothly as he side-stepped with anticipation.

Torren's sword was nearby. He retrieved it and joined his adversary in their inevitable confrontation.

Not one descendent present knew of Adelia's prophecy. She loved both sons of Jaegar, but knew before her own child arrived to the world that the two would be at war. When a father only loves one of his children, the other grows with feelings of rejection and hatred even when the separation is not the child's fault. Adelia was to blame for this shared threat upon each of the young warriors' lives.

Torren lingered, poised for defense.

Lukah stood very still, his sword low, his spine straight.

Galeena was crouched, balancing most of her weight on her non-injured foot. Blood continued to flow from her wound. She covered the gash with her hands and squeezed as the pulse in it throbbed. When her hands were damp with blood, she wiped them on her white shift then grasped her foot again. Her need to tend the opened flesh prevented her from being able to intervene in the clash between the two.

Torren waited, ready. Lukah glanced toward his little sister and saw that she had been harmed. Not knowing how she had been hurt or where the blood oozed from, he charged his enemy.

Each brother swung, struck, blocked. The clang of their swords colliding echoed about the cavern and pierced Galeena's inner ears. Both seemed to be possessed by demonic forces. Their eyes sought only death of the other.

Torren was larger but Lukah was quicker. Clearly they had been trained by the same man, Styrke. Lukah's successes in battle had always been due to his brief experiences with his Norse grandfather. Torren grew suspicious of his adversary and his style of fighting. Neither relented and neither slowed their attack. As one neared the other, blows were thrown and landed with fierceness.

Ignoring her pain, Galeena finally bound to her feet and began calling for a cease between them. She limped, desperate to keep her ailing foot from being pressed too firmly onto the dirt beneath them.

"Stop!" she demanded in Anglian. "Du skal stoppe!" she yelled in Norse.

The first few interruptions were ignored until she was able to finally place herself in front of Torren.

Streams of perspiration flowed from Lukah's brow. His neck glistened. His tunic damp.

Torren's back was to the rock wall. Galeena leaned against him. Lukah pointed his sabre at her. "Remove yourself. Tis a treasonous act to protect an enemy from receiving his sentence." She did not respond. He continued, "I see he has hurt you. You are soaked with blood. This Viking does not leave here with breath."

"Lukah, I injured myself. I lost a dagger, then found it."

Panting, her brother attempted to withhold a smile. "No boots?" he asked.

Torren was somewhat amused that she had been warned by others to cover her feet.

"If your desire is to kill him on my behalf, then you may release yourself from the act of retaliation." Galeena attempted an absolution.

"Tis my responsibility to remove him from Northanglia. His purpose here is to end, now."

Galeena ordered, "Leave him to me."

Torren rested, listening intently to the pair. His secret relief was that even though the words Lukah and Galeena exchanged were seasoned with care and protection, the actions of their bodies were not. They kept a respectable distance. Lukah made no attempt to touch her in any manner. Galeena continued to place her balance and weight upon him. He also noted her hand held to his thigh. This gave Torren hope that regardless of the history between the Northanglians, perhaps she did maintain a deeper connection with him.

"If your fellow comrade is not going to kill me today, I'd like to return to Castleton with haste." Torren spoke as if nothing had happened.

Galeena replied, "You'll need an escort. Wait for me to ready myself."

"Your services are not necessary. I shall pack provisions, and find my own way back. I believe the instructions are: proceed west until I reach the king's road, then go north being sure to stay out of sight. If children can accomplish such a task, certainly I can do no less."

Placing only the toe of her lame foot on the ground, Galeena shifted and turned to face the now indifferent man. The loss of affection for her shone in his eyes. She braced herself by pressing both of her palms to his chest. She advised, "Take the horse."

"I can walk faster than she can run. Additionally, moving whilst remaining unseen will be much easier without a large, snorting, clopping, mare beneath me. When our paths cross again, which should be soon, I will be sure to tell Olivia that her dear companion still lives, though not for long."

Lukah and Galeena both cringed at the thought of Torren's access to their grandmother. A man who shared no blood with her was permitted to contact her, yet the two children born to her only daughter never knew how or where to find her.

"Lukah, please leave us."

"No. Whether you take offense or not, I'll not leave you alone with him. You cannot be trusted."

"My decisions are none of your concern. Please leave."

Torren addressed the man who stood with them, "You have nothing to fear. My absence is only moments away. Your partner is safe."

Lukah stared into Torren's eyes. He looked for their father, their grandfather, and all other fathers he would never know. When he felt he had collected a mere fragment of a link to his unknown family line, he lowered his chin and walked away.

The desperation her brother felt to be a part of the family to which he truly belonged hurt Galeena's heart. "Lukah,"

He stopped and looked at his sister.

"We are forever. We are family. We belong together."

He offered a half smile and exited.

Before returning her attention to Torren, Galeena slipped into a daze. Her guest watched thinking the two were orphans and truly had never had any other family aside from each other.

Her silent pondering was broken when Torren said, "I'll wrap your wound, help you dress, and then I leave. Do not come to me again. All protections of you that I held amongst my people will be removed. Stay with Lukah and your troops until you are in Solsworth. King Boersen's daughter will be on a ship aimed at White Crested Cove within days. Get on with your marriage and your life. Leave this battle to the men."

A subtle chortle was released. "Get out," she viciously whispered.

Chapter 22

"My compliments and gratitude to the baker." Torren held up the loaf, tore it in half, and took a bite. Just before he disappeared into the woods, he pointed toward the cavern and said, "She is once again your responsibility. Make sure she keeps her feet covered and that wound clean. It will fester and the stubborn woman will die because of her own carelessness."

Lukah laughed. He imagined what it would have been like to have grown up in Torren's shadow, the little brother of a full-blooded Dane. He wondered if the Viking would have shouldered the responsibility of protecting him as he had with Galeena.

"Ice-lander?!" Lukah called out.

"Speak, though loudly, my progression halts for no one now," echoed from the forest.

"If I were from your land, would we have been friends?"

"Never, Anglian!"

Lukah felt a sting of disappointment. Then he heard, “We would have been brothers!”

Out of view, Galeena listened. The disappearance of the Viking filled her with sadness. He had taken possession of her heart and her body.

“Galeena?”

“I’m here Lukah, you need not shout.”

“Henry has arrived; he rests within King Wilhelm’s walls. Tis why I traveled here all night. You are to be presented to him and all others tomorrow before dusk.”

“Why does father expedite this courtship and wedding?”

“He wants you out of Northanglia as soon as possible.”

* * *

The children of the king were ushered into their father’s fortress at the darkest hour of the night. The conversations of their journey revolved around an unfailing plot to achieve victory. They knew their father would be waiting for their arrival. What they did not anticipate was finding him in their mother’s study instead of his own.

The door was closed and King Wilhelm said, “Have you kept your promise and protected the bound documents you took from this cabinet?”

Perplexed by his topic of interest, Galeena responded, “Of course I have father, though I do wish to maintain possession of them for a while longer. I’ve not had opportunity to finish reading them. Why do you ask? Why are you in here at this late hour?"

Wilhelm held up several scrolls. "These are why I am here. More memoirs have arrived via Henry and his entourage. They've been scripted by your Grandmother Olivia. Instructions were that they join these other volumes. Oh, the stories those two women have to tell. My heart wonders and my heart rejects."

"Father, Grandmother and Mother only want to be remembered. They crave not infamy. They merely long for their children to never forget them. Be not afraid of the events they record."

"Thank you for the reassurance, Galeena. Would you care to review these new messages?"

Lukah spoke up, "Why have you never shared the stories with me Galeena?"

"You are never around long enough, nor have you asked. The only moments we have together are always filled with strategy and warfare. Each papyrus wears the ink of one common day in the life of our mother or grandmother. Many are ordinary, some are interesting, most are seemingly insignificant."

She addressed their father, "I would like them, yes."

Wilhelm tossed them onto the foot of the bed upon which he rested.

Lukah shrugged and asked, “Are we allowed to sleep now? Let us discuss the events that are to transpire in the morn. Details will be lost if I try to explain all Galeena and I have decided at this moment.”

“You are both invited to retire to your upper chambers after I hear the brief version. Galeena, you’ll sleep in your suite. No escapes this night. I have the maidens coming to dress you after the sun has risen. And, did I detect a limp?”

“You did. Do not worry about that. Slippers and plenty of medicine cloth will ease my injury.”

Wilhelm noticed Lukah raise his eyes to the ceiling and shake his head in frustration. He did not ask any further questions on the matter. He simply inquired again of their thoughts.

When his children’s ideas were heard, Wilhelm ordered Galeena to personally deliver an invitation to her betrothal banquet to Torren. “You will hand him a sealed request after you have been preened and appropriately groomed as a representative of your king.”

“Father, I am not a messenger,” Galeena argued. “Send Robert.”

“They’ve seen you in their midst. They’ll not hold you hostage or attempt to harm you.”

“You are incorrect, Father. Most call for my execution or servitude.”

Lukah begged, "Father, please do not send her from here alone. Command that I accompany her. She is not capable of entering then departing Castleton without incident."

Her brother's objection changed her perspective. Galeena spoke on her own behalf, "Actually, I thank you for your confidence and trust." She looked to Lukah and said, "After hearing your point of view, I have changed mine. I will be delivering a message to the very same man who has not attempted to kill me even though he has been given numerous opportunities. I need not an escort. I believe the Dane will agree to protect me in exchange for an audience with our king."

Lukah continued his argument, "History insists we not trust those people. Our own queen was beaten, tortured, and held prisoner by them. Why would you be treated any differently, Galeena? Our mother was a princess, their own heir, and she was abused. You are to be a mere messenger, a messenger who defeated one of their commanders and killed many of their guards. Therefore, it is even more likely you would be taken by them. They will show you no honor and no mercy."

"Your logic could work against you Lukah. As a mere messenger, I could be seen as valueless. And, in response to your concerns surrounding the extermination of their fellow countrymen, some may fear me."

"Be not so arrogant. Do as you wish. Father, tis time for me to sleep. This has been a trying day."

"Lukah, my son, my heart is yours. Thank you for the love you have for Galeena. I'll see you in the hall at dawn. You'll be joining me as host for our guests."

"Galeena, you get plenty of rest. You'll take your morning meal in your chamber. Do not emerge until you have been fully cleaned and are well presented. Also, please do not seek Henry. I want your first meeting to be at the announcement ceremony."

Galeena was curious as to why she was to be the messenger. She asked for honesty, "Tell me Father, why do you send me?"

"A Styrkeson cannot refuse a Daughter of Boersen. This man, Torren, could suspect my invite to be a hidden opportunity for ambush. He would most likely deny my request to meet him. However, if you arrive and request a public meeting with him at the center of the village, he will not be able to resist you. Now go, sleep well. My deep love to you both."

The scrolls were collected into Galeena's arms and she kissed her father good night. Her soul felt his sorrow. Wilhelm missed Adelia.

* * *

Waking up the way God intended, which is naturally and without harsh disturbances, was invigorating for Galeena.

The servants' bell was at her side as was a small porcelain tea pot. The sun lit her room and a small fire warmed it. Not even the aching of her wound could dim the glow of her disposition and the brilliance of all that surrounded her.

Galeena stared and smiled at each candelabra, each portrait, and every piece of furniture that was adorned with ornate gold accents. The walls and ceiling had been painted the palest blue to resemble the sky, and the moldings that framed her fireplace and doorways were so white they reflected the rays all about her. The moments she was sent to her room were her most cherished.

Ting, ting, ting, ting. The high pitch of her bell sang to her maids.

Four young women entered, each with an important task to be completed. One was to ensure Galeena ate. One was to ensure that she bathed and was sprinkled with her private scent. One was to dress her and style her hair. And one was assigned the chore of cleaning up after all the others.

They all envied their mistress, though none would have wanted to live like her all of the other days she was outside of King Wilhelm's care.

Galeena had been dressed in a pale green, silk gown that swished and glimmered when she moved. The jewels that trimmed the neckline were selected because of their resemblance to the iridescent sparkles of the foams that are delivered to the shore by the hissing waves. Her hair had been combed, and the sides had been plaited and tied back away from her face with fine strips of cloth that matched her gown. Snakelike curls hung loosely from her temples to her jawline, and the remaining long, waved tresses, caressed her shoulders and draped down the entire length of her back.

Nothing could force one to believe that the delicate, styled, beauty was not herself descended from royalty. She was almost too perfect.

The final touch to the princess' presentation was her slippers. A nurse wrapped her foot, slid the flat shoes into place, and she wished Galeena the very best at hiding her pain from the public at her presentation that evening. "Forgive my jest Lady Galeena, but watching you dance will be quite entertaining. I'll either be most impressed or most embarrassed for you."

Galeena laughed and said, "I believe I shall do all within my power to avoid participating in any rhythmic interactions."

They concluded their conversation, "Your horse awaits. Here is the king's sealed correspondence to the leader of the Norsemen. Now off, and don't provoke the Ice-landers! Return in this exact state. It will make preparing you for this evening much quicker for us all."

The nurse received a proper curtsy as a reply.

In the courtyard and seated, Galeena sauntered her horse to the gate and paused just below the guards' bridge. Claremont was built atop a stone ridge, and the weather of the day afforded her a clear view of her village.

Four men were at attention and observing the area that faced the direction of Castleton.

Galeena asked, "What happens there at this moment?"

“There is much noise, laughter and yelling. They were quiet last night, yet all morning they have been celebrating something.”

Galeena knew they would be celebrating Torren’s return. His arrival would inspire them to continue each of their missions, and if he promised them all restrictions that pertained to her had been lifted, they would definitely be rejoicing. The Vikings would be readying themselves mentally and physically for upcoming victories. Drunken ramblings would certainly be the preamble to focus and planning.

The guard’s claim was supported, “Yes, tis apparent they are most jubilant.” After watching what little she could see, and listening to the faint roars with the occasional piercing yelps, she smiled at the men and said, “Tis a shame I will have to kill so many of them soon. I suppose they should be allowed a night or two of pleasure.”

The guards shared her sentiment. “We agree Miss. They sit far too close for our king to ignore them. If they do not choose to leave, they will be advancing to their eternal homes very soon.”

“My king’s message will not reach its recipient if I do not proceed. Good day gentlemen. Fair thee well and please keep a keen watch upon me. I should much like to arrive back here intact to meet my soon-to-be husband.”

They laughed and nodded as she exited the garrison riding like a princess on her way to meet her honored guests.

Chapter 23

Commotion and ruckus traveled like a wave upon the road from the entry of the village to where Torren stood with Gunnar at the center of Castleton. Both men turned their attention to the gathering, then parting of the crowd.

"There she sits, Torren, your rabid little pet of a woman."

"She defends her home against invaders. You would do no less. She just happens to be on the wrong side at this very moment. Although, twas not wise for her to amble so proudly into our village."

"Why do you believe she is exhibiting such bravery?"

Torren strolled to the center of the dusty road and planted himself in a solid stance with his arms crossed. Gunnar joined him at his flank. He replied, "Galeena is always brave. She is either here to collect something important to her that was left behind upon our acquisition of this little town, or she arrives with a warning. Neither matters to me. We shall allow her to come and go with freedom."

Disappointed and appalled, Gunnar argued, “You removed protections, we can do with her as we please.”

“Not in my presence. She is causing no harm at this moment, and I am curious. I’d like to learn why she graces us with this visit.”

Galeena smiled at the men who surrounded her and her horse. The few women she noticed, made their animosity or indifference to her known with turned backs or deliberate disregard.

As her pathway to the man she had rejected cleared, breathing became labored. She attempted to take long, slow draws of air so she didn’t appear as afraid as she truly was. Galeena feared not the company about her, she feared the sorrow of regret. The last strides to reach Torren had her thinking only of how desperately she wished they could disappear... together.

What everyone saw: a humble smile, a gratuitous demeanor, a beautiful guest.

The gentlest tug stopped her horse. Torren reached for the leather strap of the bridle, then stroked the velvety nose of the admirable animal. He raised his eyes to Galeena’s and offered a sultry and tempting half smile that let her know he owns a very private part of her. To the woman sitting high upon her horse, the Viking asked, “Care to lower yourself to our standards, Galeena of Northanglia?”

"I do prefer to stand on equal ground with the political delegates I meet."

Torren translated her comment to Gunnar.

Gunnar replied, "We are not equals. You are the reason she isn't dead."

Unbeknownst to her enemy, Galeena understood his threat and complaint. She offered a gentle and seemingly innocent smile. Torren allowed her feign of ignorance.

"Do you have a gentleman present who can assist me with my dismount, Sir Torren? On any other day I would not make such a request—"

Aware of her ailment, Torren interrupted, "Say no more, Miss." He stepped to her side and held up his hands to ease the jolt of her landing.

With sincerity, when she stood face to face with him, Galeena said, "Your kindness is appreciated."

Before asking why she was there, Torren first admired her. He squinted with intrigue. Having expected to see a well curved warrior, Torren had to allow himself a moment to accept Galeena in her feminine form. Her brown tresses framed her face and draped her shoulders in long ringlets. Her honey-toned skin was like silk, and her eyes were like the amber stones he had seen embedded in rare jewels. Dressed for daily tasks or battle, he found Galeena to be alluring and irresistible, but standing formally in the rays of the sunlight, she was untouchable.

As he assessed her regal and virtuous stance, he wondered if her disposition had altered as much as her presentation. In Torren's experience, most women of his lands dressed in either trousers or drab frocks. There was rarely cross-over of their preferred styles. The object of his secret obsession proved she could enrapture him regardless of her presentation.

Galeena was proud, sly, devious, and very wise. Yet, this late morn, she waited politely before him in a soft and demure pose, one worthy of royalty.

He finally spoke, "There now, a new creation has blossomed. The lady who stands in my midst surprises me with her transition. I approve. Now, care to explain your presence?" He waved his hands to acknowledge his countrymen as he added, "We all see that you have abandoned the challenge of making your way through our streets undetected."

"Would you prefer I leave?"

"I prefer you share why you are here."

"I arrive on errand for my king."

In Norse, he said, "Your king sends a woman into his enemy's camp? Does he fear delivering the message himself? Are his carriers equally afraid?"

Torren and his cohorts all began laughing with much gusto. Galeena studied the only one she knew. His roar was a bit too loud for her comfort.

She scolded, "You are drunk."

"No my love, I *was* drunk. I am no longer in such a state. Judge not. Have you never been under the mercy of a potent drink?"

"Why would I? I have no reason to partake of an excess of wine or ale. I enjoy not fermented beverages. A mild mixture of brewed herbs is more suited to my taste. Tis quite soothing, as are other non-contaminated liquids King Wilhelm receives on occasion from foreign traders."

Torren chuckled at her snobbery. The change in her was astonishing, and he wasn't sure it was welcomed.

"Speak your task. We are all anxious to learn of King Wilhelm's needs."

His jest was irritating, but she had to remain placid.

Galeena extended her hand. It held a small folded parchment that bore the king's seal. She explained, "King Wilhelm has scripted an invitation to be delivered only to you." She paused, then asked, "You do read don't you?"

Her insult did not go unnoticed. He offered a slightly amused smile and responded, "Yes. I am educated. Tis more surprising that *you* have knowledge of the written word. This nation does not have a reputation for holding girls in high enough esteem to allow them access to teachings of literacy."

"I am unlike any other woman in our kingdom."

"You are correct again," he agreed.

Torren opened the private note and read:

Torren of Danemore,

Your presence is requested at Claremont this evening. Please join me in honoring the arrival of Prince Henry of Solsworth to Northanglia. We shall be celebrating the union of his nation and mine.

King Wilhelm of Northanglia

Torren looked suspiciously to Galeena and said, "You arrived here dressed in someone else's finery to deliver a petition from King Wilhelm. The only assumption I can make is that your king is desperate for my attendance. He must have something interesting planned for me."

"There is no trickery in this personal request. And these are my clothes."

"There is no reason for me to believe you. Tell me, what purpose could I possibly serve? Why would your king invite an enemy into his home?" Torren wondered if he would be walking into a snare. The soldiers could easily imprison or execute him if he was unaccompanied, and most likely unarmed, inside the garrison.

His ego was the target of her next message. "You are the one who rules Castleton now, correct?"

He was not moved nor accepting her attempt at baiting him.

She continued, "You lead these people. Your father is the new king of Danemour. You have the authority to call upon the troops of Dornwold. All of these descriptors and powers make you important to my king. Any visiting royalty or ruler would receive an official invitation. Will you come or not? Speak your reply."

"This is the only reason my attendance is requested?"

In case anyone in their vicinity spoke Anglain, Galeena lowered her voice so none of the onlookers could hear, and she said, "No Torren, I also wish you to be there."

Although they had parted ways and he was firm in his commitment to maintain a distance from Galeena, Torren was pleased by her confession. He was happy to receive the invitation. This situation would enable him to enter the fortress and search for the concealed daughter of King Boersen. He would also be able to take measure of the man who was to marry the woman in whom he had staked a particular interest. He replied, "This night will satisfy many of my curiosities. Thus, with great joy I shall attend."

"Tis a pleasing response. King Wilhelm will be proud to introduce you to his representatives, guests and citizens."

"I'll not be walking into my final meal will I?"

"Not to my knowledge."

"Does he want me to meet Henry of Solsworth for a particular reason?"

Galeena shrugged. Her father did want the two men to meet. The voice in her head told her the introduction was meant to show Torren what he will never have: a kingdom and Galeena. Their enemy's identity would also be known to all.

The crowd never lost interest in the conversation of the two. They watched and listened, trusting that Torren would be forth coming.

Knowing they could hear very little and interpret even less, Torren said in a lowered voice, "I crave stability of mind. After walking all night, I arrived to your home and fell into a heavy sleep. Not enough time of rest was allowed though. A nightmare reoccured. Once again I lie on a feathered bed distressed over the premonition that I shall take my own life."

Her head tilted as she said, "Peace of mind shall be yours soon. And Torren, I do not interpret your dream to mean what you are believing. Jumping from a boat in a storm does not have to mean you wish to take your own life. All decisions are yours to make. Perhaps return to *my* bed and close your eyes. You've had ale, you should be able to capture a dreamless sleep. This will be a late night, and you'll need your strength for all that is to come."

"What is to come, Galeena?"

"A night filled with dancing. Also, King Wilhelm wishes a private audience with you upon your arrival. That could mean anything. You'll want to have your wits sharp and at the ready. Just join us and enjoy the festivities and banquet. Now, you should go rest. Will you assist me in regaining my seat?"

"Gladly," he replied.

Torren carefully lifted Galeena as she pulled herself onto her saddle. When she was set and her gown was situated for show, she said, “I shall see you soon.”

“You shall.” His reply was distant.

Galeena turned her horse, then before parting Castleton, she recalled another message for him. “Torren?”

“Hm.”

“Olivia has contacted King Wilhelm.”

He gaped. Then asked, “What has she to say?!”

“I have not read the correspondence. Perhaps I will be privy to such information upon my return, and I will share with you this evening.”

“That would be appreciated, Galeena.”

“Oh, Torren?”

“Yes.” She had more of his attention.

“How are my chickens?”

“Delicious.”

“You are evil.”

“I look forward to hearing what my grandmother has to say. Depart and use that rare learning you’ve been awarded to translate then reveal.”

“Til the sun sets, Ice-lander.”

The stallion was nudged into a trot.

Torren watched her until she could no longer be seen.

“She beguiles you,” Gunnar said with disgust.

Torren tapped the handle of his cutlas with the tip of his finger. He called angrily to Gunnar and his entire crew, “Does my reputation lead you to believe that I will overlook what she has done? Do you wish to confess that you think me ignorant? Do you believe I have forgotten our purpose here?"

He waited. Eyes lowered.

He warned, "Do not question me. Do not accuse me. Do not whisper when my back is turned. That woman arrived on her king's errand. One that will be used to my benefit. We sit surrounded by legions of weaponed soldiers, farmers, even children. If you wish to return home, you will wake up. Be not fools. Do your part of retrieving that for which we have come. Gudsfelt and Danemour will cease to exist if this family stakes their claim on our lands. There is a woman in that castle who has been declared ruler of our nation. She will arrive with her ships, her guards, her weapons, and her neighbors' armies. Your wives, your children, your farms, your ancestry will all be eradicated if they challenge her decisions. The last daughter of King Boersen has rejected every offer for negotiation. She will be given an opportunity to remove her name from our lineage, or she will be forced aside. We will have diplomacy, or we will have death. The Daughter of Boersen chooses. You all must remain alert and ready."

Torren's speech was met with cheers from all except Gunnar, and that did not go unnoticed.

Chapter 24

"I'll take my noon meal in my suite," Galeena informed her waiting maids upon her arrival through the doors of Claremont. "My... uh... our king should be notified that I wish not to be bothered until tis time for me to be dressed for the evening's events. It would not be a terrible idea to deliver the exact message to Lukah as well."

Her final comment was met with giggles. The girls would no doubt have an argument over which one was to address the king and which would receive the pleasure of hunting Lukah for a private audience. Galeena could see why her perceived circumstance was held with such high regard. Her marriage to a prince, meant there could be hope for all of them. Although Lukah was not a known royal, they aspired to be worthy of assignment to a king's royal commander.

Oh the lies they all lived.

Their whispers caused a momentary pause. Galeena pondered that Lukah was her equal in every way. For even though he was not born of a marriage blessed by the church, he was the only male heir to a line of kings. His lineage could very well be argued to hold more significance than hers. After the conclusion of their concealments, many meetings would be had over declaring the rightful heir. Galeena was a woman and Lukah was the son of a Viking. As a young woman who was nine sleeps from her sixteenth annual, Galeena was finally realizing that perhaps she would have to share her claims. Adelia had bore two children. The titles of Queen of Solsworth, Queen of Northanglia and Queen of Gudsfelt might not all be in her future. Did she crave power over or peace with her beloved brother?

A finger flick commanded that one of her maids follow. A hint of disappointment was detected that the girl she selected was out of the competition for what could be a time consuming search for Lukah. Galeena hid a smile and shook her head at the girls and their longings. She then proceeded with determination aimed directly for her room and Olivia's scrolls.

The silk gown was removed and a luxurious robe was draped about her warm skin. The maid's exit was awaited, and the parchments were gathered and placed upon her bed. She began reading every word.

An attached notice scribed in Anglian was addressed to King Wilhelm. It read: *Beloved Wilhelm, These histories are to be joined forever with those belonging to Adelia. I trust you will keep them safe.* All else was written in King Boersen's private script.

A year has passed since Fredric, our crew, and I sailed for Solsworth.

I settled my affairs with Jaegar as they pertained to Gudsfelt. Twas made clear to him that since his successful conquering of Danemour was complete, he would have temporary rule of Gudsfelt. Jaegar had followed my father's commands and his father's lessons with perfection. He liberated Gudsfelt and our citizens from the constant threat of the Danes. My dear Jaegar had been born in all the right circumstances to all the right people. I hope he someday will realize that his placement was not one of coincidence. It was directed by God.

One fear remains as it pertains to my son; his wife, my sister Annika, has recently passed leaving him with no known heir to our King Boersen. Torren is loved as my own, but alas he is full Dane. Our people want Adelia's daughter, as it is written, for their monarch. My hope is that the loyalists will stand firm. There is plenty of power to be distributed. Princess Helene's claim is hers to accept or deny. Should anyone else apart from Jaegar, Torren, or Helene step forward to take rule, my wish is that the negotiations be amiable, respectful and discerning.

The one thing I wish I could tell the Olivia who craved only her father's throne at age six and teen is that titles, gold, silver, ships, servants, and guards became meaningless to me once my child arrived. Though some continue to crave and seek dominance for themselves, living a simple life with my Styrke taught me that the truest love and comfort of a home and a husband were all I needed. Setting armies to fight for me and what I felt to be my rightful claims to all I could see and imagine, was not a life that would lead me to peace and accomplishment.

Adelia however, wanted her father's nation. She wanted to oversee the protection of the borders and shores of her home. She wanted security for her people. I hope that all she had to sacrifice for that hard earned peace brought her true joy.

After living a full life on our farm these past thirty and more years, my heart has led me back to the green and fertile land that held me captive so long ago. I have arrived to Solsworth.

The coastline is far south of Northanglia, but nearly identical. With anxious disposition, I found myself watching soldiers line the docks and the sands with weapons ready. The sight of our Norse ships hold many of them prisoner. Both Danemour and Gudsfelt have viciously attacked these people, though not in equitable distribution.

I watched. Fredric moved into a position before me. His now massive substance blocked my view. I said to him, "Fredric, these men will be far less likely to release their arrows if they see that a woman leads this ship."

"You are all I have, Olivia."

I smiled at how he has given all for me. My hand touched his shoulder and I said, "Tis not too late for a man as strong as you to seek a wife."

"Who will keep you in line if not me?"

"I will keep myself in line."

We laughed together and he moved to my side.

Nearer and nearer our ship drew to the waiting soldiers. My heart began to feel as if it were rising into my throat. What would this morning bring? I returned to the west with purpose, but also with one regret; I could not cherish a deserving man who gave me two of my most prized gifts, Adelia and his undying love. Tis my hope that he will find a place in his heart for me. For I must make full confession, I never stopped loving him and he never left my thoughts. As circumstances forced my heart to grow away from him, seeing his smile upon our child's face and hearing her whispered pleas for his arms and his voice, my broken bond with him rejuvenated.

Styrke had me and I had him. I knew he was my home, but it saddens me that Alexar maintained a relentless hold on half of my soul.

Our ship sidled to the wooden beams and planks. Ropes were cast and when nods of approval were given, servants I perceived to be fishermen or workers of the wharf, secured us to the pier.

We arrived with no armor or shields, nor did we display any other device that might imply our visit was one of aggression. My troop and I were escorted through a growing horde of inquisitive people. Some scowled though most simply ogled. Any uninvited or unannounced visitor would surely hold the interest of onlookers. A deviation from a normal routine is sure to invigorate all living beings.

Whispers and mutters of, "No, she's a queen," were heard causing Fredric and I to exchange smiles.

I guess I was, or am, a queen, and I have been for a very, very long time.

Once we were led into the gates of the Solsworth fortress, more soldiers surrounded us, and we were taken to a damp and dreary room on the ground level of the castle.

Within moments of a strategically orchestrated distraction, I was listening to this, "Your return to my chamber with such speed had better be to bring a favorable announcement to my ears. For I cannot be convinced that you made your way to our prison and back here with a thorough gathering of information from my commanders about the arrival of another ship filled with Norsemen. What promising news doth you deliver?"

Post growl, that I assumed to be addressed to Wymer, Alexar waited, continuing to face away from his entry as if he refused to welcome anyone.

I spoke. "My hope is that news of the arrival of one Viking will ease the temper and distress of the King of Solsworth."

Stunned to complete silence, Alexar turned at the sound of my voice. Disbelief, anger, sadness, and longing, were words and emotions spoken only by his eyes.

The sight of the pain I had inflicted upon him nearly stopped my heart for all time. I had to quickly justify my reason for leaving him. He left you. He married another. He needed to reign. He had a role that you would have destroyed.

"Step no further than the threshold of this chamber, Olivia. Do not move." He commanded me with an irate glare.

I obeyed.

"There you stand… the woman who saturated my every thought whether awake or asleep. The woman who has been like a plague to me has found her way to my home. I will present the very same question to you

that was meant for Wymer, what promising news doth you deliver?"

"I'll not be subtle nor mysterious, Alexar. I expect nothing but an honest reply. I've come only to tell you that I can bear not another breath apart from you."

With apparent anger, Alexar's eyes closed tightly as his fingers pressed to his forehead then slid through his silvering hair. He walked to the backside of his ornately carved chair and held onto the spires that adorned the top rail. After a pause there, he stepped from behind his work table and moved very slowly in my direction. He stopped out of my reach, but near enough for us both to feel the other's growing need for touch.

"You are truly here."

"Yes Alexar. Though, I do wonder, how much time do I have before your guards notice the only woman onboard the enemy's ship has evaded their grasp?"

"Still one for sneaking about, huh? Tell me, how did you escape?"

The cunning side of me answered. "My men gathered about me and created a moment of confusion, acting as if they themselves searched for me. When the guards stepped into the crowd to find me, I slipped through. I heard Fredric demanding that their queen be immediately returned to them. He released accusations and threats of retaliation upon your men if I were harmed. Bewilderment increased. Then, I was out of range and am now ignorant of the outcome."

"And finding your way to my private chamber, I suppose I need not ask. There is no doubt that our daughter sketched a direct and unhindered path to me."

"You are correct."

"So she put my life at risk with a correspondence that could have ended up in anyone's hands before it reached yours?"

"Fredric was the courier. Details as to how and when I was receiving notices from her are now irrelevant. Worry not, Adelia was blessed with many gifts."

Not wanting to give energy to the past, Alexar complimented with an adoring tone, "Perfection, she was."

I had no wish to state the truth as it pertained to our daughter, which was, she was human, like us all. Instead, I nodded with somber agreement, and said, "Our daughter was perfect, as are her children."

His interest was piqued. "You know she has more than one child?"

"I do, as did Styrke. We've kept her secret."

"We?" He still hated the sound of the word coming from my lips.

"Will you listen to me?" I asked as I made an attempt to approach him.

Alexar held his hand up to bar my moving forward. I was not yet accepted. He said, "Since we are not being attacked and tis my assumption that Wymer has found his way to Fredric's company, we have time. I'll hear what you have to say."

No time was wasted in expressing my feelings to him.

"I hated you, Alexar. My husband died and you replaced him. Then you married another."

"At your very own command, Olivia."

"It could not be avoided. You knew you had to marry Khara. When all that transpired stole you from me, I planned my return to Gudsfelt. Then, you came to me before I left Northanglia. I boarded a ship with Styrke dying for a glimpse of you. The hatred had to increase within me or I would not have been able to face where I was meant to be and with whom I was meant to share my life."

"I did not call you back to me, Olivia. I had nothing to offer you. I knew your father, your mother and Styrke were better for you. I would not hold you as a mistress and our daughter as a... I cannot even speak the word."

"When Adelia grew, I hated you again for the love you held for her. She wanted you and only you. I lost

her when I sent for you to join us for rituals. That time together reminded me how deeply I still loved you."

"And you had to continue to reject my love?" He asked not understanding my decisions.

"Of course. I do thank you for the secret moments in your arms, but I could never have said that back then. Alexar,"

He raised his chin for me to speak.

"I despised you from the moment you faced me in the forest and then tried to purchase me as a slave."

He laughed, as did I.

"Is there an end to all you cannot bear about knowing me?"

"The end is this, I have fought to free myself from the echos of your voice, the memories of your scent, and the gentleness of your touch, but I cannot."

"Olivia, all I hear from you is that your husband has died and you now need me."

"No. No. Though Styrke was meant to be my punishment, he was my equal, my partner. He held my heart. He was the one who would forsake the entire world, all expectations, titles, belongings, and even his breath, just to be with me. He did not care that my father was a king. Tis why he took me away from White Crested Cove to our farm. He wanted me, and he wanted me even after I gave birth to another man's child. Styrke has passed. A sad, despairing,

deteriorating death stole him from this world. But he and I both knew that you never left me. There was a place within me that could only be filled by you. A year has passed—"

"Another year of mourning your Norseman," Alexar muttered as a memory not as an insult.

Tears fell before I spoke again.

He watched, refusing to console me. I wiped my eyes again and again.

"The hatred Olivia. What of the hatred?"

"Twas all a shield. You know that. I've returned to you to ask for forgiveness and time. If you have another wife, I shall leave you. However, if you have time for me, I would very much like to be at your side as much as possible for the rest of my life."

"Before you say you want me, you must know that I've prayed for Styrke's death since the moment he took you and my daughter away from me. You may have hated me, but I hated him."

"Forgiveness is for sins my love. No exchange between us shall ever be considered a sin, a weakness, yes, a sin, no."

Alexar opened his arms to me, and I stepped into the comfort of his hold.

"Shall I reclaim you as my wife?" he asked with his lips and nose pressed into my hair.

I looked into his eyes and said, "I can wait no longer. You have my promise that you will not be disappointed. I am yours as often as you desire. Any and all dreams you have had you are welcome to pursue."

"So, you are now Queen of Solsworth since our marriage has never been contested nor annulled. Welcome to your new home, my love. Allow me to show you to our bed."

"Allow me to show you its proper use," I teased.

Surprisingly, we were not interrupted.

As my husband made love to me, I had no recollection of ever having been apart from him. Being beneath him, having his hands, eyes, and lips reclaim me as his own, it was as if I'd been with no one else in all those years. My body craved only him. It accepted him with longing and intense passion. He entered me, and we satisfied one another as many times as we could until rest was necessary.

Looking back to that afternoon, I am glad my Styrke had chosen Heaven over haunting. He was with God. And I was given the gift of being alone with my husband.

A click captured Galeena's attention and she was unable to complete the reading of Olivia's letters.

"You were not announced," she chided as she neatly placed the unrolled parchments one atop the other in front of her.

"This has been settled. All is mine," Wilhelm chuckled lifting his proprietary hands.

To that, he received the innate reaction that all children offer to a domineering and intrusive parent. Galeena's eyes rolled before returning their focus to her father.

"Is it time for me to be dressed?" Her heart fluttered and she actually began to feel fear.

"It is, Love. I have come though because Olivia sent notice that your wedding is to take place in Solsworth. I will announce this during your presentation and I did not want it to come as a surprise."

"Matters not to me where the ceremony is to occur."

"Your grandmother demands that you and Henry leave tomorrow. She wants you in Solsworth days prior to the arrival of your sixteenth year. As queen of the region, she holds significant power over this union. After all, you are being joined to their lineage."

Gaping since revealing she was to leave tomorrow, Galeena immediately argued. "I'll not be told when or where I am allowed to travel. I have no issue with Olivia hosting my marriage ceremony, but I'll not leave tomorrow."

"I am not ignorant as to your reasoning for refusing her orders."

“This has nothing to do with Torren. You know I want to go to the Applewoods.”

“While I do believe you are eager for the peace you’ve yet to have these past days, I have to say, us Northanglian men tire of the Boersen women and their relentless attachments to the Styrkes. Tis my opinion you have formed an attachment, and the interference of those men in your lives ends now. You’ve been given a mandate and that is final. Tomorrow, you depart with Henry.”

To his statement Galeena fumed. She bit her bottom lip. Her mind raced.

Seeing her fight back all instincts to quarrel, Wilhelm added, “I thought you’d be happy to see your grandmother.”

“Do not make this about a pleasant visit with a dear relative, Father. May I please be left to my preparations.”

“Galeena, I do love you. All that has been designed is for your benefit. Once you are revealed, Olivia will see to your appearance before the Gudsfelt assembly. If you do not accept this path and Jaegar or his deceiving son get you, you will be ruined or killed.”

“They do plan to kill King Boersen’s granddaughter.” She thought her statement to be new to him.

Wilhelm replied, “Although I knew this to be true, my gratitude is yours for the honest confirmation.”

Chapter 25

King Wilhelm and Galeena stood behind a curtain awaiting the announcement of their entrance.

Careful to remain hidden while peering through a small opening in the drapes, Galeena extended her arm outward toward the incoming guests and asked, "Father, where is my brother? If I must endure being paraded and exhibited before all of our court officials and Henry's, then certainly Lukah should be required to accompany me."

Wilhelm smirked at her defiance and lovingly said, "My dear daughter, Lukah is not the one being married. He will be coming and going throughout the evening. Having both of my military leaders in one room makes you easy targets and leaves our kingdom unprotected. Everyone here would be appalled if you and Lukah appeared side by side for an entire evening. Tis expected that you patrol together or fight together; tis not accepted that you enjoy leisure together. You will see him during our meal."

Galeena shook her head, not at her father, but at the frustration of having to spend such a momentous occasion without her dearest confidant.

"You need not fill your thoughts with Lukah's whereabouts, you are to think only of Prince Henry and assure him of your devotion. You are also to be graciously accepting all of the well wishes from your guests."

"*All* guests?" she stressed.

"Do not tease in reference to the Ice-lander."

Galeena giggled. Irritating her father was always a rewarding form of entertainment for her.

Wilhelm reminded her, "You have been placed and named by those who hold power. Whether they be of Northanglia or Solsworth, these people are your constituents. I dare say, should Jaegar's son someday decide his citizenship is with Gudsfelt, he too can be considered one of your constituents."

Galeena listened, then asked, "And what of Lukah? Your assignments to thrones never reference my brother. We are of the same lineages. Why must the awarding of all of these titles fall to me?"

"Solsworth will not pass to Lukah because Henry has exclusive claim. As for Gudsfelt, King Boersen scribed your name as his successor. Lukah is in line behind you for Northanglia because he is not of *my* blood. He has my undying love and respect. He also has my father's undying love and respect, but Lukah has stated he wishes to maintain his freedom from the burden's of being a monarch. King Alexar was willing to place your brother before you here in Northanglia, but he refused the offer."

She asked, "What of Gudsfelt? When they learn of his existence and the truth of his father, tis possible he could have that throne?"

"You mention a circumstance on which I cannot speak. I have no foresight on Lukah's heart for Jaegar or possible secret desires to usurp your claim to Gudsfelt. All I know of Lukah's thoughts is that he repeatedly vows his allegiance to Northanglia, just as did your mother. My final assessment of your brother's role is that Torren, should he live long enough, will have claim to Danemour."

Galeena accepted her father's explanations even though she doubted that Lukah would just relinquish all claims to five nations, including Dornwold. She had never been adverse to shedding her weighted blanket of concealment and accepting her role as queen to any of the lands from which she descended. Her only apprehension was that she was feeling a sense of deviation from the intended course that was on the horizon.

Her doting father wrapped his arms around her shoulders like a warm shawl. He said, "Imagine my love, imagine, and confess your true feelings to me, does the sound of: Helene, Queen of Solsworth, Queen of Northanglia, and Queen of Gudsfelt, not entice you?"

Galeena tilted toward her father for a kiss to her temple. She did not smile yet. First, she asked, "How am I to rule a nation that sits across the North Sea?"

There was no hesitation in his reply, Wilhelm stated, "The very same way any *king* would, with the loyalty of your advisors, your citizens and your armies."

She then asked, "And you feel Henry is the optimal choice of husband for me to rule three nations?"

"With absolution daughter. He is a fair man who has the affections of his people. You will see how his charisma is like a magnet to everyone he encounters. You are the leader. He is the politician. Henry will never attempt to overtake your rule. He will only love you, support you, and negotiate for you."

Pulling from Wilhelm's embrace, Galeena released a sigh of amusement.

"What entertains you my love?"

"Father, he sounds like he has the loyalty of a hound!"

"Galeena Helene Stefania Styrkes! Desist with your jest! You have yet to meet the man! Your knowledge of and affections for one another will grow. You have my promise. Be patient and withhold your judgements."

"One week, huh?"

"Aye."

Needing to erase the strain of all that was to come, Galeena rested the back of her head on her father's strong shoulder.

"I was assigned the task of killing the one who commands the Vikings, remove them from Northanglia, learn of Henry's personal traits, prepare for my official presentation as Adelia's daughter, accept my relocation, secure the loyalties of the citizens of three nations, *and* ready myself for marriage all within the next nine days?"

King Wilhelm roared with laughter. His amusement was so loud the gathering audience heard him. He lowered his voice and replied to his daughter, "Some will take more time, but yes! I know no other who could ever master all of those challenges with grace and success apart from you." He kissed her forehead and commanded, "Now, go forth. I am anxious to begin. Brace for your first official political presentation as one who will soon be queen, instead of one who is being promoted as a warrior."

Bells chimed. The crowd silenced and turned their attention to the platform at the far wall of the banquet hall. Two men were summoned to pull the gold toned, velvet barriers from before the king and his ward. The curtains opened and Galeena, the future Queen of Solsworth, took one elegant step toward her admiring guests. The solo movement reminded her of the nagging injury. She squeezed her father's hand, but he pulled his fingers from hers, "Proceed my child," he whispered.

King Wilhelm breached all etiquette and followed a commoner during this royal event. His decision was taken as a symbolic gesture; a gentleman was escorting a young woman deemed to be worthy of reverence and respect.

Thankful for slippers and not boots, Galeena ignored her pain and flowed with grace to her marked place.

Time was given for the guests to stare and comment to one another about her appearance. Galeena's father had invested a great deal of his tradesmen's time into finding the perfect silk cloth, woven of pure white that was embossed with flowering vines. For any other to have worn a similar gown would have been unimaginable. The dress had a heart shaped bodice and long, sheer sleeves of lace that revealed her shoulders. The lower portion had a flattering flare and a train that swept only a bit behind her. The pureness of her features combined with the customized garment being the personal choice of the king presented Galeena as nearly worthy of worship.

Moments of whispers, smiles, and ogling were allowed before Wilhelm spoke. Galeena smiled and feigned that she had not been throwing daggers merely days prior to this glorious evening. She practically glowed like a heavenly spirit. There was no sign that she still had tasks to complete as a vicious soldier. Tasks that were only possible because she was also a Viking.

So many eyes were upon her. She tried to acknowledge every onlooker with a nod or bow. As she scanned the multitude of faces further toward the back of the room, she saw him. Torren stared with arrogance. Their attention to one another became exclusive, and he was sure to remind her that he alone knows her intimate secrets. Her heart fluttered and returning to the mindset of being her king's puppet was difficult.

Wilhelm knew something had halted Galeena's current of greetings, so he stepped to her side, placed his hand on her lower back, and announced, "My countrymen, you know, trust and adore Galeena of Northanglia. She has lived amongst you for nearly ten and six years. She is one of you. She is one of us. She is one with this world." He paused for the cheers to settle. He then turned to Galeena and proclaimed, "You have earned honor because of your love for God, love for country, love for king and queen, and love for justice and protection. There is no one more worthy to be sealed to our sister nation than you."

She maintained eye contact with her father as he spoke. Another pause was allowed for further cheers to be quieted.

He then concluded, "Galeena, I present to you Prince Henry of Solsworth." Wilhelm stepped aside and from behind the same curtains where she had just waited, Henry advanced accompanied by a priest of Broodenshire.

Though she beamed, before Henry was near, she seethed through her smiling teeth, "Father, why the priest?"

"Merely a formality dear. Fret not."

The fear of having to take immediate vows nearly buckled Galeena's knees. Nothing had ever terrified her as deeply as seeing Otto escort Prince Henry to her. And, as her betrothed reached her side, she actually swooned. The tightness of her dress, the momentary lack of inhaling, the shock, and a debilitating thirst all weakened the princess.

Fearing a public collapse, Henry embraced his bride to be about the waist, then pulled her to him.

"Dear Galeena," he whispered. "Miss," he whispered again.

Her eyes saw that his lips were moving, but she was regaining her strength.

She finally muttered, "Do they stare?"

A very handsome man peered at her with concerned eyes. He said, "Of course they stare. If it were even possible to remove their attention from you it would be considered disrespectful."

"I am not certain I can join the gathering without assistance. I have never needed the grasp of a man to stand on my own, but my head suddenly grew heavy. How many witnessed my embarrassment?"

Henry chuckled and gave the most honest reply. "Only every member of the courts of two nations, many soldiers, several priests, and countless landholders." He then added, "Oh, and me."

"I shall never show my face again!"

"Be not so injured. You have merely shown that you are vulnerable, a lady. I believe they will all have more respect for you now than they've ever had. They admire your strength. Allow them to admire your humanness as well."

Galeena replied suspiciously, "Your Highness, you should know I shall never marry someone who tells me only what I wish to hear."

His touch to her cheek was not despised nor resisted as he said, "I require that you use only my name when addressing me. Call me Henry. You should also know, I've told no lies. My words are for your encouragement. No longer worry not about what they think of you. From this moment forward, they think of *us*. We are two people who represent the success of our traditions, two who honor our calling and are learning to fall in love."

Galeena was liking the man a bit more. She had listened to every single word he spoke with undivided attention. When he completed his thought, she pinched her eyes closed and said, "I am not vulnerable. I have never been vulnerable. And, I will not be seen as vulnerable."

Henry smiled and shocked her with his next thought. "Would you rather the public perception be that you are with child?"

Her eyes widened and she seethed at his brazen words. "What evil shall befall you for speaking in such a manner in the house of our Lord and King?"

"No evil my dear, for I believe tis our Lord who has blessed me with my wits."

Galeena placed her palm to her midsection and moaned, "Uh, I need water."

Henry nodded to a waiting maid and asked her to retrieve a refreshment for Galeena. With haste a cup was delivered.

King Wilhelm soon stepped forward to offer guidance. "Time for you to right yourself and join your people. Tis rather unorthodox to be hosting a celebration in your honor and neither of you is attentive. I have guests who have arrived from no less than six nations awaiting their meal and their entertainment. You lead the progression of all that is planned. Let us move on with it."

Galeena was vague when she made her emotions known to her father. "This man caused a momentary lapse of sanity with his shocking words to me."

Wilhelm spoke with great care directly to Galeena, "Your shenanigans have amused me for many years. However, this is not the day for you to crumble beneath the weight of a fate you have been aware of for the past three years. Proceed!"

Wilhelm smiled and waved to their guests as he marched from the platform. His departure forced the new couple to follow.

An arm was offered and Galeena took hold. Her mild limp did not go unnoticed. She whispered with a broad smile, "I stepped on a lost knife."

Henry snickered and said, "Ah, a story with a happy ending. Tis comforting. I mean to say, at least you found it."

Galeena decided she liked him.

He then asked, "Before all we have to say to one another is heard by strangers, tell me, was your near state of unconsciousness induced by a resistance to marrying me?"

Her father had been correct. Henry was kind. He was also compassionate, amusing, accepting of her, and remarkably handsome. She replied with delicacy, "No Henry. Tis my best guess that my loss of balance was caused by my own unpreparedness, or perhaps my feelings of being unworthy of you."

Henry smiled and reassured her, "Dear, I care not about your name or your lack thereof. Your reputation as a warrior who also protects all she holds dear is what I honor. The added benefit of your matchless beauty of face and figure are mere rewards from God for my loyalty to our promises. King Alexar and King Wilhelm selected us for one another. I would like to say, I shall never doubt either of those men again so long as I shall live."

The pair laughed in unison.

"I openly confess, I am no longer against those men making choices for me either. You have not disappointed. Also, your compliments and willingness to attend to my needs are much appreciated. Thank you, Sire."

"Again, my name is Henry. Now, let us go and greet our visitors, Future Wife. I have heard there is even a commander of the Danemour army in attendance."

Galeena gasped. She suddenly remembered she had not been as protective of their expected loyalties to one another. She had allowed another man, an enemy at that, access to all that was to be held only by her husband. She silently prayed that Torren would hold all they had done in confidence. Oh how she instantly regretted her decisions of the previous week.

Chapter 26

Their places at the table were set. King Wilhelm sat in the center. To his left were Christiahn, Khara, and two of their advisors. To his right were the vacant seats for Henry, Galeena, Lukah, and Torren.

As the people of honor were called to take their places, Galeena asked of her father, "Why doth Torren have a seat beside me?"

"Galeena, he is the son of a king. Torren's father rules Danemour, Dornwold and he has current power over Gudsfelt. He should be seated beside me, but I'll not place him above Prince Henry."

With frustration she added, "He sits above Lukah?"

"He is positioned above an advisor, as he should be. You are to be polite and proper. Introduce him to your brother."

"They've met. It was not pleasant."

"Then introduce him to your fiancé."

"I'm not certain that is a safe idea either."

Her father closed his eyes and shook his head trying to avoid any images of his daughter's dealings with a Styrkeson.

"King Wilhelm, Monarch of Northanglia," was announced. The king stepped forward and Galeena watched his regal welcome.

Henry approached her. "I shall be next. Would you prefer I break all rules and enter at your side?"

She looked to him then behind her. Torren stood with one eyebrow raised and a smirk upon his face. Lukah was far back, not wanting to be anywhere near his half brother. Galeena surmised he was seeking a viable reason to abandon this part of the events. Her eyes caught his and she shook her head at him as if she were his superior. Torren followed her gaze and smiled at the way Lukah seemed to accept the command that was given.

"Prince Henry of Solsworth."

"Decide Galeena."

"Go Henry. We'll play by the rules."

"For now," he whispered into her ear allowing his lips to graze her cheek.

Galeena wasn't sure if she should be offended or enamored. She was developing a genuine attachment to him. Before he left her side, she grasped his arm and replied, "Where were you last week?"

He smiled and said, "I don't want to know what that means. My love for you begins today."

He was as Torren had described. She was to marry a man who admitted that he wanted her just as she stood.

When his back was to her and he was walking to his place beside her father, Galeena took another glimpse of Torren. His scowl reminded her that he was not there for her benefit. He was there to kill her.

"Galeena of Northanglia, Commander of King Wilhelm's Army."

A princess and future queen entered the banquet hall to clapping hands and bows. None needed to acknowledge her with such respect, but they did. She lowered her eyes and smiled at as many men and women who were within her line of sight. Her eyes met Henry's for but a moment, and she nearly laughed out loud at the sight of him pointing to his own foot. Walking with grace was not as painful with her thoughts on everyone else and not tripping on her gown. He placed his hand over his heart sending the message that he was already proud of her.

As she arrived to the table, Henry stood and in place of the servant, he pulled her chair.

A nod of gratitude was offered. Galeena took her seat. And she waited with dread for Torren's announcement. Her fear was his humiliation. He stood alone. He had no one there, apart from her, who knew his heart and his affinity and pure desire for love and peace. The Viking was at the mercy of his king and father, exactly as she was.

"Prince Torren of Danemour and Dornwold."

Not one jeer was spoken. Muted claps were offered. He made no attempt to look at any face except Galeena's. She gifted him a very soft smile. He remained expressionless. A servant assisted him with his chair as well.

Lukah was the final guest of honor to be announced. His title was identical to Galeena's.

"Lukah of Northanglia, Commander of King Wilhelm's Army."

His hatred was tucked away and he entered the room like a future king. Lukah had colored his white hair with die from tea leaves or perhaps a diluted black walnut mixture. The summer months working without a top covering had afforded him a darker complexion. Galeena nearly grinned at his arrogance or was it confidence. It was definitely both.

Torren did not watch the soldier's approach. He watched Galeena's reaction. "You should save your smiles for your prince. All will question where your heart lies if you do not ease your attraction to that man."

Her head snapped to him, "You are very new here Icelander. That man and I have been at each other's side for a lifetime. We have been paraded publicly together on countless occasions. There is no shame in my outward joy over his name and presence."

A yielding bow was given. "My apologies," he conceded.

Lukah took his seat and immediately asked of his neighbor, "Will you do me the favor of withholding all manner of conversation with me this evening? You may direct your attentions to my—"

"Your what?" Torren asked quickly.

"My friend." He pointed to Galeena. Not wanting to speak anymore, Lukah turned his attention to the platter that was placed before him.

Torren suspected that Lukah did love his partner, and he did not approve of her being given to another man.

Respecting the request that was made of him, Torren did not look his way for the duration of the evening. Polite nods and delicate discussions of the weather, the names of attendees, or close of the summer season were had.

The only moment of discomfort that arose was when Torren whispered to Galeena leaning a little too close to her ear, "Do you approve of your king's choice?"

She accidentally pressed her forehead to his when she replied, "He is very kind, Torren. Very kind."

"Does he know that you are not?"

Her eyes widened and her shoulders pulled back. She looked at him preparing to chastise.

He snickered and said, "Twas a compliment with a hint of a jest, Galeena. Be not offended."

She defended herself in a hushed tone that held urgency, "You do not know me, Torren."

"I know you far better than he ever will."

Henry's interruption ended their exchange. He addressed the Viking, "Becoming acquainted with Queen Olivia has been a pleasure. You two have relations, correct?"

"Uh, yes. She is my grandmother. She raised me."

"You two share no blood though. Is that also correct?"

"Blood is not needed to be declared family, otherwise no wedded pair would ever be considered relations."

"Point taken," Henry replied with a nod.

Torren asked, "Galeena, you informed me earlier that Olivia sent a message?"

Before she was able to speak, Henry answered. "We leave tomorrow for Solsworth. Queen Olivia wishes to host our ceremonies."

"Henry, I am able to converse with my guest."

"Of course." Henry offered his hand as invitation for Galeena to respond.

Torren found the situation to hold humor. Lukah was listening and unknowingly shared his brother's opinion. Galeena marked the intrusion as one of normality. She felt Henry was truly being a gentleman. She had never experienced life as a lady at a man's side. Her father, brother, grandfather, and the soldiers who existed in her life gave her liberty to be independent and speak freely at all times.

She turned from facing Henry to facing Torren. "Queen Olivia has requested that we marry in Solsworth."

Hearing the news from Galeena closed Torren's heart even tighter to her. He replied, "Sounds like the perfect situation for you, uh, for you both. If you think of it, please send a greeting of undying love to my grandmother on my behalf. Congratulations."

"Thank you, Torren," Henry replied as he raised his cup to him.

The entire party resumed only polite chatter until they completed their meal. Galeena took each bite of her food wondering if Torren truly meant what he had said.

All were soon led to the gathering room for music and dancing. Galeena's only partner was Henry, and after a few variations of dances, knowing she was most likely in pain, he escorted her from the center of attention.

The man she was to marry held her complete interest. She thought not of Lukah, King Wilhelm nor Torren. Henry was seizing her. He may not have been known for his skills in battle, but he was keen in the ways of attracting her heart.

"I am in dire need of a private moment with you Galeena. Will you grant me this wish?"

"There is a room nearby. If we can disappear without instigating rumors, then I see no reason that we can't have some privacy."

Henry was led from a side door into a public passageway. They strolled as if they were simply cooling from the energy they had expended. Others passed them. Greetings were shared.

A door appeared. Galeena sought prying eyes, but none were around. She led Henry into a room that was lit with torches mounted on the walls and a mediocre fire. Adjacent from the main entry, there was an exit to a courtyard. He followed her through and out into the fresh air.

"What have you to discuss with me, Henry?"

"I was in desperate need of companionship and conversation. The crowd, the music, the noise of tonight's party was becoming too much. We have a life ahead of us of only the other's company."

"We are not the last two people in the world. There will always be others to join us or even come between us. However, I appreciate that you seek conversation. Shall we?" Galeena motioned toward a bench in the garden.

Henry did not accept her offer. Instead he moved to her so they touched, and he said, "As I look at you, what I see is a marble statue of a goddess. One cannot share warmth with a statue. I wish to see the woman who is to be my wife. Will you allow me to release your veil of curls so they can have their natural freedom. I have no desire to rejoin the celebrations in our honor. I much prefer learning more of you and knowing that you are mine."

"Tis inappropriate Henry. The evening has not come to its conclusion."

"King Wilhelm can make his final announcement without us. He is a discerning bureaucrat; pardons will be made on our behalf. After this night's sleep, we take to a carriage and proceed to our life. You are going to adore Queen Olivia. She is beyond anxious to see you. She has admitted that you are already accepted as her very own."

Galeena took a step back and a deep breath. "Henry,"

"Yes?" He closed the space between them.

She did not move. She said, "Henry, tomorrow will arrive very quickly. I've decided I agree with you. This night has come to an end for me. I have much to think about and do before first light."

Without an invitation, nor denial, Henry kissed his bride.

The intimate connection to him was intense and immediate. Galeena shared in his energy.

"How am I to wait for you?" he asked.

"We are merely days away, Henry."

"No. I've already waited years for a wife."

She snickered, "Then a few more days will not cause you any harm."

Another kiss was pressed to her cheek then her lips.

Torren listened. When he heard silence, he leaned for a glimpse, then returned to his discreet position.

Galeena pulled his hands from her waist and said, "Tomorrow Henry. I shall see you tomorrow. Are you able to find your way to your guest suite?"

"Without error."

He left her in the small garden.

Torren was humored that a man walked past him and didn't even sense him in any way. When the absence of the prince was assured, he stepped from his place just inside the terrace door.

"Did you find our exchange to be amusing?" Galeena asked without turning toward him.

"You knew I was there?"

"I knew the moment the door opened it was you."

"You heard that?"

"I felt the shift in the air. A mild breath of a wind traveled inward. When my father's voice didn't immediately call for me, I knew the intruder to be you. Did you find what you sought? I presume you've been relentless in your search for Princess Helene."

"Is she here?" he asked.

"She is. King Wilhelm orders gowns for all of the young girls so they are equal in presentation. She is quite beautiful. Did you dance with any of the young ladies?"

"None."

"Well, I speak with great sincerity when I say, I am sure the girl is most disappointed. I danced one dance with all of the maidens. Did you witness that? The princess was present."

"I regret to say I did not witness the display. Prince Henry's relentless proximity to you was somewhat of a repellent."

Galeena replied with one exaggerated nod.

"So, you are to leave tomorrow?"

"Aye. The message from Queen Olivia, did you know she had returned to Alexar and claimed her title?"

"My father and I did know she and Fredric were going to Solsworth."

"So your schemes were plotted after she left Gudsfelt."

"No. Our decisions were made upon her departure. We knew she would not be returning, probably ever. Was there more to share of her message?"

Galeena finally turned to face Torren.

The woman who stood before him stole his vision of all else aside from her. The image his mind now held of another man kissing her stung. The sound of the Prince of Solsworth requesting she diminish her presentation for him stirred an anger which he suppressed. Galeena's freed tresses had been his covering for three nights, and he suddenly wished he would be enjoying their sweet aroma and luxurious cascades again.

"Olivia's orders that I arrive to Solsworth before my sixteenth day of birth and her declaration of her love for Alexar are all that was sent."

In a tone that was on the brink of fury, Torren said, "I can scarcely believe you still intend on marrying their prince. You have thrice awoken in my arms. My hands have caressed you. My eyes have seen you. My lips have known you. My tongue has tasted you! I know of your religion. My knowledge may exceed your own. Are these not sins to your God?"

Distressed, Galeena chided him. "Huh! You stand before me offering a sermon filled with chastisement over my actions when your new found indifference to me has been made quite clear. Additionally, dare I review a list of names of men and women who have fallen victim to your conspiracy."

"This moment is about you and me, no one else."

"You are wrong. Every moment of my life is about *everyone* else and now that includes you."

Galeena stormed past him back into the portrait gallery.

Torren followed.

Stopping in the middle of the room, Galeena looked up. She studied the walls. Torren's eyes followed hers. She pointed. "Tis my mother."

His attention turned to the portrait. "Your mother? I thought you an orphan."

Galeena suddenly felt a terror like she had absolutely never felt before in her lifetime. She calmly corrected herself, "I've always told myself that Queen Adelia was my mother. A childhood fantasy. A dream."

"I too dreamed of having a mother. Your Adeila resembles Olivia."

They both looked to the wall where a portrait of Olivia was displayed. Then, returning their attention to Adelia, he mentioned, "That is how she looked when I met her."

Galeena stated, "I believe the reason King Wilhelm dotes over me is because before his wife passed, she asked him to ensure I was cared for."

"Tis most likely true. I remember her telling my father to take special care of me. It seemed that she loved children."

"As did Olivia?" Galeena asked while making a special point of remembering to revisit her mother's histories.

Torren's smile exhibited a great love for his grandmother. "Yes."

He looked to Olivia once more, then to Galeena.

She suggested, "You should retire for the evening." Before he could acknowledge her, she quickly asked, "Oh! Did King Wilhelm pull you for a conference?"

"He did."

"Do you wish to share?"

"You will probably be enlightened by him, so yes, I'll share. King Wilhelm said it is imperative that I know his daughter will be maintaining her rights as Queen of Gudsfelt, and she has his full support which is accompanied by the support of their ships and forces. He reminded me that any rightful ruler would be useless on all accounts if they were willing to give up their claim to a nation. Especially when they are more capable and more powerful than the current commanders. Your king did not fully take into consideration that I have the armies of three nations supporting my pursuits."

"So he offered a gentleman's threat?"

"In a manner of speaking," Torren affirmed. He then said, "I was incensed by his insult, but perhaps tis more a statement of ignorance on his part. I told your king that my father and I are far more capable of ruling the Northlands than a girl who has only left this island once!"

"My king has an extreme distaste for all things Jaegar and Norse and now Torren," Galeena informed him with an amused glint in her eye.

Torren walked past her, caressed her cheek with his finger and touched his lips to hers. He then said, "I'll always remember you, everything about you. For a very short time, you were all mine. The time has come for you to forget me. It brings me comfort to know that you will not be in this castle for much longer. Go rest woman, for tomorrow you begin your training as Queen of Solsworth."

The sound of the word 'tomorrow' was driving her to madness. Or, was it his touch, his scent, and his charm, that caused her to fight succumbing to insanity?

Chapter 27

"Has the Norseman departed?" Galeena called up to the guards.

"He has. You'll not catch him. He'll be near the village by now."

"Open," she commanded and two soldiers obeyed.

Clicks and jabs with her heels set her horse into a gallop.

"Tis not safe, Galeena!"

She ignored the warning and soon disappeared into the trees below the ridge. Galeena was not going to Castleton; her destination was her cottage in the Applewoods.

At the top speed she could travel, the distraught princess thought of nothing apart from fleeing her assigned fate. She was not ready to be loaded into a carriage and transported to Solsworth before the sunrise. If she could not be located, she could not be forced to leave.

The road to Castleton came into her view and she slowed her horse for only a moment. Torren had made his position clear to her. She was not to seek him. At the intersection, Galeena stopped. Torches, lanterns, and fires cast a glowing dome over her home. "Your residency is soon to end, Icelanders." She continued toward her destination.

The farther Galeena traveled away from Claremont, the darker and narrower the path became. Warnings were spoken to her from the spirit world. She replied, "I hear you, Mother. I shall take great care. I'll be alert."

Only half of the moon was available for light and it did not have the potency to illuminate her surroundings through the canopy above. Galeena pushed her companion as hard as he would allow. With the distance back to Castleton increasing, she was feeling more at ease.

"Umph!"

The unforgiving gravel was suddenly beneath her. Understanding what had happened was impossible, for she could not find the strength to breathe in a much needed gasp of air. The fall had compressed her back and chest, and she lay on the ground with her arms crossed over her ribs. Galeena looked up but saw only blackness. Her knees raised as she rolled onto her side. The beautiful marriage gown kept her face protected from the soil and rock that had welcomed her like a mallet. Finally, a cough, then another, forced her body to receive the night air.

Was someone nearby? How did she fall? Where was her horse?

Galeena could neither hear nor see. A piercing ring was all she could detect. After a few breaths were taken, she realized she had hit her head, but it didn't seem to be anything more than a decent smack.

Two hands, one under each of her arms, lifted her body and placed it upright. Her head swooned and she suddenly felt as if she were floating above the scene.

"Shall you depart or shall you remain?" a calming voice inquired.

"I wish to fight, Mother. I will fight for myself this night."

Her head raised and she peered to her left and to her right. Gunnar and an unknown Norseman held tightly to her. Before her and behind, others encircled.

Galeena twisted and wrenched her arms trying to free herself. The men beside her barely seemed to struggle to maintain their hold. She realized they were too strong and numerous.

A quiet rasp in Norse was all she could manage, "You cannot harm me. You are of Gudsfelt."

"I am to protect only the daughter of my king. You are a soldier who killed my men. You are an enemy who hinders our mission," Gunnar replied.

A rope was tied to each of Galeena's wrists and her arms were pulled apart. She jerked and twisted once more, but she was at their mercy.

"Will you take me to my own village to execute me?" she asked.

"No. Torren is too soft as far as you are concerned. Though he declares his indifference, he'll not allow any harm to come to you. He will probably release you back to your army. No. You die here."

"My guards know I am out here. If it has not already commenced, a search will soon begin for me."

"Is it out your routine to part the fortress unattended?"

No reply was given. Nothing Galeena did was part of a routine. She remained silent.

Gunnar stood in front of her, and two others still held her arms out. "Did you just wed or are you running from a ceremony? Is that why your speed seems to imply an escape?"

"I did not marry. I was presented to our citizens as the future Queen of Solsworth. My exodus is an attempt to find some time alone before being bound forever to a man I do not know."

"Hm, it seems that the events of your life do not hold my interest." Gunnar then addressed his men, "Let us move this atonement from the road into the forest."

The men controlling the ropes tugged at their prisoner. They would then ease their hold, and as Galeena's arms would lower with relief, they would immediately pull the bindings taut again. They walked faster than she could comfortably advance due to the gash on her foot, the cumbersome dress that wrapped her legs, and the pounding of her head. If she stumbled, they would catch her before she fell by tightening the leashes. One even lifted her by her hair. All laughed at her clumsiness and torment.

Galeena thought only of a way to free herself from the situation. Although there were a few blades hidden in pouches of her dress, she had no means to collect them. And, she knew she could not defeat every Norseman who surrounded her.

Into the woods they moved. Two trees were selected and Galeena was tied between them. All of her captors stood before her, some gawked, others stared as if they were vultures.

Gunnar moved in first. Before he spoke, Galeena whispered, "Are you a man of honor?"

Her question intrigued him. "I am," he replied.

"You have come to ensure the safe retrieval of the last daughter, correct?"

"Yes."

"Are you aware that Jaegar aims to execute her?"

"He will not. You are a liar."

"I am Princess Helene. You can do no harm to me. You are my servant, my soldier."

"A desperate woman will say anything to save herself." Gunnar appeared to have had a revelation. He reached down the side of Galeena's dress and felt the weapons she had hidden within the layers. "You lie. You wish to convince me you are the one we seek so you can gather your trusty blades."

He drew nearer and whispered in her ear, "I admire your attempt to fool me. However, since you are not my queen, there's no reason to prolong this chatter. I'll not bridle my private intentions. I know Torren has already introduced you to the matters of men and women." His finger tugged the fabric at the neckline of her gown. He ogled into the depths at her nearly exposed self. The same tip of his finger reached downward and slid its way up to the bone of her breastplate.

Galeena had kept her head turned and her chin pressed to her shoulder. She knew it was far too dark to reveal her mark. Thus she retorted, "I prefer death. Be done with it."

The vicious hand of the contemplative man grabbed her jaw and wrenched her face toward his. She wondered if he was going to crush her. When she tried to twist from his hold, he only held tighter.

He stared into her eyes. She was simply not afraid of him. He released her and landed a slap with the back of his hand to the side of her head and cheek.

"You don't even bleed when a strike as powerful as mine lands upon your pretty face." Gunnar then added, "I've decided everything about you repulses me, though I know not why. We do have a purpose here and treating you like a cornered dog does not interest me this night. There is no glory in torturing something so weak. Death is better." Gunnar pulled his dagger from his belt and raised it to her neck. "Your heart pounds. It will stop soon."

All were silent, watching, waiting. By the light of a dimly lit lantern, the point of his knife pressed the pulsing, fleshy, blue ribbon that ran from below her jaw to her collar.

"I am not afraid," she muttered.

A hand gripped her throat, and their leader's face appeared just above her shoulder from the blackness that was behind her.

Without removing his weapon, Gunnar justified his position, "You declared that this woman no longer held your protection."

"I've changed my mind."

Torren cut the ropes and pulled Galeena to him with his arm about her waist. With her out of Gunnar's reach, he ordered, "One of you bring her horse."

A man appeared from the shadows leading Galeena's steed.

Her savior's lips pressed to her ear and said, "Go my love."

"Come with me," she replied.

"Absence from my army is not wise. I've no utility at your side."

"Your actions prove otherwise, Torren. Please, join me."

"You must go."

Torren signaled for the horse to be brought closer and he assisted Galeena with her mount. She situated her dress and said, "Thank you. You know where to find me." Her horse was prompted to part their company with haste.

The man who sought to be King of Gudsfelt ordered his troop, "This shall all be forgotten by morning. Return to Castleton at once and prepare for our second attack on Northanglia. I've been within the walls, I have noted the locations of the king's chamber as well as the private chamber of Princess Helene. An entrance has also been discovered. Gunnar, send a message to Dornwold that we shall be arriving before the fourth sunrise. Our ships are to be stocked and ready for an immediate return to our homeland."

Each man stood with pride, acceptance and zeal. None had expected their leader to have been able to act so quickly to complete their task. They all turned north and west and marched through the trees toward Castleton.

Gunnar was enraged by Torren's weakness. He grabbed his leader's arm and asked, "You found the private chamber of our Queen?"

"Yes. I know where she sleeps."

"To save her own life, that woman you just freed tried to convince me that she is the one we seek."

"Impossible. I've seen Helene. She is much younger and she is fair like a natural born woman of the North. Galeena bears no resemblance. Her words were an attempt to overpower you."

Satisfied that his instincts were accurate, Gunnar marched onward.

Torren paused and looked back over his shoulder into the blackness of the forest. He pondered what had been shared.

Finding the claim to be impossible, he followed his men back to their village.

Chapter 28

The gait was slowed and Galeena dismounted. She fell to her knees upon the ground, clasped her hands, bowed her head, and she prayed.

"You were so near, my Lord. I thank You for release from death. I thank You for guidance. Our way is blessed by You."

Her hands shook. Her legs were so weak, taking her seat upon her horse was nearly impossible. In the saddle and aiming toward the south, Galeena heard the hammering of hooves approaching behind her. She guided her horse into the trees.

"Lukah, Lukah," she whispered from her location off of the path. Whilst patting the neck of her horse, Galeena shushed him to keep him calm and non-reactive to another equine.

A man charged past her. All she could see of him was his hair. Concerned that the rider could be one of the Norsemen Torren dispatched to Dornwold, Galeena made her daggers ready for ease of grasp, and she charged after the man.

Nearing him, he looked over his shoulder. "Woooooah..." he called as he pulled and spun to face her.

"Torren!" Galeena yelled with relief.

Once sidled to him, he leaned to her for a craved kiss.

"I've come to ensure you reach Broodenshire. Some of my men have decided to hunt you. Let us hurry. We have much distance to place between us and those who still believe you owe us your life."

No rest, no slowing, for hours they proceeded to the cave. Then, prior to the sun's rise, Galeena and Torren were listlessly lowering their bodies to the earth. The Viking ambled down and hurried to the aid of the woman he loved. Galeena graciously accepted his assistance. She had lost feeling in her legs and when her sore foot landed upon the solid turf, her knees buckled.

Torren lifted her into his arms and said, "Either the assortment of foods you enjoyed last night has added to your substance, you have rocks hidden beneath this mass of cloth, or the jewels of this gown weigh more than you. So, what is to blame for the significant increase in your size?"

Galeena laughed and nuzzled his neck. "Perhaps the fault is with you and not me. You could have grown weaker."

"I doubt that."

"Just get me to my fur mat without causing any further damage to my body please. My head hit the road first, then my back. My arms still ache from being tied and nearly quartered, and I do believe I should refrain from walking for a number of days."

"Please know how deeply I regret what was done to you."

"How did they pull me from my horse?"

"Someone looped you with a cord. Tis my experience that the victim generally falls unconscious and has no recollection of the binding."

"Ah, that was a new experience for me. You Norsemen are astute at inventing remarkable torments."

Once Galeena was lowered to her bed, Torren informed her, "I shall eat, take only a short rest, then return to my army as quickly as I escorted you here. I'll be riding your horse back to Castleton."

A silence fell. Instincts told him he had erred. He stood over Galeena and placed his hands upon his hips. "Look at me."

Her eyes would reveal her thoughts. Galeena rose to her feet and stepped cautiously away from Torren.

"What... have... you... done?" He asked very slowly.

A window to her soul opened. He knew. "Speak!" He demanded.

"You followed me here, Torren. Why? Why are you here? I have made you no promises, yet you refused to leave me. You chose your fate and the fate of the men who serve you."

Without losing his glare, Galeena said, "You knew when you left your camp unattended, they would be vulnerable. They could all be slaughtered."

"And have they?"

"If you would not have released me from Gunnar, Lukah and my army would have. I am confident that they withheld attack because they must have seen you drawing near to me."

Torren suddenly realized that although his aim had been to weaken Galeena with his presence, she had weakened him with hers. Their first visit to the cavern was a test. This second one was part of a plan. She was to lure him away from the safety of his troop, and she succeeded.

He shouted at her, "Why have you brought me here? What is the fate of my comrades in this moment?"

"Those who did not surrender, have been eliminated. Those who chose life, are in King Wilhelm's prison cells far north of Claremont and Castleton. The men from Solsworth increased our capabilities. You were not going to be successful."

"And the messenger I sent to Dornwold?"

"If he did not surrender, then he has been relieved of his soul."

Frustrated, fuming, then desperate to just complete his mission he yelled, "Where is the girl, Galeena? Where is she?"

"You and Jaegar have done everything wrong. You two do not get to decide the fate of Princess Helene or Gudsfelt."

"King Wilhelm made the decision for her. He refused every attempt we made to negotiate."

"You did not wish to negotiate. You demanded that he release Gudsfelt on behalf of his child. You still do not wish to negotiate."

"She doesn't deserve to rule in the North. Now where is she?"

The echo of his violent bellow helped her fulfill her promise to her father and brother. She could be trusted.

Galeena withdrew six daggers, three in each hand, and she held them by her thighs. An eyebrow raised and her lips tightened.

Torren glared through squinted eyes and taunted her, "Throw them. Throw every one that you have hidden within your garments. Move forth and aim well. I trust your accuracy. I will even kneel before you. My position will be held firm. You cannot miss. Do it… DO IT!"

A barely detectable rock from side to side aided Galeena in her focus. The blades were being shifted between her fingers while she debated her choices.

Torren coaxed, "You have no loyalties to me, and I have none to you. You have no reason to spare me. My own plan has been to clear you from my path. I've come to take an entire nation from the grasp of someone you have pledged your life to protect. This is a serious act of aggression, one punishable by death. I will not lie. If I get my hands on Adelia's daughter, my father will kill her. I've been trying to ease your concern with the possibility that she could just release her claim and walk away. No, she dies. Jaegar hates her. So choose Galeena, my life or hers."

Distant, cold eyes approached him. She said, “Your death shall be honorable if it comes by the Boersen dagger.” One hand was vacated and held out to him.

Torren withdrew it from its case to place it in her hand.

She took it and dropped the remaining blades in front of him. Standing within a killer’s reach, Galeena raised her mother’s knife to plunge it into him. She then lowered it so the point would pierce his core.

Torren kept his promise, he did not move, nor attempt to stop her. He stretched out his arms, and whispered, “I love you.”

Her stance did not alter as she replied, “No, you do not. You loved what you thought you could gain from me.”

Then, he saw her heart. She was done thinking of Helene, discussing Helene, protecting Helene, *hiding* Helene, and she was done fighting, killing, and chasing.

“All I ask, before my soul parts, is this, does Adelia’s daughter live? Am I hunting a ghost?”

The only thing keeping Galeena from admitting who she was to Torren was his relentless desire to overpower Helene. She did not want to even risk revealing herself to him so he could simply marry her and take his place as king. She wanted to be enough for him. He needed to want only Galeena.

Deciding not to share her identity, Galeena replied, “You know nothing of your prey. A skilled hunter of beasts or man you may be, but on this quest, you were destined to fail. She lives. She is strong. She is wise. She will take her own army to Gudsfelt and claim her throne. Your hunt is not in vain."

Torren's hands gripped her at her hips. His forehead, then lips pressed to her abdomen.

Galeena lowered the symbolic weapon. She said, "I no longer feed thoughts of what you can do to me, my king, or my nation. And, because of you, I believe more exists to this life. Simplicity is what I desire."

He looked up to her and asked, "Will you tell me this, why am I here with you?"

"For reasons I wish not to share, Lukah was to kill you himself, but I couldn't allow that. He would be unable to live with the regret."

Torren found her statement to be most odd, but he did not question it.

Galeena held Torren's face in her free hand as she said, "There is nothing left for you in Castleton. Dornwold is not far from here. Board a ship there and return to your father. Tell him he will not be King of Gudsfelt."

"Where will you go when you leave Broodenshire?"

"I have another home in a place called the Applewoods. Tis there I long to be. I will collect a respite then find my own way to Solsworth. Wilhelm, Alexar and Olivia have chosen my fate."

The informality of her listing the names of regents was noticed. So many of Galeena's behaviors had been out of what he believed to be ordinary or expected. In that moment though, all that mattered was that she choose him. All else would be resolved in time. Torren asked, "Will you join me, Galeena? Will you come with me to Dornwold, then to Gudsfelt? Forsake the plans that others made for you without your permission. Join me."

"I am to be married. Henry awaits. He is kind and he is real. Our planned union may not have been made by me, but I accept it."

"It shall never be," Torren argued.

"You, nor I, can alter the decisions that have been established."

There were no doubts that Galeena was considering his request. With confidence, Torren stood and raised her skirt as he did so.

Galeena softly smiled and shook her head.

"I promise my loyalties to you, Galeena. I promise my heart to you. I promise my love and life to our children. And, I promise, you will be freed from battles and hunts and the commands of kings and queens. You and I will belong solely to one another and no one will ever separate us. Can you make the same vows to me?"

"Not all. Your visions are not possible, Torren."

"They are. We marry now, Love. We marry now. Think never again of that man. I am to be your life."

"Nothing is that simple."

"I believe all is that simple. I believe we have been tied like knots into the complicated schemes of those in power. I believe we should forsake them all and marry. We decide."

Galeena considered all he said without looking away from him. Torren was sincere. He meant every word. She knew he could be trusted. His proposal and his promises were accepted.

She asked, "Am I forgiven?"

"No. You need no forgiveness. You had orders from your king."

The woven laces that held her dress closed were pulled until her shoulders were exposed. Torren then slid his hands inside pressing his palms to her warm skin. He placed a kiss at her neck and moved his lips to every part of her that was being revealed from behind the heavy curtain. When all was removed, his eyes absorbed the full vision of the woman he chose to be his wife.

Galeena tugged the hem of his shirt and lifted it over his head. She then loosened the bindings of his trousers. He looked down at her hands and loved the sight of them setting him free. He stared.

Looking at him, Galeena admired his nearly colorless locks. It was as if she was seeing him for the first time. She had always imagined Norsemen to be unkempt and barbarian. Torren was clean, coiffed, chiseled, fair, and his masculinity piqued her body's yearning for his touch. She could never have dreamed that such an outstanding example of a man existed.

Yet there he stood, wanting her, marrying her, and soon, he'd be making love to her.

Torren lifted her chin. He teased her tongue with his. "Please," she begged.

A deep, filling kiss was uninterrupted as they lowered together to their bed.

Galeena reclined and he observed how she lay below him. Her hair sprawled like a halo. Her bare form created a hunger in him. The full length of her legs to her feet was exposed and smooth. He was in awe of her pampered and flawless skin. His fingers twitched as they prepared to caress it.

Torren was so enraptured by the gift that was now his, that he did not notice her observing his study. With his gaze fixated on her, she asked, "May I close my eyes? Have I your undying guardianship? Tell me I can trust you."

"I shall never betray you, Galeena. Never. Please rest."

He lowered and touched her center. He then moved upward accepting every single measure of her.

Galeena placed a leg on either side of him. Her hands reached to his waist, eased down, and they pulled.

Needing not another invitation, nor wishing more time to pass, Torren moved from a kneeling position to one of readiness. Galeena remained very still while he placed himself over her. He held each of her shoulders in his hands as he pushed forward. The wrinkle in her brow and the loss of her breath told him all he needed to know. She was his, forever.

Chapter 29

Nothing in her life had ever given her the feeling that she got from Torren, the feeling of truly belonging. She belonged to him and with him, and he belonged to her and with her. They would never seek another for comfort as long as they lived. The bond that was formed between them was sacred and entirely satisfying. Every event that had been established for her by someone else would have to work itself out without her participation. Galeena had made her own decision about who she would share her life with.

"This is love isn't it?" she asked innocently.

"This may be more than love, my sweet. We are one now. That surpasses the emotion, the word, that is love."

"All is healed between us?" Another innocent question was asked by his wife.

He sensed that she had changed from a confident, independent warrior, to a woman with a husband. Her heart and mind would forever be concerned with another, a man, a husband. He assured her, "All is healed. You will never have to worry about my thoughts toward you. I promise you will always know that I love you and I am yours."

"Thank you."

Galeena turned onto her side. The dulled fire warmed her face, and Torren pressed his body against her back. Her thoughts were of wanting to believe him and of hopes to keep him with her. She wondered if he could keep his promises or if he would again seek to complete his mission.

Torren felt an irresistible affection for the woman lying in his arms. His world had unexpectedly changed. He thought of how upon his arrival to Northanglia his single focus was on callously capturing a young girl and returning to Gudsfelt with her. All emotion placed on that task was suppressed, nearly gone. He lay there with an enchanting woman who had absolutely no connection to the kingdom's princess he sought, and this was where he preferred to remain. His soul was bewitched. He buried his nose in her hair and inhaled.

"How many days have passed, Torren?"

"Tis still today. We rode all night whilst our armies battled. We arrived here only hours ago."

"I hunger and thirst. All of me feels as if I have been trampled by a horse."

"Every ache will be healed soon, but tell me, what is next?

"We eat, soak, then ride all night again with the same vigor as the last. We will arrive at my cottage in the Applewoods as the sky sees its first ray of light. Then, we shall sleep."

“Will we be having guests?”

“No. Not a soul. It will take days to escort those who have survived to the northern prison. The captives will be on foot, so they will be given ample rest. They will also be fed twice a day. Once everyone has been relocated from Castleton to their cells, the soldiers will begin their return to Claremont.”

“And Lukah?”

“He has a farm a half a day to the west and south. I am confident, he will go directly there when he leaves the north.”

“Does he believe me dead?”

Galeena tightened her hold on the arms that encased her. She kissed the back of one of Torren’s hands. No reply was necessary.

“Sleep, Love. Your body has been beaten. I shall prepare a meal for us.”

Galeena had no recollection of Torren leaving their bed. The moment she heard the word ‘sleep’ she closed her eyes and obeyed.

His efforts to arouse her failed many times. He had never seen anyone fall into such a deep state that seemed near death. When she would not even acknowledge his attempts, he wondered if she had suffered some unseen injuries. It was apparent that she needed the rest more than she needed the food.

The daylight hours came and went and Galeena still had not awoken. When darkness covered their world, he forced her to sit and take water. She sipped and nibbled, walked outside for refreshment, then returned only to sleep again.

In his mind, Torren laughed at her, because she was never truly aware of what she was doing.

Their fire was livened only a mite, he removed the trousers he had worn during his hours of caring for her, and he draped his warm body partially over hers for the night.

Feeling him next to her, Galeena nudged at him with her own unclothed limbs and his eyes widened with anticipation. "Are you awake, Love?"

"I am awake enough," she muttered pulling his lips to hers.

Torren smiled and eased atop his wife for another intense yet tender interlude.

"More tomorrow," Galeena whispered when they were both weakened by the experience. She turned onto her stomach. Torren studied her every curve. His kisses upon her back soothed her until she once again left consciousness. Utter disbelief that he had stolen such a prize from all of his enemies consumed his thoughts.

"I care about nothing but her now," Torren shared with the world.

* * *

Boersen daughters always awoke before rays painted the skies so they could bathe in private. Galeena opened her eyes, scooted from their bed, stoked the fire, slipped a small tunic over her body, then stepped lightly out of their shelter. After an extended soaking, she twisted her waist length hair tightly into a roll and tied it high on her head. Replacing only her shift, she strolled to the shore.

When she reached the waves, she tested the water's warmth. Was too frigid to stand in that early. Dragging her toes in the sand, Galeena backed away from the sea's reach and studied the breezes for signs of the season's change. After a prayer of gratitude was offered for her solitude and health, she sat, raised her knees, examined her wound, buried her other foot in the sand, then finally braced her hands behind her so she could recline.

"The chill consumes the warmth now, Torren. You should seek refuge in Dornwold. You'll not be allowed to return to Castleton with or without me. You will never leave Northanglia alive if you do not heed my instructions."

He had arrived and stood behind her. He listened, then sat so no space was between them. Each of his legs appeared at either side of her, and his arms encircled her waist. He nuzzled her neck and inhaled the sweet perfume she always touched to her skin and sprinkled in her hair.

"We've chosen marriage. Join me. I already sense that you carry my first child. You will live no where apart from me. I am not my father."

Galeena turned her face so he could press a kiss to her forehead.

"Sounds simple," she said with a smile.

"It is, Galeena. Just because you are finally alert to all that has transpired, does not mean that we are no longer united forever."

She softly shared her reasoning. "Jaegar nor Wilhelm will welcome me. Wilhelm will see me as a traitor and Jaegar will kill me for not revealing my nation's secrets. I'll not be bait for an enemy nor will I be a public disgrace for my king."

Torren assured her, "You are not bait. I love you. My father will not even consider harming you if you arrive as my wife. You know that sea travel will soon be treacherous. We must sail for Gudsfelt. The winds will be arriving and no one will be able to pursue us."

Galeena was quiet. It was the first time she had heard herself called a wife and it comforted her. Still resting against his chest, she asked, "Why does your return to Gudsfelt suddenly seem to be so urgent? You've been resistant."

"Because *you* will be joining me. I do not want Lukah or Wilhelm to provide chase. If our timing is optimal, we will part ahead of the season's storms. I want you to trust me, Galeena."

"Shall we trust one another?"

"We shall. But please always be truthful with me?"

"I have been, Torren. I've told you not to return to my village home. I've told you I was assigned as your assassin. My exodus was to be seen as a flee from my marital commitment, but was intended to lure you. The men who hid along the road were not anticipated, but all ended up on course. I have even offered you safe passage to your people in Dornwold. Truth has been shared."

Torren asked, "I request another truth from you. Did you lure me to spare me or did you fully intend to kill me?"

"The plan and the orders were to kill. My life's work has been to defeat not offer excuses. Alas, when it was you I faced, I could not."

She lifted from his arms, turned to face him and said, "Please, tell me once more that I am enough, not for now, but for always. Tell me you have forsaken your hunt for Helene?"

"She is forsaken until the next sailing season returns."

"Choose me, Torren. Promise me you will tell Jaegar that you have chosen me, our love, over all else."

"You are asking me to admit weakness, treachery, or defiance to my father. To please you, I will have to admit to loving an enemy soldier more than Gudsfelt or Danemour."

Then silently, Torren pondered his position. He realized, from what he knew of Adelia, she had chosen country.

He added, "Your queen, Adelia, she was not so unlike me at this moment. She had to choose between Northanglia and my father, an enemy, but an enemy she loved dearly. I've watched my father suffer every day of his life without her. Therefore, I choose you, Galeena. We shall face our adversaries together."

In that moment, Galeena threw her arms around him. She turned and climbed onto his lap. She beamed at the feeling of securing him. Her next words were going to be her whole truth, her full confession, but when she opened her mouth to speak, they would not flow. The broad smile she wore faded. She had hidden for so long, that she could not admit to anyone who she truly was. A better time and place would present itself. What she said instead was, "I believe we are both traitors."

"No my sweet. We are probably now both farmers."

"Will we be executed?"

"No, Love. Appointments to monarchies may be withheld, but we have an equally desirable option."

"And that is what?" she asked curiously.

Torren smiled and said, "We will be banished to my childhood home."

His bride thought that to be a dream.

"Shall we seal our love *again*?" he inquired.

"You need not ask that."

Galeena took full control of him. "Welcome to my dreams of you, Torren."

His eyes closed tightly. Salacious moans from him sent energy up her spine. She would make sure he never went hungry again… at least not for too long.

Chapter 30

A clearing in the forest revealed an idyllic little home made of stone. Not wanting to divulge the route to where they would be staying for an undetermined amount of time, Galeena led Torren in a varied path.

"You do not fool me with your winding directions." His tone sent a clear message that he found her attempt at disorienting him to be one of absurdity. "The coastline is near and our direction was south. Is this locale that sacred to you?"

Galeena giggled. "Our proximity to the sea and our general placement as it relates to Broodenshire are not secrets. You will see for yourself as you venture out, there are no distinct markings to guide you here. My quaint little home is very well hidden."

There was a corral for livestock behind the house. Galeena dismounted, so Torren did as well, and she led them to the grassy yard. Both took their saddles and leather satchels from their horses. The gate was latched, and after their gear was situated, Galeena walked to the empty chicken pen. She picked up a container, scattered feed, then pounded the metal ladle on the wooden panel of the henhouse.

Torren looked at her quizzically and said, “There's nothing to feed.”

She informed him, “They'll return… if they are alive.”

“You have trained your chickens?”

“Trained is not the word I would use. Instinct is a better descriptor of their behaviors. They return if they have been smart enough not to get eaten. They come back here because they are hungry and prefer the safety of being cooped up behind this fence and in this house.”

“When were you here last?”

“Six weeks, perhaps. My plan was to come here the day you arrived. However, your unexpected appearance sent my life into a whirling tunnel of wind. In seven days I will see my sixteenth annual finally arrive. I was not to be introduced to Henry until then. I was supposed to be enjoying my final days as a free woman here. All has been expedited.”

Half of Torren's mouth smiled and one eyebrow raised. “So marriage means the death of freedom?”

Galeena had no reservations about her response. “Yes.”

“Do you not feel you have traded solitude for companionship? Tis my thought that marriage brings more freedom. We are free to make all of our own decisions now. You have left your position as commander for your king's army, and I have chosen you as my wife. These decisions cannot be undone, and no one can force us to fulfill their commands."

"Torren, you cannot believe all you've just said. We can still be beckoned and called upon by anyone at any moment."

"Not if we cannot be found," he smiled and placed his hands upon her hips.

"I can be found. Your presence is a mystery."

He shrugged, "Come, show me the inside of this perfect little abode."

Galeena looked up, the gray above them was blending with the sun's glow, and the ombre of faint blue, yellow and orange was just beginning to paint the skies. She accepted his personal touch and nudged her head in the direction they would walk.

Just behind his wife, Torren stepped into her cottage. Galeena immediately sought a strike to light a lantern. He watched and observed all he could glean of his temporary home.

"Another man lives here?" he asked with irritation. "You said this is your home?"

"Yes. I share this cottage with another. He sleeps in the loft, there," she pointed to the large platform above them.

"Lukah?"

"Of course." Her nonchalant response was given without removing her attention from the fire she was igniting.

"He will not come here?"

"No. He will go to his farm, as I have said. This is my cottage."

"If this is your's, why does he have his own place to sleep?"

"He comes and stays with me or alone on occasion. Now, will you please desist from asking questions to which you already know the answers? You tire me. Sit. I will serve you a small meal so we can rest. I do not want to sleep for very long though. We need to reset our patterns after traveling for two whole nights."

"Sleep?"

"Only sleep."

The two proceeded through their plans and took to another one of Galeena's regal beds. When Torren's curiosity was once again awakened by her lavish belongings, she reminded him that not only men were skilled at trading. She also restated that she was often rewarded with payment in goods instead of gold.

They sank beneath her silk and linen covers into a feather filled mat.

Hours later, the sound of clucking aroused Galeena. Torren was curved to her back with his hand placed on her bare hip. She reached to his ear and twisted his soft curls with her fingertips. The delicate touch eased him awake. Before he opened his eyes, he of course nuzzled her hair. She knew he was letting her scent stimulate his senses and bring him to life. He slid her hair and tasted her neck with the very tip of his tongue.

"This will have to wait. I wish to bathe." Galeena's tone was nearly a whine, but more of a plea.

“Understandable,” he rasped.

“I have much to show you. Let us rise. There is still much daylight.”

Galeena and Torren dressed and stepped into what was to be their own world. She escorted him to the stream for a soothing and refreshing bath. She then led him to the apple tree. As they wandered, he noted animal beds throughout the forest. And finally, she walked him to the shore.

Gazing at the expanse, he asked, “How long do you wish to stay here before we move onward to Dornwold, then sail to Gudsfelt?”

“Can you not allow me the pleasure of this day?”

“Tis allowed, but you must also be thinking of our future. Our first child shall be born in the North. I do not want to risk missing the opportunity to safely travel by sea.”

“Torren, I will be sixteen in less than a week. All discussions about where we will live can wait until then.”

“I accept.”

“For now, you learn to live my life.”

* * *

The need for meat, meals and intimacy guided their schedules. The newly wedded couple became inseparable. Galeena didn’t even want to spend her morning routines alone. She wanted her husband beside her, beneath her, or atop her at all times. Torren’s expectations were no different.

During the following six days, they lazed in the abundance of nature. Two very skilled hunters found birds and rabbits galore to prepare for each meal. They enjoyed the stores of herbs and foraged for other edible leaves to accompany their main dishes. Galeena had containers of wheat for cakes, and she had crystalized honey that they set over the fire to warm and return to its liquid state for consumption. They needed nothing from the outside world.

Sunday, the day before her annual, they stirred in unison. Galeena peered from their bed to the window. Their forest was dark. "We shall have a dreary day, Torren."

"Matters not to the larger game. I've decided to hunt today. I crave something more than birds, eggs, or rodents. My concern is that our activity these past days and nights will have sent the deer elsewhere."

"I shall join you. You could easily find yourself off-course and unable to relocate my cottage. You must believe me."

"You need not worry. I shall not travel far and as long as I can find the sea, I can find my way back to you."

"We had this discussion once, but I must ask, have you ever been lost, Torren?"

"Lost?" he replied.

"Yes. Lost. I know you have heard the word before now."

"I know the meaning of the word. Seems an odd question. I will not stroll idly in the woods. You stated that if one knows the direction for which they aim, the are never truly misplaced. I shall be well."

Her instincts had her concerned, but she did not argue. Being alone would give her time to complete some tasks, and it would also give her time to devise a plan for revealing her identity to her husband. The premise of their meeting had honestly escaped her during the time they had been reveling in what it means to be newly married.

"Shall we enjoy a send-off exchange?"

"We?" she asked with a giggle.

Torren nodded whilst his hands coaxed.

She stopped him, "Before we frolic in our warm bed, tell me you'll be quick about your return and promise me you'll not go far."

"Fret not, Love. And hinder not my cravings."

Another giggle and a soft leg over his hip welcomed him back to her.

Chapter 31

Greeted by a new chill and a blanket of steady rain, Torren walked through the front posts of Galeena's property. His aim was to seek game north of their lodgings since he and Galeena had been more active to the south.

Thankfully, the first morning they arrived, Galeena had ensured that the only two Boersen symbols in the vicinity, those her mother carved at the entrance, were covered.

With Torren absent for a length of time, she also thought about another task she had postponed. The desire to revisit her mother's parchments had nagged at her. Galeena had hidden the leather sack containing the documents in a cupboard of her greatroom. She fully intended to retrieve those and finish reading the story of Adelia's first meeting with Torren.

"A meal is to be prepared. Animals need to be tended. Wood shall be brought in for drying. A plan shall be established for telling Torren I am the heir he seeks. A bath, even in this dreadful rain, is needed. Hmm..." She thought. "I could clean some small items of cloth and hang them by the fire. I believe I have much to do. All will be accomplished."

Realizing there were too many chores to complete, Galeena decided she would find another time to withdraw the papers she held so dear. She wanted that task to have her full attention. And many hours could pass without notice if she were to fall into the trance of reading her mother's histories.

What could be considered the day passed by quickly. Galeena was relentless in her work. She even found other jobs that needed to be completed. One included collecting apples so she could treat her husband to a sweet delight upon his return.

As dusk was creeping its way over the faint daylight, she began to look for Torren. *He should certainly be returning before dark*, she thought.

"Perhaps he has killed a deer and is sluggish in his return due to its size."

Galeena decided that if Torren had not returned as the last light was consumed, she would take her horse north to search for him. She maintained her busyness about her cabin until no more work remained.

Later than she planned, because the air was cold and the rain fell harder, Galeena bridled her horse, led him to the fence and climbed upon his bare back. Her mate carried her into the densely set trees to seek her husband.

Many hours passed and no vision or mark of Torren could be found, so she returned to her home. She dropped her soft night dress over her head and sat by the fire until her hair had mostly dried. When she felt she could sleep, she retired to her bed.

"One night out there won't kill you. However, if Lukah lurks about, he might."

The night's sleep was rather peaceful.

The light of day energized the wearied soldier turned spouse. The sun lifted her spirits. She fully anticipated her husband finding his way home.

Galeena started a pot for tea and a pot to boil for a cloth bath. Post nourishment and cleansing, she dressed in her leggings, boots and black silkened shirt. Her satchel was packed with provisions and she exited her abode in hopes of finding Torren.

Her thought was that he would definitely go directly to the coast at daybreak, so she would begin there.

Standing at the water's edge, Galeena declared, "I have two directions and an equal chance at finding you no matter my choice." She looked north, then south. "Would it be the wrong decision to just wait here I wonder?" She sat. Her mind could not and would not settle. No clarity could be found. "I have never suffered from an inability to choose. My heart always guides me. Today, I have no direction."

The strap of the bag she carried was beginning to irritate her shoulder so she hooked her thumb beneath it and lifted. As she was removing it, Torren appeared to her right. The bag was replaced about her and Galeena bound to her feet.

She fought the reaction of running to him. Instead, she crossed her arms and glared.

He approached with a smile, but was met with a scolding.

"You arrive from the south?"

"I have passed this way many times in the woods. I found the stream but could not make my way to our home."

"My home," she corrected.

He ignored and reached to collect a kiss. She turned.

"Why do you not have a slain animal?"

"I saw none," Torren defended and attempted another kiss.

"Forgive me if I don't believe you. For a lone stag marched proudly past only moments ago. I could have claimed him six different ways, including returning to my corral, gathering my saddle, and forcing him to subject to my commands."

Torren laughed with gusto. Through roars and gasps, he asked, "So, why did you not kill him?"

"You were the one craving venison, not me. Therefore, twas your responsibility, not mine. Where have you been, Torren? I searched late into the night for you. The heavy dampness began to burn in my throat and chest. I feared sickness and returned home."

"You should not have looked for me. I have spent many, many nights out of doors, Galeena. And, I have simply been lost. As I said, I thought the stream would lead me to our cottage. The ways to walk from it are enumerable."

"You say nothing that is unknown to me. The stream is useless unless you know the precise point of westward direction to my land. The Applewoods are dense. I warned you." She paused, thought for a moment, then said, "I recall you saying you do not get lost."

"Accept my sincerest apology. I was severely mistaken. When all hope of finding my way back had vanished, I found a large tree and curled up against it. I slept and waited for light."

He observed and pinched his brow, "Why do you carry your bag? Did have plans to abandon me?"

"No. It contains my weapons. I thought I might need them. The days I have spent with you, I have not carried my blades. In your absence, I decided it was best for me to be prepared to protect myself. It also contains dried bread, apples, and hardened eggs. My bladder of water is here as well." Galeena held up the small pouch. She continued, "I did not know if I was going to have to go search for you. Food was necessary. There is enough here for us both."

"Allow me the embrace that leaves me starved."

"I am furious." She shoved him.

He barely budged.

Torren grasped her face again and said, "The return of your fighting spirit humors me. I have missed the anger and fire that lives within you. This makes me wonder if marriage is the best state of being for you."

She squinted with disgust. "Are you saying you have a mind to leave me?"

"Never. I am merely saddened by the observation that when you are at peace, you are so very docile. We have not faced the world yet, you do not want to lose your might, your skill, your drive for survival. The many moments of making love to you these past days have led me to ignorance of the woman I first met. I love both of you. Do not allow one to conquer the other."

"You need not worry. I'll not lose who I have been my whole life. You see, I now have a babe to care for. *His* survival is my singular concern now. As you are well aware, your absence has caused me much strife this entire night. I wish to be alone. You should return to my cottage. Dry, warm, eat, and rest. I'll join you after I've regained my peace of mind."

The Norseman gaped. The deep and loving kiss he took was met with no opposition. Another and another and another embrace was pressed to his wife.

At a moment of distance, Galeena gave Torren a much needed smile.

"When do you believe it happened?" he asked excitedly.

She thought his question to be a bit immature for a grown man who was now a father, but she replied with her unhindered thoughts. "While the countless moments in bed were memorable, and the times I floated across you in the pools and was met with your very interested advances were more than pleasurable, I will boldly confess, I felt that our son came to me before you ever breached my surface. Twas my feeling you contaminated my innocence with your over zealous explorations before we even declared ourselves married."

"Contaminated?!"

"I need not be so descriptive with you. You were there. You know what you did."

"We slept without barriers for three nights. You also knew the risk."

"It matters not. We've chosen and we've committed. Our son will come. You should go rest."

Torren looked out to the sea, then back to Galeena. His face shone an expression of deep thought, many questions, and mild concern.

She repeated, "Tis apparent you need rest. You should seek our bed. When you wake, I'll be at your side."

Softly he replied, "How can I sleep now? We have a child joining us."

He'll not be arriving today. You will be quite useless as a father if you don't regain your strength each and every night."

"He?" Her husband's eyes were beginning to lose their liveliness.

"Styrkes always sire males. You shall be no different."

"Tis a girl I desire."

"Tis a boy I desire," Galeena stressed with a teasing smile. "I shall be next to you soon. I wish to sit on the sands and absorb the sun's warmth. There are not many days left of it."

A very long, passionate embrace nearly led to the removal of their clothes, until Galeena pulled herself from him.

"Do not disappoint me. I now fear for you. Come soon," he begged.

"You need not worry. I'll see you after prayers."

Torren's eyes lifted to the seas and the skies. He kissed his wife's forehead, and he walked toward her cottage in the Applewoods.

When his absence was assured, Galeena's hands raised to the heavens and she said, "And thus, I am the last Daughter of Boersen, for I have married a man who is worthy in my grandfather's eyes. My children are Styrkes."

Chapter 32

Longships appeared, gliding quickly atop the swells. Galeena had never seen a fleet of Norse vessels. Each war boat carried what she estimated to be forty to sixty men, and there were ten ships within view. Her heart pounded. *Torren found his way to Dornwold, then readied a crew to sail us to Gudsfelt,* she thought as she waited, watching in awe their approach.

She did not fear. She felt only anger that he would have decided the moment of their departure without her consent. Galeena looked behind her to see if her husband approached. An hour or more had passed since he left her alone on the beach.

The men must have been invited to her private locale; they showed no aggression from their places within the boats.

Then, only one ship was beached while the others remained offshore. From that ominous seafaring craft, eight men carrying shields with swords drawn began jumping into the knee deep water and marching toward her. The man in the lead was of an advancing age, but well built. Three were of middle ages with thinner frames and formidable appearances. Others were young, perhaps her age, and much less intimidating. Galeena had battled Norsemen and sought familiarities, thus her instinct was to study each possible adversary for potential challenges and weaknesses.

"You are here for me I presume?" she called to them. Her survival instincts suddenly screamed for her to flee. The beat of her heart pulsed hard in her throat. She panted. Countless enemies she had faced with a leveled head and steadied hands. In this encounter, she hid the trembling she could not control.

"We know you are the Northanglian commander of King Wilhelm's army. We've been dispatched to retrieve you from this shore."

The precious satchel that was draped diagonally about her was gripped. She slid her hand inside, retrieved three daggers, and she flung them at one man. Her attack had not been a surprise, and it set them in pursuit of her with much more vigor. The water and the sand caused the men to lumber for only seconds. When they cleared the waves, Galeena was disappearing into the trees.

She ran one direction, then another. The shoreline was too far from her cottage for her screams to be heard. She would have to fight for herself. She ran, she hid, she stepped as lightly as a feather.

The men called to her, “You need not make this difficult. You will be leaving with us, Miss. We smell your fragrance. You cannot hide.”

Galeena assumed more Vikings had joined the hunt. From a lowered position behind a tree, she listened. Their footsteps crackled as they stomped upon the littered floor. *Why do they chase me?* she wondered. Desperate for a plan and quickly being engulfed by the Ice-landers, Galeena knew she had to wait until absolutely necessary to climb or scream for Torren.

She gasped and thought, *What if he sent them? What if he won’t come for me?*

Nearer they drew to her. The aroma of her perfume would inevitably lead them directly to her. She climbed the tree that held her upright. At least from above she would be able to kill ten, or perhaps fifteen of the men.

“You are one of them,” she whispered to herself. One dagger landed in the neck of an enemy. She waited. Another dagger pierced the center of a man. She hoped it was his heart. A third blade was released, but it was embedded in a leg. That miss caused her to be located. An arrow, then another impaled the tree trunk.

“Tis our intention to miss, Commander. We have orders to deliver you alive. Come down.”

“Torrrrreeennn!” Galeena screamed.

“Come down,” their leader ordered.

Galeena lowered with grace and ease just as she had ascended.

Placed before the man in control, she said, "You have made a mistake. King Wilhelm has no quarrel with Dornwold at this moment. However, any attempt to abduct me will cause a war you cannot yourselves defend. All Anglians have been kind to allow your residence. You are surrounded to the north by my army and to the south by Alexar's army. You do not want to do this."

She looked again through the trees seeking Torren.

"Though earlier than advised, we are here for you. Nothing you offer will change our course. We've been informed that your armies are preoccupied at this moment. We will not be pursued until word of your departure is able to reach the King's ears. Our ships return to Gudsfelt now because the autumn storms threaten to stir sooner than usual. Your ships may not even be able to follow us for weeks or months. Now, make haste, back to the ship." Two men grabbed each of her arms and jerked her in the direction of the sands.

"Torrrrreeennn!" she screamed again. "Are you not going to wait for Torren?" she asked the leader.

In a gruff and irritated tone, the lead man answered, "Tis my understanding he'll not be part of our crew this voyage. Therefore, Torren is not my concern. He arrived, told us to be here, collect the commander, and depart."

The paranoid Viking strained to see if any other Anglians or guards were lurking about in the forest ready to ambush his crew.

Sickened with a mounting fear, Galeena tugged against her captors and asked, “If I refuse transport? If I choose to fight?”

“You’ve already made that choice and it got you right here with us. If you resist again, I will have to take you by way of a less pleasant force, and you will not be well for the weeks ahead at sea. You will not prevail against us all no matter how skilled you are. We are to deliver you to Jaegar. He plans to trade you. Now, you can walk or we can carry you. I make this vow, you will not like our method, so I suggest you move.”

I am bait, Galeena surmised.

At the open shoreline, she turned and looked to the woods once more, weighing her options. How far could she get if she tried again? Certainly she could fend off the two men who held onto her. This time she could just run. How fast truly was her fastest? How fast was theirs?

“Make no more attempts to prolong our stay here by fleeing again.”

Showing no fear, with fury and defiance she wrenched her arms from their grips and shoved the two nearest to her. I am capable of walking without aid. Surrounded, Galeena followed the men to their ship.

Before stepping over the gunwale, she muttered to herself in disbelief, “He betrayed me.”

"It would appear so, Miss."

A hand was extended for her to proceed.

One last glance to her Applewoods was captured. Men lifted her aboard. She sat where instructed and placed her satchel at her side. They were in motion. She watched fixedly the entire scene with her hand braced to her belly.

"He betrayed me," she repeated.

Countless tears fell.

Chapter 33

"The fragrance overwhelms," Torren muttered before he had even entered the cottage. "I shall rest with an unobstructed portal this morn." He turned the knob, pushed, then placed a wedge at the base of the door. Galeena had left remnants of her meal on the table so Torren partook of an egg and bread, and he sipped the tepid tea. Satisfied enough to rest, he stepped once more onto the porch and looked and listened for his wife. Confident she would soon arrive, he retreated to their bed, disrobed, reclined, and covered his lower half.

The moment Torren walked away from his wife on the beach, he had decided his interest no longer included seeking Princess Helene of Northanglia. His new mission was securing a life with Galeena and only with Galeena. The new awareness sparked an impatient energy within him. He fell asleep conjuring images of their child and their family in Gudsfelt.

A restless slumber stirred once again his recurring dream. He jumped from the boat into the angry seas and heard his wife's screams as he entered the unforgiving waters. From the violently rolling waves he lamented at the sight of his wife in the boat surrounded by guards with Jaegar's sword pressed to her core.

* * *

"Uh! I have told her not to brew her flower water here. I can follow the aroma from miles away. And, she has left the door open. Tis no wonder the scent is so powerful."

Lukah stopped at the gate. No sounds came from the home that he and his sister shared. She would not have ventured far with the port unattended. Pests would enter and wreak havoc on their stores of food. They would soil their floor and bedding. They could hide or dig unknown tunnels. No, Galeena should be near.

He stood and studied the path to his home. A sickening rage grew within him: the presence of another. Quietly, he advanced and entered.

Torren opened his eyes from what had been a restless sleep. Accustomed to Galeena peering at him when he awakened, he at first barely gave the one in his company any notice. However, soon he realized twas a Norseman who stood over him. Focus was an unexpected challenge. He did not recognize the intruder.

Lukah allowed the unwelcome man a moment to wake and decide if he was going to need to defend himself.

No signs of fear were sensed. Jaegar's eldest son was actually quite at ease with the stranger in his midst.

Aware that the man in his cottage was coherent enough to communicate, with his arms crossed and no weapon drawn, Lukah asked, "Why are you alive?"

"The heart of a warrior has softened." Torren's eyes were then opened. He knew who loomed over him. He said, "Your knowledge of this place does not instill curiosity. However, your appearance does. Which countenance is your natural one?"

"This is who I am, Torren."

"You're Norse?" The Viking's entire face shown confusion. He checked the sheet for coverage.

"I am more than Norse," Lukah's vague confession instigated another deep pondering from Torren.

"You are a traitor?"

"No. I am more loyal than you. Tis apparent you have found your way into your enemy's bed."

"Are you a spy for Dornwold?"

"No."

Torren was disturbed. "I have no interest in being taunted with riddles." His declaration was met with silence. He then grew fearful for Galeena. "Where is Galeena?"

Lukah informed him, "She did not return to Claremont before her annual, which is today. Thus, I've been sent to collect her. Her future husband awaits. And, from what I see here, it would be best if she get to Solsworth as quickly as possible. I am taking her there. We leave at once."

Torren reached for his trousers and while maintaining modesty, he slid each leg in, stood, and turned his back to fasten his breaches.

The mark on his left shoulder held Lukah's attention. He asked, "I would like for *you* to tell me, where is Galeena?"

The door was still open. Torren turned to study the outside and muttered, "What is the time of day?"

"The sun has past its high point."

He had been asleep for hours. Torren ran his fingers through his hair then sought his tunic. He responded, "I left her at the water's edge for prayers. I shall go to her now."

As he reached his arms into his top covering he said, "Tell me Lukah, why do you declare that you are more Norse than I?"

"For the reason I stated. You have found your way into your enemy's bed. Tis not your fault. I knew Galeena would not be able to kill you."

"Then why did you send her to do the job you would have accomplished?"

"I have reasons you would not comprehend. One of them is, I knew there was a possibility that she would have compassion on you. I knew she wanted you... for some reason."

"Your tone is seasoned with jealousy. You need not concern yourself with her. If I would not have arrived, she would have married that man, Henry."

Lukah's next words nearly caused Torren to lose his balance. "I'll lie no more; Galeena is my sister."

Silence was his first response. Torren thought about Lukah's claim. He wondered if the two considered themselves siblings because of their history. Lukah remained silent awaiting Torren's next question.

Torren looked around the room. He could see Lukah's influence, but he also became keenly interested in the furnishings and supplies. Nothing was plain. All was of extreme finery. He looked at the pot of brewed perfume. He recalled Galeena referring to Adelia as her mother. He thought about her betrothal to a prince. The night of her presentation, King Wilhelm's proximity to her was excessively personal. He whispered in her ear, he doted on her, he passed her hand over to the Prince of Solsworth, then kissed her cheek. Her fluency of his native tongue made sense. And finally, the meaning of her name 'Goddess of the Seas' made all perfectly clear. No Anglian would be given such a name. The Vikings are tolerated, though detested, by the Anglians. She would not have been given a Norse name unless she had a connection to the people.

A veil was lifted. "Tis her... Tis her! Galeena is the daughter I seek." Every encounter, spoken word, and false lead sharpened in his mind. Torren had put all information together and realized that Galeena is the Queen of Gudsfelt and the Princess of Northanglia. "That which I have sought has been in my grasp since the morning I arrived?" His eyes raised to Lukah's, "Galeena is the Princess Helene isn't she?"

Lukah replied, "She is one of them, our mother was another, as was the deceased daughter of Olivia and Styrke."

An exhale of relief was immediately followed by anger, fear, and more disorientation. "Who are you?" Torren asked with a hint of a growl to his tone. "You've called her your sister."

With great pride Lukah said, "I am the son of Adelia and *Jaegar*." He then pulled his own tunic to reveal the antlers dripping blood that had been stained on his left shoulder at the age of three.

"You are the son of Jaegar?"

One nod was given.

"You are a son of Boersen?"

"No. Grandfather Boersen declared Jaegar worthy. I am a Styrkeson. As the daughter of Wilhelm, Galeena is named and documented a Daughter of Boersen."

"What does Olivia know of this? What does Alexar know? What does Jaegar know?" Torren's tone grew louder with each question.

"Olivia knows all. She and Styrke both know of my existence, though King Boersen did not. Wilhelm claimed me upon my birth as his own, though Adelia kept Galeena and I both concealed throughout our lives. She did not want Jeagar finding either of us. Her choice was wise. This became apparent when we learned that Jaegar's intention, and your own, are to kill Princess Helene."

"Why reveal all now? Why have you waited?"

"We have reclaimed Castleton, imprisoned those who wished to remain alive, and we established our plan for claiming Gudsfelt. Galeena is to return there and share all that proves her worthiness as a leader in the Norse. I was also to be revealed as one of their leaders so she could return to Solsworth and accept her position in that nation as well. All was to transpire, though it was expedited by your arrival weeks ago. Jaegar had been instructed to oversee Gudsfelt until the true heir took their place. His greed for power may cost him his family. Grandmother Olivia does not yet know of his invasion. I suspect she will not be pleased. Jaegar managed to gather a loyal army, and he has been able to reveal his lifelong relations to King Boersen without losing their trust. Tell me, is having reign over Gudsfelt a condition of keeping Danemour?"

"My father has the right to rule Gudsfelt. He has earned the respect and trust of the people of both nations."

"Tis a false trust. Olivia may have relinquished her hold, but Galeena has not, nor have I. Answer my question, will the Danes only allow his continued placement as Overlord if he also secures Gudsfelt?"

"Jaegar is a Dane with a mighty blood line. He has fought for and conquered Danemour. He will not lose that nation nor will he lose Dornwold."

Another realization shot through Torren. Lukah had a stronger claim to Gudsfelt than he and Jaegar. And the joined forces of Galeena and Lukah would leave him and Jaegar completely exiled from rule. He questioned, "At this moment, Gudsfelt belongs to the Daughter of Boersen, not a son of Jaegar. What plot do you foresee?"

"I am the only male heir to King Eichmann, King Alexar, and Queen Adelia. I still have a voice and much power in both nations. Wilhelm has many years of life before him. He will be King of Northanglia, I will be Regent of Gudsfelt, and Galeena will be Queen of Gudsfelt and Solsworth... unless some other path is disclosed."

Torren sensed Lukah's suppressed desire to make his own rights known to all. He asked, "And Northanglia's future?"

"That has not been decided. The church and Alexar have yet to solidify what is to occur postmortem of Wilhelm."

"Your family seems to have made decisions without the consult of others. This is precisely why Jaegar claims Gudsfelt. In this moment though, naught can be resolved standing here. Alternative paths have already appeared; Galeena is my wife now. She carries my child. I need to go to her." Torren sat upon a chair and shoved his feet into his boots. He exited the cottage, jumped from the porch to the ground, and ran with Lukah following toward the coast.

Into the forest, across the stream and nearing the open shoreline, a body was seen. Both men stopped and peered. They neared the corpse and recognized Galeena's daggers. From where they stood, they searched for her. Another body was seen. That man was approached as well.

"Galeena!" Torren called.

"Galeena!" Lukah yelled as he ran for the beach.

Their hearts raced as did their feet. Emerging from the woods, they scanned the horizon and the sands. Another corpse lay within reach of the waves. Drops of blood were found and tracked to the place where footprints showed signs of a scuffle. Impressions from Galeena's small boots created a path into the hissing, rolling crests.

"They have her," Torren whispered.

Both men panicked, paced, and groaned with anger.

"Will they kill her?" Lukah worried, and his voice nearly revealed the despair he truly felt. "Will they kill her?"

"If she tells the truth, yes. If she hides her identity, eventually," Torren confessed.

"She will not reveal her name to Jaegar. She will not." Lukah continued pacing and searching as if some mistake had been made. "You said she is with child?"

Appearing laden with guilt and utter confusion, Torren pressed his hand to his forehead and replied, "Yes, my babe, she carries my babe."

"Then she will take death. Galeena knows that all will be revealed to Jaegar and having to face that he killed his own grandchild will be more painful to him than losing a crown. I fear she may even provoke him."

"Does your king have ships?" Torren asked with urgency.

"We share our seafaring vessels with Solsworth and that is where they are docked at this moment. Tis a three day ride south. We have no hope of reaching them any sooner. What of Danemour?"

"Though premature, their departure would have included all of our longboats. They should not have left yet."

Torren looked to Lukah, "We depart for the south. Storms come."

"No. I choose both directions. I'll ride north, you ride south."

"We stay together!" Torren demanded.

"My father will have you locked in our prison. If you are taken in Solsworth, Olivia will collect you from Alexar's."

"Your father?" Torren's tone was one of cynicism.

"My mother chose Wilhelm. *He* is my father."

"Perhaps, but your God chose Jaegar. I believe His voice is the more honorable one to heed."

"You've known of our relation for mere minutes and you are ready to claim me as your brother? Tis needless to discuss."

"I respect my father and all he has suffered. There will be no more lies, no more deception, no more threats. Reconciliation is at hand. You approached and stated you wished to deliver Galeena to another man so *my* child could be raised as an Anglian. It makes me wonder if you wish for me to go south so you can retrieve Henry and Wilhelm and part for Gudsfelt without me. Your lack of willingness to name Jaegar as your father raises a concern within me that your intentions are not to resolve matters in my favor, nor in Galeena's."

The accusations infuriated Lukah. He yelled, "All I do is for Galeena's promotion! My life's work has been to ensure she is to be recognized for who she is. You know nothing of me and my intentions. You came here to either kill, or deliver to be killed, my sister. Why should I trust you simply because you managed to lead her into a bed?"

That remark was met with a solid blow to his jaw. Lukah braced his hands to his knees while he regained his wits and readied himself to return the unexpected punch.

Torren pointed at Lukah and commanded, "Do not retaliate. You deserved that and if you argue, you'll receive another."

The younger stood prostrate. Before he spoke, Torren added, "Our father gave his life for Adelia's promotion. I know all there is to know of postponing advancement and relinquishing that which you hold dear. You suffer no curse that has not befallen others. This will be resolved. We will not separate. We go south."

"Your selfish ambition is to blame for Galeena's circumstance. You don't have the authority to give orders. I am trusting you to go to Solsworth, ready our ships, then retrieve my father and me at Broodenshire. We sail together."

"Do you send me into a trap?"

"My mother once said to me that she professed to Jaegar that her son and his were destined to battle. Tis time that our battles end. Your dead body was not at Broodenshire. Priests said they saw you leave with Galeena. I wasn't certain if you had continued to Dornwold or if she brought you here or if she planned to be rid of you along the way. I came to the Applewoods to get Galeena, but I secretly hoped you lived. When you parted Broodenshire and I called to you inquiring if we would be friends, you said we would have been brothers. My deepest desire was to confess the blood we share. I did not though, because we were not certain that you could be trusted. I have been honest. Do not fear that I send you into a trap. Go, gather Olivia. She may be awaiting your arrival. She may be awaiting my arrival. Father sent a messenger to Solsworth. We now have only one aim, retrieval of Galeena. As you mentioned, paths have now changed."

Though Torren's initial tension had been eased, hearing Lukah's subtle word revived his alarm. Torren placed his hands low on his hips, scowled and questioned, "Retrieval? What do you aim to do with her?"

"She'll be brought back to our land, then be sent to Solsworth. Our aim to have rule of Solsworth has not altered. Alexar may be the temporal king, but Henry will take his rightful place. Galeena will be at his side."

Utterly disgusted, Torren asked, "And what happens to my child?"

A callus reply was given, "Henry will raise it."

"Lukah, you just led me to believe that we were joining together for cause: to remove Galeena from Jaegar's wrath." He quieted. Another realization was upon him, Lukah was more like Jaegar than even he himself was. Power, greed, schemes... all in the name of controlling a throne. Torren said to his brother, "Time has come for Galeena to make her own decisions. Time has come for her to listen to her own heart. Tell Wilhelm she decides, not him and not you."

Lukah advised, "Though you are now privy to two truths, there is still much you do not know. Do not sail for Gudsfelt without me. Do not."

Chapter 34

"The calm before the storms, Miss. Yesterday's torrential downpour was a sign; today was meant to be. Appears as if our travels will be smooth. Perhaps you'll bring us favor from the gods."

"I don't believe in your gods," she insulted.

"Your beliefs don't affect mine. What's your name?"

How she hated to answer that question in that moment. "Galeena," she stated with derision.

"Goddess of the Seas. Appropriate."

Galeena replayed his words. She asked, "What did you say?" then she listened acutely for his reply.

"I said that yesterday's torrential downpour—"

"That. Torrential? What does it mean?"

"Overflowing, abounding, abundant... do you know those words?"

"Yes." She quieted.

"I know why you asked. Tis similar to the name of Jaegar's son, Torren. That word, like his father's name, means great hunter. The words are similar."

"If given the chance, I shall tell him that someday." She pondered their future then said, "Perhaps not. I suppose I should break my thoughts of him, huh?"

"I'll not be getting involved in your affairs, Miss. I've been hired to do a job for my king. Tis all."

"Why do your words sound strange? I know people of many lands. Some of your words and the way you say them are unknown to me."

"My parents raised me apart from civilization. We had our own language."

"Very odd..." she muttered. Then she gasped, sat up, then slumped again.

"Have you something else you'd like to say?"

"Yes, tis the day I am supposed to be celebrating my birth."

"Ah, what number?"

"Six and teen years I have now lived."

"Sorry you're having to suffer the loss of your freedom on such a momentous occasion." The captain spoke with sincerity and lowered his eyes. He then raised them to the horizon. "Look back, Miss."

Galeena watched her homeland disappear. More tears welled, then rushed down her cheeks.

"Those will do you no good. Might as well get it out and be done with it."

Galeena cleared her throat and asked, "What is your name?"

"Tis Cinad."

"What?"

"Sin not if you want to know more. Mi mum had great hopes for her last born son."

"Huh, yet here you are in the employ of a tyrant nabbing someone who has done you no harm."

"I've worked my way up by being faithful to Jaegar. He freed me from the Danes."

"You sit amongst the Danes. This is not freedom."

"I could go elsewhere if I choose, but I like the voyages. I have food, a bed, an occupation."

"Why not return to your family?"

"One's purpose is not to return home, it is to follow our own path. I'm doing well. No complaints."

"You seem to be a decent man, I simply don't understand why you are committing *sins* for Jaegar."

Cinad laughed, "You've never sinned, aye?"

One eyebrow raised and Galeena turned her attention from the man in charge to the rowing crew. All aboard dipped, pulled and glared. She knew it was a matter of time before she would be seated at an oar as well. She was an enemy, not a guest and not a princess.

"Does progression ever cease?" she asked.

"Nay. We row. We sail. We shift."

Galeena stood and looked outward. "Are all of these ships aimed at Gudsfelt?"

"Nay. Some will continue on to Danemour."

Taking her seat upon a wooden box again Galeena counted barrels and crates. "Will I be fed?"

"O'course. You are to be set before Jaegar alive."

"So I am to be traded?"

"I'm not certain of your worth; although I doubt that you, a soldier, are as valuable as a queen. However, your confidence is admirable." Cinad laughed as did all of the men within range of their conversation. Galeena watched his statement travel to the ears of the farthest pair at the bow. Orphan, soldier or slave, none of those titles mattered to her. She was content with just being Galeena daughter of Adelia and Wilhelm. That thought caused her to squeeze the strap of the satchel that still remained by her feet.

"Whatcha got there?" one of the nearby men asked.

There was no reason not to speak. A lack of response would only make her bag more intriguing. "Tis food and documents."

"Show us."

Her shoulders dropped with annoyance and her head cocked to one side. She lifted the parcel, opened the flap and withdrew an apple, an egg, a water bladder, and then her mother's parchments.

"Are any of you learned?"

"None," replied Cinad.

She looked over her shoulder and up at him, "What about you?"

"Nay."

"So does that mean I will be allowed to keep my scrolls?"

"Will you tell us what is scribed?"

Galeena lied, "I don't know. They are written in a foreign script. I stole them."

"Ah, so you do sin!" Cinad's declaration was met with more laughter that traveled to all present.

"Forgive my lack of amusement. I am not able to find much joy in this day."

"Your circumstance is familiar. I have sat right where you sit. I chose not to battle the circumstance either. Nor did I find it to hold entertainment. You may be freed from service someday as I have. Jaegar will most likely find you useful in some way."

"I doubt that," she scoffed.

"If you don't give him a reason to kill you, in time, you could be farming one of his parcels of land."

"Or attacking innocent people," she inserted.

"We all have a purpose. Torren arrived in the night, said to collect the King's commander and get back to White Crested Cove. He wishes only to save us all from a foreign king and his daughter and their armies."

Galeena wanted to say, “Speak not the name,” but she did not want to raise suspicion. Back into hiding was where she retreated.

The day crept by with no more conversations. When evening came, the crew rested and all ate.

Only half of the men were assigned to continue rowing. With a great distance placed between them and Northanglia, the shifts were to begin. Cinad directed Galeena to a resting place for the night, and he tied her wrists and ankles with ropes.

Before the final rays of light were consumed by the darkness, Galeena peered once more behind her. With certainty, storms were gathering.

“Will the rains reach us?” she asked Cinad.

“There is a heaviness that we believe will protect us. We keep moving.”

The change in the weather meant that her father would most likely not be able to come for her. Galeena also knew their ships were docked in Solsworth. She wondered what Torren was doing. Had he returned to Dornwold to gather more troops? Or, would he seek Olivia knowing she would undoubtedly shield him from all threats?

The only thing that was certain was that Lukah or Wilhelm would be seeking her within a day or two. She was to return to Claremont by her sixteenth annual to join Henry.

"What thoughts possessed you, Galeena?" she whispered to herself. "What did you believe you were going to do?"

Galeena pulled her satchel beneath her head and used it as a pillow. She closed her eyes and tried to find peace in the sloshing of the waves that rocked the boat. The water was her comfort. "Perhaps I am Viking, Mother," she mumbled.

Chapter 35

An unwelcome, yet familiar, sensation caused Galeena to awaken.

"I'll ask only once for you to remove yourself from such proximity to me."

Instead of a distance, she received increased pressure. The man's gruff voice asked, "Are you married? Know you the pleasures that await?"

Galeena turned only her face toward the invader. She smiled. He smiled. She planted one of her daggers in his throat, then immediately withdrew it. "Shhh..." she continued smiling at him as he gasped and choked. "You were warned."

Very carefully, she wiped the blood from the blade onto her victim's black breeches and slid it beneath her waistband. The moment she felt him against her, she had eased her hand into her satchel and hid one tiny knife in her palm. Quickly, and with as little motion as possible, she sought a blade upon the man she had just killed. When one was found hanging from the belt at his back hip, she collected it, soaked it in his blood and gripped it tightly before her.

She waited. A new day had arrived so another shift should be occurring soon. So many needs she had in that moment: relief, food, water, motion, and removal of the body that was still half draped upon her.

After what seemed like hours, someone arrived and kicked the dead man. "Up! Up!" He called. Receiving no response, the corpse was rolled off of Galeena. Shock, then disgust. Galeena met the eyes of the one who stood over her. No remorse was felt. She was lifted to her feet by the rope that bound her wrists. The knife was snatched. In Norse the stranger scolded, "You killed, you row!"

Galeena was stunned at the lack of emotion they felt for their fellow Dane. Two other men were called upon to help toss the body overboard.

Cinad looked at Galeena and said, "A slave. You have chosen."

"I was destined to slavery in your midst. That man got what he deserved."

"I am confident that both statements are true, Miss."

Galeena worried that she would be beaten, starved, and given no opportunities for care. She asked, "What of the next thirteen days and nights?"

"Food and rest only once from sun up to sun down."

She nodded, then thought, *my babe will never see this world. Torren you have killed your own child.*

* * *

Lukah and Torren had parted ways and advanced to their destinations with as much haste as each, and their horses, could muster. The gates to Claremont were opened and Lukah was welcomed with an abundance of curiosity. All wanted to know why Galeena was not at his side. He boldly announced to each who questioned, "She has been taken by the Danes," as he never halted his progression to the king's chamber.

Torren made his way across Dornwold with no interference, stopping only at their fortress to trade his horse, eat, and collect a short rest. Directions to the Solsworth garrison were explained, and he once again took his seat to ride south. Crossing the entire nation to reach their southern most port was going to take two days, and he knew it was not likely that he'd make the entire trip without being questioned. Thus, he was prepared to speak only the truth; he sought an audience with Queen Olivia to deliver the message that Prince Henry's betrothed had been taken from the shores of Northanglia.

Once a lone Viking could be seen riding with intent on their king's road, messengers were dispatched to call upon the guards.

As was expected, Torren was stopped.

Four soldiers blocked the road. He slowed his horse, and when he was near them, four more guards appeared from the forest and created a barrier behind him. Each withdrew their weapon. “What affairs have you within our borders?” one asked.

The imposing rains had come. With great projection, Torren offered his rehearsed justification for his intrusion. Many more queries followed, and ultimately, Torren had to confess that he was Olivia’s grandson and he meant her, nor King Alexar any harm. Not wanting to risk having to confess the killing of their queen’s grandson to her, the eight men agreed to escort Torren to the prison where Olivia could make her own decisions about the man and his claims. The soldiers received only agreement.

With the passage of another rainy day and night, Torren and the soldiers arrived in Solsworth drenched and chilled.

Their approach was solitary until the constant showers ceased. Then, as if all had been informed that the skies would clear, people emerged from nearly every doorway. The city miraculously became active. Torren noted how it was much more populous than the regions of Northanglia. It reminded him more of the port at Dornwold and White Crested Cove. The citizens gawked at the Dane who seemed to be a prisoner of their guard. Torren noted that there were three ships. They were far taller and more rounded than the Norse vessels. The central masts were accompanied by two small masts, one forward and one toward the stern. All appeared to have quarters or storage below the main decks.

The eight guards were joined by several more armed men and Torren was led into the gates. Once inside the lower halls of the fortress he peacefully took his placement in a cell and awaited his beloved grandmother's arrival.

The tapping of quick steps preceded, "Insight about your escapades has reached me. Torren, what have you to say?"

A natural smile of endearment and amusement appeared and would have been impossible to suppress even if he did try.

Torren watched for the woman who was his home to show herself through the small opening in the wooden door. At the sight of her, he said, "Grandmother, may I please have food and opportunity to dry. I've been soaked for three days."

"First, you will declare what you have done and erase what I hope to be rumors and lies." She pointed to the lock for a guard to open that which barred her from one of her children.

Able to fully face one another, Torren informed Olivia of Jaegar's desires. "Father sent me to retrieve the last Daughter of Boersen. His aim was that she release all claims before the counsels and leave. Any refusal would result in her death."

"Our citizens would never allow such an act of treason." Olivia chided.

"The deed would not have been made public. Nothing I have spoken would have been conducted before others. No one knows of Princess Helene's appearance. If a refusal was her choice, then she was to be eliminated. For the sake of the public assembly, an unknown girl would have been presented as the last daughter, then her quiet return to Northanglia would be witnessed by all."

"How dare he! Why has he chosen such a course? Does he believe I would remain ignorant to all?"

"Grandmother, Father does believe you will be ignorant to all. We knew of your return to Alexar. We knew of your departure to other nations. Jaegar feels you have given him power to choose what he feels is best for Gudsfelt. King Boersen, Styrke and you have always sent him off to deceive and fight for what he wants. He is the creature you all molded."

"Jaegar was to secure our nation from Danemour threats. He was given that land. He does not need another."

"Father disagrees."

"And what do you feel about all of this, Torren? You are here, therefore you must be in agreement with him."

Torren paused, then admitted, "I was, but now I want my wife and my child. I've changed."

"You have married? And, she is with child?"

"Galeena and I have chosen one another. Tis done. Tis final."

"Do not rely on that, Torren. Come, I shall rectify all that flows like a waterfall with no end."

Torren followed Olivia from the frigid, dark halls up to the courtyard. She led him to a room and called for clothing and a meal to be brought. Inside the small chamber, Torren said, "Grandmother, I saw no longships."

"No. They're en route to Gudsfelt. Fredric has returned to the Nord."

“Shall you send two vessels to Northanglia so we can leave at once for home?”

“No, Torren. We will travel as one to retrieve Galeena from Jaegar. She is Wilhelm’s daughter. He is the only one with the right to barter for her.”

“She is my wife. If I arrive first, Father will have no choice but to release her to me. As my wife and the mother of my child, she is free from harm.”

“She is not your wife just because you say it is so. She is Anglian until she accepts or denies the crown of Gudsfelt. Jaegar will not hear of you claiming a woman he is holding prisoner. If you, or he, shares that she is their queen, he will look a fool or he will stand trial as an enemy. He will kill her regardless of your wishes just to save his own pride. No. We arrive as one. There is more to be revealed.”

Olivia’s claim was similar to Lukah’s. Torren asked, “More? What more is there to know?”

His question was met with a stern refusal, “Do not ask that of me again. I will receive no questions and no arguments from you. You are now under my command.”

* * *

Alexar accompanied the servant who delivered the clothing and food to Torren. Olivia’s heart still raced with joy at every sight of him. The two shared a gentle kiss, then Torren was introduced to her husband. The vision of the woman who raised him standing in the arms of anyone other than his Grandfather Styrke caused a mild discomfort to stir.

Torren witnessed the exchange that Adelia prayed for yet dreaded, because she too loved Styrke dearly. He lowered his eyes and turned his side to them.

"You'll have no choice but to give me your attention when I speak," Alexar advised.

The young guest respected the king's position and did as requested.

"We need time to ready all ships for sailing. Provisions must be stocked and men will be called from their farms. We have to consider the protection of our land while manning our ships."

"I have asked Grandmother for one ship. She has refused."

"Our fleet sails as one. Tis safer. A lone ship in a storm risks being lost. I'll not jeopardize my soldiers by sending them out alone. They could also be easily attacked by others. A three cord is stronger."

Torren asked, "Is it possible to expedite the preparations?"

Olivia spoke, "Torren, Galeena is our granddaughter. Do not believe that we are not doing all within our power to depart."

"I shall help. Send me so I may be of use."

"That we can do."

It took one full day and night to gather supplies and men for the journey. On the second morning, all was in order.

Torren stood on deck watching the last of the crew board from the small rowboats. From the waters just beyond the wharf, overlooking the village, he saw an entourage approaching. His hands rested on the smooth wooden rail of the gunwale. The regal group arrived and walked to the very end of the pier. The removal of one man's helmet revealed Henry. Torren watched Olivia and Alexar over his shoulder; he felt sorrow for Styrke. He then imagined his father having to see Adelia and Wilhelm in each other's arms. This future king seemed to know that his armies were to retrieve his bride. The Prince of Solsworth glared pridefully at the Viking.

Olivia stood beside Torren and placed her left palm on his lower back. She waved politely to Henry, then held her grandson's arm with her right hand.

Alexar took a stance on his wife's other side and informed Torren, "We'll not be porting at Broodenshire. We travel to Claremont. Notice has been dispatched to Wilhelm."

Torren knew the weather was going to bring about treacherous seas which would cause a cessation of their journey in Claremont. He feared Olivia had too much faith in his father. He feared every decision he made would lead to Galeena's demise.

The sails were hoisted. The rains began to fall.

Chapter 36

For two weeks, Galeena rowed. Cinad had compassion for her. He knew she would most likely be facing a harsh greeting. Thus, he allowed her rest and extra portions of food. She had consumed all she carried within the first few days, then small quantities were provided from the stores reserved for the crew.

Galeena's hands were blistered and bloodied as were her wrists. Her lips were cracked and her soft skin bore rashes from the salty spray. The appearance and external woes were painful, but internally she was strong and her babe still lived. No evidence of its demise had been seen. For that, she was not sure if she should be grateful or sad. The seas would not be navigable for very long. She could be held in a merciless prison cell for months. Galeena knew she would have to set her mind to accepting death.

The peaks of White Crested Cove stood proudly in the distance. She remembered this vision from her childhood. Seven years prior to this moment, the cliffs seemed majestic and welcoming. This morn, they were dreary and forbidding.

"We'll dock soon. Let us get you better prepared." Cinad unleashed her and helped lift her to her feet by one arm. He lowered his voice and said, "I'll watch and listen for you, Miss. And, when we reach the shore, if I can be of any help, I'll intercede."

Galeena was escorted to the platform at the stern where she was given the opportunity to revive. A pail of water awaited her and she first drank from it. Cinad held a drape so she could remove her clothes for rinsing. Prying eyes were sought before the small dagger was removed and hidden beneath the pile of cloth. She washed. Replacing the soaked garments was a miserable experience, but she was grateful to have been allowed water and a comb for her hair. When all was reset for presentation, she noticed her leather sack had been crammed behind some crates. She reached for it and draped it across her body. The dagger was secured inside her waistband once more.

"You may lower the barrier. Tis not much more I can do," she announced with humility.

"You'll sit for the passage of these last minutes."

"May I keep my bag?"

"It hasn't caused me any harm, but you know Jaegar will have the authority over that request."

Jaegar... she was moments from facing the infamous Jaegar. The man her mother dearly loved. The man Torren dearly loves. The man for whom her own brother holds a secret affection. All of these people are so willing, no anxious, to please him. The fascination was, well, fascinating.

There were five ships that sidled to the docks before the one upon which she sat entered the cove. Galeena's heart wanted to pound, but she forced a steady beat. If her blood flowed too quickly, she would lose her ability to think or react with wisdom.

Men, women and children gathered to greet their friends and family members. Twas apparent that Jaegar's reign had joined many of the people who had been lifelong adversaries. The boat that Galeena was on even held a blend of Danes and Gudsfelt citizens.

Nearer and nearer they drew to the shore. Celebrations and cheers welcomed all seafarers. Their ship docked, ropes secured the vessel and men were bounding to the solid platform. Cinad held Galeena at her elbow. She was of an unassuming size so many did not initially give her notice. Once it was apparent that a stranger was being guarded, attention fell to her.

Cinad and Galeena walked the length of the pier to the sandy beach. She looked at every face within her view. Some admired, some worried for her, and all wondered to whom she belonged. Side to side she peered. A tear nearly formed as she remembered experiencing this place while in her great-grandfather's arms with her brother. Not wanting to appear weak, Galeena looked to Cinad, he forced a smile for comfort. She then looked ahead.

A subtle pause of shock was followed by a deep inhale.

There he was, walking toward her. A handsome man whose strength was evident yet he was ideally proportionate. Their leader politely acknowledged others and was revered by those who trailed him. He was the king of three nations, and he knew no one could alter all he had earned. Jaegar was captivating. He commanded everyone's attention without even making an effort to do so.

A list of questions she had about him were all answered before they had even been introduced. Galeena no longer wondered why this man was allowed to do as he pleased with no accountability. Her mother's inability to resist him was no longer a mystery. The powers that his sons had over those they met were clearly inherited by their father. And, she no longer wondered how Torren had captured her heart and trust so easily.

Jaegar was enchanting. He was a magnificent man. His eyes lured her into his realm. The structure of his build could be likened to one of the mighty gods he worshipped. He even smiled at her. She knew he saw past her tiresome exterior. She knew he could see her true beauty that was fogged by deprivation of sleep, lack of nourishment and absent elegant covering.

In Norse Jaegar spoke, "Cinad, you deliver a child to me? What am I to do with her? Is she to be a slave or a wife? Where is my son?"

Galeena replied in his native tongue, “I am of very little importance. I am a mere soldier, a soldier who is perhaps to be held for ransom?”

“My address was directed at Cinad. You’ll be forgiven for the interruption for now. Since you are versed in our language, tell me, are you that valuable to the Northanglian king?”

Galeena replied with only a slight shrug.

“Now I receive your silence. Answer, do you discount your own value to save your life?”

Again, Jaegar received a barely noticeable shrug.

He studied her. “What is your age?”

“Sixteen.”

A deep sigh was released in response. Jaegar seemed to be at a loss by her deliverance. After a few more moments of staring, his interest turned to that which she clutched. He asked, “These men allotted time for you to gather belongings?”

She smirked, almost chuckled. “No. This was already in my possession when they arrived to my property.”

“How is that they found you?”

Cinad began to speak, “Sir—”

Jaegar’s raised hand stopped him from continuing. “I wish to hear from the woman.”

Galeena obliged, “Your son, Torren, led them to me.”

“Why did you feel the need to name my son? I have only one. I know his name.”

He had made a very valid point. Galeena had always thought of Jaegar as having two sons. She defended, "I simply forgot to whom I am speaking. Was an innocent oversight."

Jaegar ignored her comment. "Tell me, why did Torren know of your residence?"

This she would not be able to hide. Galeena had had two weeks to come up with a response to this question, yet she had no misleading excuse to offer. She stuttered, "He, he had followed me thrice."

"He left the security of his men or he *and* his men followed you?"

"Only Torren followed me. The first time, he retreated to Castleton almost immediately. The second time, he returned to Castleton after he was nearly beheaded by one of my comrades, and the third time, he completed his mission. He trailed me, then continued south to Dornwold to have me taken. I was caught completely unguarded. The arrival of your army was so unexpected that I didn't flee at first sight. I just stared in awe."

"What is your name, and why have you been selected by my son to be held by me? This time do not lie. If I have to ask one of my men, you will find it very difficult to speak for a long time. Torren chose you and he chose to remain in the west. What is your value?"

She did not hesitate, "I am one of two of King Wilhelm's commanders. I am betrothed to the Prince of Solsworth by the command of Kings Alexar and Wilehelm. I was days from meeting Queen Olivia, who was to host my wedding. I have been under the care of Queen Adelia and King Wilhelm for many years. They hired a governess by the name of Dreisel to care for me until I was ten. Upon Adelia's passing, I was no longer governed. The army took me and trained me to fight, defend and survive. My value may be in the investments that have been made to ensure I am capable of keeping Northanglia, and someday Solsworth, safe from Ice-landers. Torren found me to be a threat to his mission. Thus, he sent me here to be guarded by you."

"So you were enough of a nuisance that my son sent every ship back to our shores with only you as a reward."

Cinad spoke up again, "Sir,"

"Yes, you may speak now."

"She is quite astute. She had to be bound for the duration of the voyage. Seeing the damage she can inflict with my own eyes, I can understand why Torren would want to be rid of her."

"Why would he not simply kill you?"

Galeena offered a half smile, "Perhaps he wasn't capable."

"Astute you say?" Jaegar suddenly grabbed Galeena's left wrist. She winced. He pulled her sleeve and revealed a dagger. She wrenched, dropped one from her right sleeve and swung at him. A man caught her arm before it reached their king.

Jaegar laughed.

An evil glint shone through her squinted eyes. "I'm not as quick as usual. Hunger and exhaustion weaken me."

"Should I kill you now? Miss?"

"My name is Galeena. And, I can't say if you should or should not kill me."

"Will you seek my harm again?"

"Only if given the opportunity."

"Now that is the honesty I seek."

Jaegar crossed his arms and pondered what to do with the talented woman who had been sent to him by his son. "Tis so disappointing that you cannot be trusted to fight as a Norseman. Your skills are remarkable. You do remind me of—"

She reminded him of Adelia. He asked, "You knew my wife?"

"I knew King Wilhelm's wife."

"Adelia never loved him. She merely fulfilled the duty Alexar expected of her. She only married Wilhelm because I orchestrated it to keep her safe from the men I eventually conquered. I could not be a husband, a father, and a spy."

No argument was given because there was no reason to battle a man who loved her mother as much as she did. His pain was evident and Galeena had no desire to drive a hot iron into his unhealed wounds as they pertained to Adelia.

"Are you to kill me or not, Sir?" she asked.

He did not answer yet. Instead, he asked, "What are the contents of that sack you hold so dear?"

Hearing that, Galeena backed. The man who had halted her strike upon Jaegar bumped her with his chest.

"Hand it to me."

She gripped the strap and the folded flap.

"Place it in my hand or lose one of your own."

The bag was lifted over her head and she held it out to Jaegar. "Please, I beg you, please do no harm to what is in there."

He took it with grace and opened it. A nod instructed Cinad and his cohort to restrain her. Three blades were removed and tucked into his own belt. Then, Adelia's parchments were carefully withdrawn. Jaegar looked at them as if he knew what they were. The bag was dropped. The leather binding was opened and each page was reviewed. Galeena could have sworn he was reading them. His expressions changed a few times. Finally, he looked at her. She knew his next question. "Where did you get these?"

"I stole them," she responded.

"Shall I separate you from your tongue? Your lies are beginning to frustrate me. Where did you get these?" he yelled.

"Do you know what they are?"

"Annika, my most recent wife, revealed secrets. She admitted that she should not have, but she felt sharing her words would be harmless. I never thought I'd be seeing them from any other daughter. Thus, yes, I know what they are. Now answer me. From whence do these come?"

"I stole them."

"Why?"

"I stole them because I saw Torren's name scribed within the pages. They belong to Adelia and I hoped Olivia would translate."

"Why would my mother tell you her family's secrets? Was your intention to manipulate her, lie to her?"

Galeena was strong and even toned, "Torren—"

"You have found that my son holds your interest?"

"He saved my life. Just as he followed me three times, he saved my life three times. The night of my engagement announcement, I found these parchments in a cabinet. Torren's name appeared several times. I took them."

"Why would he save your life?"

"I can only surmise, it was because he thought I could be traded for Princess Helene. Will you return those to me?"

"I will not. They belong to my wife, not to you."

"They belong to Adelia's daughter, not to *you*!"

"Oh Galeena, you are a brave one for such a young woman. These are useless to you. The script is a secret language."

Jaegar's interest had left the girl and turned to the writings of his beloved. "Take her, search her, then lock her. She'll receive another visit from me soon. Until I emerge, I shall not be bothered."

The Norse king was far less appealing as he walked away with her mother's scrolls.

Chapter 37

Secluded in his private chamber, Jaegar lay the bound parchments on his work table. This was the first moment he had ever felt joy about having married Annika. Though she was a kind woman, she never had the same fighting spirit with which Olivia and Adelia had been blessed. Annika had been sheltered by her parents after the death of their two sons. Thus, she was always more frail and less interesting than her sister and niece. Her untimely death due to a contracted sickness did not surprise Jaegar. He felt sadness for her, but never for the loss of her. Their marriage was intended to be his opportunity to bring forth a male heir with Boersen lineage. Olivia approved their union only because she knew Jaegar would not, nor would he ever allow anyone else to, mistreat her very young sister. In those months, the reason Jaegar held control of Gudsfelt was because of his approved marriage to a Daughter of Boersen. Sitting before his true love's memories, he finally saw the value in convincing Annika to teach him their secret language.

"Well my love, speak to me. I pray your words resound a message that will fill me. I pray your voice echos all around me. I pray your memories deliver me back into your arms."

The first page was lifted.

Torren then said with disappointment, "I shall be punished for my disobedience. I was not to return here without my father. He was to bring me home after thirty nights. Only eight have passed."

"You shall not be punished my sweet. Your father will have to cross me to collect you."

Jaegar imagined Adelia's playful scowl as she spoke to his son.

I chose to leave the pool's edge, my safe haven from temptation, because Torren's smile was not to be resisted. A pressure in my throat made it difficult for me to breathe when he said, "I have always wished for a mother who would overpower my father when he has set his mind to punishing me."

I knelt, took both of Torren's hands in mine and said, "I may not be your mother, but I promise you, I can overpower your father."

We both giggled at my confident declaration.

"Come, both of you," a deep and familiar voice commanded.

My new acquaintance and I gasped in unison and turned to see Jaegar standing nearby. Torren gripped my hands in fear, but I eased his nerves by caressing his cheek once more before placing my warm palm below his chin. I whispered, "You've nothing to fear. He loves you, I promise."

Torren nodded only once before lowering his eyes in shame. He had disobeyed his father by running all night to return to the only home he knew.

I looked at the stave manor that was my childhood home and saw my mother standing, staring. She knew her sons had returned. I waved, confident my own children would be cared for in my absence. Still holding Torren's hand, I turned toward Jaegar; his smile poured sunlight into my soul. I released the angelic boy and walked into the arms of the man I had loved my entire life.

Jaegar's lips pressed to the top of my head. I clasped my hands behind his back and held tightly. I heard him inhaling my unique fragrance.

"My spirit has returned," he said, not removing his lips from me.

The erect posture I had carried in my shoulders for many years oozed down and my body attempted to lower to the ground with it. Jaegar only held me tighter.

He assured me, "I will hold you up in every circumstance, even a joyous one such as this. Rest in my arms, Love. Your burdens are mine to bear."

A silent sob escaped, but I was not ashamed, for my tears were of joy. When I had last seen Jaegar, we were at the northern border of Dornwold. He was ensuring my safe exodus from captivity and begging me to leave Northanglia as his wife. The hatred I felt for him that night removed the complication of abandoning him. In that moment, I never thought I would be able to forgive him so easily. Yet, I had. One smile, one extended hand, one invitation of open arms, and finally, one sweet embrace, and I belonged fully to him once more.

Tears were fought at hearing that Adelia had forgiven him, and she had never stopped loving him more deeply than anyone else.

Torren stood in awe of his father's display of affection. In my presence, Jaegar was calm, peaceful, loving, and pleased. It was not often that Torren witnessed his father experiencing joy. The boy smiled apprehensively at the woman he had just met and the man he respected and feared. Though a stranger to him, I smiled back and said, "I told you to trust me. Your father loves us both."

"Come," Jaegar instructed of his son.

I turned toward the beautiful child with my hand extended to him. Torren joined us, not only grateful to have the experience of a mother and a father, but also grateful he had avoided a switching.

We walked in the opposite direction of our home with me placed in the center of our trio. For the first time in the little boy's life, he was gifted with the sensation of being part of a loving family. I was not going to miss any opportunity to let him know he was loved by us both.

"Shall you sleep at our camp?" Torren asked excitedly.

I immediately glanced at Jaegar unsure of what my response should be. Jaegar raised one presumptuous eyebrow and offered a flirtatious smirk. My attention returned to Torren. His anxious and hopeful eyes could not be denied any request. I replied, "I do believe the journey back from your camp will take many hours. A night's stay will be necessary."

Torren squealed with glee, and jumped while squeezing my hand with both of his. He celebrated, "Father! Father! This lady will be our guest this evening."

"Torren, my child, this lady has a name."

"Yes Father, she is called Adelia."

"No, her name is Lillia."

"I do wish I could call her my mother."

Jaegar lowered to his son's level and replied softly, "Tis too soon my boy, too soon." He then whispered, being sure I could hear, "We do not want to scare her away. We just got her back."

The following pages painted a perfect image of the trek to their camp. All day they walked, chased, threw sticks or rocks, played games, and laughed without ceasing. Jaegar remembered never letting go of Adelia's hand or arm or waist. She allowed him to wrap himself around her, to kiss her, and to breathe her into his soul. Many times as he stood behind her, absorbing the joy of his son's stories, she turned to him and took her own much needed embraces from his lips and cheeks. Her fingers gripped his curls, she nuzzled his neck, and pressed against all of him. Jaegar remembered hardly being able to wait for the sun to go down and for Torren to fall asleep.

They reached the site where Torren and Jaegar were spending their time together. Jaegar had been very thorough to provide as many comforts as the wilderness would allow and he could carry. A fire ring was positioned in an area that had been cleared and was surrounded by only soil. Adelia surmised that was to protect everyone and everything from a precarious boy who may enjoy playing with flames when left unattended.

A large canvas was propped across from a smaller tented structure. The center gathering place separated the two. Again, Adelia smiled imagining a little boy who wants to be brave and grown, but who also may want to sleep next to the father he rarely sees.

Jaegar had constructed chair-like furnishings and covered them with furs. They rested on the earth and their backs reclined. One could sit and stare at the fire or study the stars. Lessons of their Norse gods were certainly a topic each night.

In addition to the shelters, seats, and fire place, a few clean dishes were set and ready for use.

Adelia had Torren join her on a search and gathering of white roots and edible bulbs to accompany the stew Jaegar had already prepared. They were all quite blessed that some large creature had not already consumed their meal. As a precaution, the pot had a sealed latch closure and had been hung high in a tree. Rodents could have pawed at it, but wolves or bears would not have been able to access it.

As they searched for compliments to their supper, Jaegar was glad that his son had a doting experience with a woman who was not his grandmother.

Adelia, at the time, wanted nothing more than to have Lukah there with them. She then wondered if the boys would see one another as a threat and perhaps spend their time in scuffles. She then thought it was best that she and Torren had that time alone.

Once all was eaten and cleaned, we three rested and enjoyed time as a family. Jaegar entertained us with the story of Freya.

"Her beauty was unmatched as was her love for her husband. But one day, she decided to leave home against

her husband's wishes to search for a treasure from three giants. When she finally found them, the giant women gave her a beautiful necklace. Freya went home to Asgard to show her husband the prized possession she had received. Her plan was to ask for his forgiveness, but he was gone. Freya then left their daughter to be cared for by Frigga, Odin's wife, and she sought her husband at every extension of the universe. Unable to find Odur, she returned, distraught and weeping. Standing on the Bifrost, unconsolable, Frigga brought Freya her child, Hnossa. Finding that her daughter was grown and more enchanting than any other, Freya was consoled. Thus, she remained with her child in Asgard.

"Another story, Father," Torren begged.

"One is enough. To bed my son."

No argument was given. Torren was most obedient and clearly wanted only to please his father. He came first to me for an embrace, which he received in abundance. The boy then approached his father for the same comfort. Nothing pleased me more than seeing Jaegar take Torren in his arms, pull him onto his lap, and hold him showing deep affection. Torren knew he could trust his father for comfort. There was no apprehension in him as he walked directly to the man who gave him life. Watching, my heart wished, in a very small way, that we were a family.

Chapter 38

For quite a while, post Torren's departure to his own makeshift abode, Jaegar and I sat awaiting the demise of the fire. We talked openly about so many things.

A common emotion that reappeared time and again was Jaegar's unrest about the ease of my life. He compared us many times. Having heard enough from him that I had been given ease of decisions and a life free from difficulties, I said, "Jaegar, even though you see my life as one of leisure and prominence, you are the one with freedom. You can vanish into the forests with your son. You can arrive at our childhood home for lengthy stays at will. You have the pleasure of choices, infinite choices."

He replied, "You are wrong. I gave up my freedom in exchange for your life. My father delivered me to strangers, lied about my age, and ordered me to become an enemy. My childhood was murdered by my own family so you would have protection." Jaegar's voice turned sour. His anger forced a hiss filled with rage, "Because you insisted on leaving me, I was left with no choice but to continue Grandfather's assignment of conquering Danemour. As a pair, we would have had everything we wanted. You were selfish. You left me."

He pointed to where Torren slept and said, "He should have been your son, our son. This land should be ours. This country ours. Grandfather has now declared it shall only pass to Olivia, you, or the daughter you have bore with a foreigner. I gave all to protect our king and his descendants, yet because my blood is that of two Danes, he finds me unworthy of the loyalty of his citizens and unworthy of rule."

Surprisingly undaunted by his scolding, I held firm to my claim, "You know why I left you. And I will say, you would have abandoned me here with Torren even if I would have chosen you. Jaegar, you see your past as a burden to your present and your future. However, I still believe that you are free. You can disappear just as you would have done with or without me. The only thing holding you back from complete freedom now is your refusal to give up your self-inflicted need for power. This land upon which we sit will belong only to you, then to Torren. It is exclusively your father's property. You have the ability to remain here, attend Assembly once per year, and live in peace. You know nothing of my sacrifices. I have no options. Even if I wanted to take Gudsfelt when Grandfather passes, I cannot." I paused and thought carefully before proceeding, "My daughter will live in danger. Ulfdan wants Gudsfelt, he sent Vidar for me, they will come for her."

Jaegar declared, "I did not allow Vidar to harm you, and I'll not allow him to harm your daughter. That is a promise. Ulfdan is gone and I have ensured Vidar's placement as king."

I interrupted, "Why would you do such a thing?"

"Because he will be easily removed at my whim. Tis not time for me to take control of Danemour. I need more time to build even stronger loyalties amongst the soldiers and landlords."

Although I questioned his decisions, I needed to trust his loyalty to me. I replied, "I thank you for that Jaegar, and I trust your promises, but please do not allow Vidar's darkness to become like a plague to you."

"You need not worry, Lillia."

"We have peace in Northanglia with the Danes who inhabit Dornwold. That could easily change though. Therefore, we have very special protections in place for my daughter. It comforts me to know that we have your guardianship as well."

Feeling more calm, Jaegar asked, "What is she like? How old is she? What is her name? Tell me everything about her. You have met my son, tell me of your daughter."

An immediate response was not given because his questions livened many thoughts. One of which was, is he asking so he can someday search for her? Alas no, I said I trusted him.

Though my offering did contain a lie, I finally replied, "My daughter's name is Helena. I named her out of respect for our lost sister. Four years have passed since she arrived. Helena is quite precarious. She has a viciousness that I am certain has come from King Boersen. I fully expect her to return to Gudsfelt yielding a sword to claim her land. While she is young, she is vulnerable. One day will come though when she will command honor; she will earn loyalty; she will rule."

"Is she as delicate as you my love?" Jaegar asked exhibiting a soft smile.

"I am not so delicate!" I retorted.

"The warrior in you is understated my sweet. It does not surface easily." He laughed at me.

"The warrior in me need only emerge in times of danger. I no longer experience those situations. Wilhelm is certain to over-ensure my protection. He remembers all too well the abuse I suffered prior to our imprisonment in Dornwold."

My heartbeat increased. I had revealed too much. Immediately I wondered if Jaegar heard all I had said. My eyes could not meet his.

"Repeat what you've just said," he whispered with urgency.

He heard it.

"Speak," he demanded once more.

I fully confessed. "The man you met, the priest, Stefan, he is Wilhelm."

"I released you to the man you were to marry? You lied to me?"

"I did not, Jaegar. I promise."

"The priest?" Jaegar pondered what he had done. I could see that he was thinking back on every experience. He then asked, "Does Wilhelm know that we were to have a child? Does he know about our *child? Our lost child?"*

"Of course he knows. He never left my side. I thought my secrets were being witnessed by my companion. I thought I was sharing all with my assigned priest, the one person who was supposed to hold all of my deeds and sins in complete confidence. Imagine my utter despair when I arrived at the side of my betrothed, before countless witnesses, only to find that he knew all I had prayed would remain hidden from my husband. I nearly collapsed. I hated myself and I hated you. The

man I was to marry could have had me executed. He could have exposed my truths to the entire nation."

Wringing my hands, my voice cracking from the tears I was straining to withhold, I concluded, "But he did not. All along, Stefan simply wanted me, just me. Northanglia was to be his. Wilhelm needed only speak one sentence and I would have been banished. He could have collected the exclusive rights, but he wanted me, Jaegar."

"What he wanted was your children. What he wanted was to win. That man did not want me to have you. He hates everything about the Norse. He hates your heritage, the blood that is yours, ours. His aim is to purify the lineage of Northanglia."

"You are so very wrong about that. You don't know him. Stefan accepted me knowing I had been in your arms. Wilhelm accepted me knowing I carried a child to the altar."

"What?"

It hurt me to offer yet another confession, but I told Jaegar of my other sin. Unable to look at him, I said, "Stefan's child was with me as I walked an aisle to meet the man I was to marry."

"You agreed to marry Wilhelm even though you carried another man's child?"

"I had no choice! Jaegar, you do not know me. The claim that my life is simple and free from all turmoil is so very wrong."

Jaegar rested. He touched my knee. He pulled himself to my side and kissed my cheek. He loved me despite my sins. He said softly, "Though I have much more to say, I will not. I see the hurt you bear. However, I wish to know one more thing, why did Wilhelm have his own rights to your land? Explain why you trust so deeply that he wanted you."

I wiped a tear and said, "His father is Wymer, cousin to my father. Alexar and Wymer were the two blood heirs to Northanglia. They were raised as brothers by my grandfather, King Eichman. They were inseparable. Alexar, the elder of the two, still refuses to be apart from his commander. In time, both men bore children, but Alexar bore no son. He sired an illegitimate daughter, me, and Wymer fathered a legitimate son, Wilhelm. Alexar had my position established with the church and the courts only under the condition that I marry Wilhelm."

Jaegar listened intently.

I continued, "My father was not going to force me to accept his marriage contract. He, Olivia, Styrke, and Grandfather Boersen agreed that I would always be allowed to choose. Then, upon reaching age six and ten, Father released me for a period of isolation and freedom.

When news of the Danes' search for me was reported, Alexar sent Stefan to escort me back to Castleton."

"Why was his identity withheld from you?"

"Father wanted me to choose Northanglia, not a husband. Additionally, if we would have been seen alone together, my image could have been stained. A princess, or any lone woman, escorted by a priest is acceptable and even expected in many circumstances. However, I could not have been seen with a man, even if he was to become my husband. Alexar and Wymer knew Wilhelm was the most trained of their soldiers."

"Ha, so much becomes clear. I believe though, Alexar knew you would easily fall in love. Therefore, he strategically placed your betrothed within your grasp. Your father established your path. Do not be naive."

I was deeply offended at his blatant insult that I am weak. Still in a hushed tone, I rebuked, "How dare you speak such a cruel and humiliating accusation to me."

His thoughts were almost echoing throughout the surrounding cliffs. I was not naive. Jaegar had many intentions that night, the most important one was to reclaim my heart and body, even if only for a very short time. He slid a strand of hair from my face and with a sultry voice he said, "Twas not an irreverent accusation my love. Twas a self-elevating hope."

"I shall regret saying this, but explain yourself."

Jaegar whispered into my ear, "My meaning was that you would have fallen in love easily because you had reached womanhood. I believe with all my soul that you were longing for my presence."

His eyes did not leave mine as I processed his words. He waited patiently for my revelation that I had in fact missed him. When it appeared, he pulled me to my feet and continued, "We had always been promised to one another. Not only had our family promised us, but we made promises to one another at ten years. When you reached age six and ten, you should have been by my side, in my home, and in my bed."

Unable to break away from his long ago established hold on me, I followed him into his tent.

"Will he wake?" I asked nervously hoping for an excuse to deny myself the man I craved.

"No. Of that I am certain."

Jaegar leaned toward me. I knew if I allowed him even one kiss, neither of us would turn away from this temptation.

He leaned closer saying, "I love you, Lillia. I... love... you."

"I... I..."

His hands touched my waist and slowly they moved around me. My body turned with his gentle guidance until my back was to him. Placing one hand on my abdomen and the other a bit higher, Jaegar used the hold to press his hips, then his chest, then his hips again, against me. My hair was lifted from my neck and my dress was pulled. The very tip of his tongue met my shoulder then eased its way up my neck. The laces that caged my modesty were released, and I was his.

At my own will, I turned and we both took equal part in disrobing him. Nothing kept me from the intake of his appearance. My eyes wanted to see what was mine. He enjoyed my stares and smiles and collected his own memories as well.

Lowered onto his primitive yet inviting bed, Jaegar filled my heart and satiated my longing for him.

We joined a number of times throughout the night and not once did I feel remorse. The only animosity I did feel for one brief moment was fury that his father ever thought he could force us to see one another as anything other than partners in this life. Jaegar and I had been sent from heaven at nearly the exact same moment because even as spiritual beings, we could not be apart.

Jaegar paused to dream about having regained his wife after so many years of separation. Every thought was of her in his arms. He even remembered a moment when he too was angry with his father for trying to establish them as family. Olivia and King Boersen always knew the children should be united. The curse of Alexar and Olivia in Styrke's life was also the blessing of their union in Jaegar's.

"I still love you Lillia," he muttered.

If it was possible to read something to nonexistence, then the rows of words that told the story of her joy and pleasure when in his arms, or beneath him, or atop him, would have been erased from her histories. The details she scribed should have never been disclosed outside of their private room, but Jaegar left the scrolls in tact. These were Adelia's words, her memories, her choices, her life. He would never deny the woman he loved the power she wielded with ink.

The mighty and vicious Viking softened as he envisioned that night and the love he shared with Adelia.

Chapter 39

The men who guarded Galeena escorted her to a one room outbuilding near the food storage houses. The building was built into the hill and had a stone facade with a sod roof. There were no windows and the door was fabricated of iron. The floor was dirt, the stench was repulsive, and the only offering of comfort was a soiled blanket woven of threaded fibers.

Orders had been given to search her. Thus, two of the men who had been on the boat that transported Galeena to Gudsfelt decided their task was to be an indulgence. Prior to locking her in the holding shed, they fully intended to enjoy their time without supervision.

Inside the dark cell, Galeena focused on the one gleaming crevice. She knew the attempts that were forthcoming. With her hands bound behind her, she could not retrieve the dagger she had hidden at her waist. However, if she could evade the wretched oafs, she had a chance at loosening her wrists and protecting herself.

Oh how she hated Torren.

One man stood by the door while the other approached.

"I could scream," she warned.

"Would be expected," was the reply.

Galeena wasn't sure if she should believe him. He could be telling the truth.

She lowered quickly to the ground, shuffled to the entrance, kicked the door closed, tripped the man who stood nearest to it, and she scurried quietly away. If he flung the door open, she could rush past him in hopes of one decent Gudsfelt citizen coming to her aid. If their consciences convicted them, they would seek her instead of light.

They sought her.

With no illumination from the outside, they couldn't find her. As long as she was quiet, her attackers would have a more difficult time locating her. Every move, every panicked word, enlightened her of their exact placement. Galeena wrenched her hands and crept as they searched frantically for their prey.

The moment she was victorious, she slipped a finger beneath her belt, hooked the blade, and she waited.

With a plan ready, Galeena allowed one man to feel his way to her. He grabbed her tunic at her shoulder. Not wanting to miss, she in turn grabbed his arm and sliced his wrist. In the dark, he did not know right away what she had done to him. The payment for allowing him near, a pounding blow to her cheek with his free hand.

Then, the pain, the realization of the damage she caused set in. The monster backed away clutching his own arm. The other man opened the door wide and captured the vision of his comrade's bewilderment. A call for help instigated a rush of onlookers and pandemonium.

Galeena took the moment of distraction and mounting chaos to attempt freedom. She crouched and ran past the uninjured guard. He too reached for her and received a slice to his palm for it.

Unsettled and loud voices reached Jaegar's ears. He closed the leather encasement and stood to inspect the activity of the village. Without seeing for himself, he assumed the new prisoner would be in the center of all that was happening. A few chuckles escaped through his nostrils as he imagined Torren wrestling, chasing, or seeking the woman.

As Galeena ran a bit farther from the outbuilding, Cinad stepped from the crowd and encircled her from behind. He was quick and managed a hold on her and a hold on her hand that held her defense. "You have to settle, Miss. You'll not be leaving alive. Release it. I'll keep it safe. No one need know to whence it has vanished."

She could not harm him. Her muscles relaxed, and she calmed her pulsating blood.

The former slave, appointed captain, bent her arm and pulled it behind her back. The knife was slipped from her hand, and he made no mention of it to anyone. She was then held firmly by him.

"Cinad, please do not lock me in there. It is grotesque," Galeena begged.

"I'll find other accommodations, Miss. For now, that is where you'll reside."

An uneventful retreat to the cell was witnessed by all, including Jaegar.

"You need not close her in yet, Cinad," he said.

The respectful guard stepped aside.

Jaegar looked at Galeena, "How do you feel?"

She thought him absurd, and her expression did not hide that fact.

Her cheek was a deep red and would certainly bruise. Her lip was swelling and a small stream of blood trickled from it. Jaegar took her chin gently in his fingers and turned her head so he could see the other side of her face. "And this one?" he pointed.

Galeena reached up to the bone just above her left brow. Blood flowed from there as well. "I suppose my head hit the stone wall when your *gentleman* hit my face."

"And what cause did he have for such an act of abuse?"

"He attempted familiarities with me that I was not to allow."

"Justifiable," Jaegar nodded with a raised eyebrow and downward turned mouth.

"Ladies, gentlemen, I gave no one permission nor orders to violate her. We are not animals. I shall kill the next person who has a complaint lodged against them. We are peacemakers, not beasts. She is held here for transgressions of which we have not yet learned. I trust my son's judgement. You may return to your daily duties."

All in attendance agreed with him then walked away. Cinad stepped to a distance that allowed privacy.

Jaegar was not yet finished with Galeena. "Tis my understanding that you have actually killed one of my guards. That man, there." He motioned.

Her chin raised, her head cocked to the side, her eyes lowered, then focused on his. Using his own declarations, Galeena said, "They were disobeying your command. Twas for your benefit that one is gone. If I had not been interrupted, you would be rid of them both."

Jaegar snorted, amused by her perspective. He observed her. She looked weak. "How could someone as peaked as you nearly overpower two virile men? Have you that strong of a will to survive? Have you something more powerful than fear of death that keeps you fighting for your life? You say you have no value beyond that of a trained soldier, but your actions tell me you have something worthwhile hidden in your heart."

"Jaegar, do you analyze the thoughts and actions of every person you encounter?"

"Aye. Every... one."

"Then desist from asking me questions that you should be able to answer yourself."

A loud laughter followed her comment. Jaegar was enjoying her. He defended, "Though my instincts tell me much, I cannot hear your thoughts."

"My thoughts are this, someday your son will return. He will step from his ship and come to me without hesitation. And when he does, I will kill him." Galeena's voice became stern, "You see Jaegar, I appear fragile, but I am not alone. We all suffer from something that can cause our collapse. I am *his* weakness."

"I believe you, woman. Much thought has been given to why he sent you, and the only reason he would want to be rid of you is that you overpower him as well, though in a very different manner than with blades or braun."

One shrug was her reply.

Jaegar moved backward to indicate he was done with her.

Cinad moved forward and before he closed the door to leave her to adjust to her surroundings, he said, "I'll return, very soon. Tis my vow."

"Thank you Cinad. I am in great need of food and drink."

"A delivery will arrive before you sleep." He then whispered, "Be strong."

The attachment that was forming disturbed Jaegar. He instructed, "Cinad, I'll decide what and when she eats. If you feed her, she will only strengthen. The woman is as cunning as she is skilled. Until I know why she is here, let us keep her at the edge of life or death."

"Sir?"

"I have spoken."

With defiance Galeena intervened, "Jaegar, withhold all from me. My death shall come sooner. Your misery shall be multiplied once I have escaped this world."

The provocation that Lukah fore-saw had surfaced. Galeena indeed planned to provoke her captor.

Mildly stunned with revelation, *Torren loves her*, Jaegar's intuition whispered. *Perhaps he sent her to keep her, not to punish her.* He approached Galeena once more, "Why are you here?"

There was no reason not to be forthcoming. Galeena said, "My stance before you is a result of retaliation. I lured your son from his troops. In Torren's absence, my king's armies and those of Solsworth reclaimed Castleton and killed all who resisted. Anyone who surrendered sits in prison."

"And Torren?"

"He followed me. It was my job to get him alone then kill him. Except, I failed. I held his family's blade to his heart and revealed all to him. He was accepting of death after having failed you."

Jaegar listened to all she had to say with keen interest.

She continued, “Tis not often, but I felt compassion for him. I denounced my orders and denied him death.”

“And where is my son now?”

“If he returned to Castleton, he is undoubtedly dead. If he sought refuge in Dornwold, he is safe. If he made is way to Solsworth, Olivia could have placed him on a ship.”

“Olivia’s boats returned seven nights ago,” Jaegar commented.

“Then, perhaps Olivia will protect him in Alexar’s garrison. Or, she may hold him accountable for his transgressions against her granddaughter. You know her. I do not. I cannot ease your mind. He betrayed me. I bear no affection for your son.”

“How were his actions a betrayal? Torren owed you no allegiance. You are an enemy.”

“He led me to believe we were friends.”

“Ah, smart man,” Jaegar said with an arrogant smile.

Chapter 40

The winds blew in from the west and north. They brought rain and cold to White Crested Cove. For eight days, all was gray and very wet.

Woolen bedding was brought to Galeena as was bread and water. Once a day, Cinad arrived with hot tea, of which she did partake.

The only other item in Galeena's damp and puddled room was a bucket. A maiden came to her cell each evening to remove the offensive container.

Three weeks had passed since she left the Applewoods, and at least four or five had passed since she felt the babe had arrived. To that point, no signs of loss had occurred, nor had any signs of the curse of sickness.

"Perhaps I shall see my mother before any growth or pain of expectancy are upon me." Curled beneath the meager covering, Galeena muttered, "What happens in my homeland?" To keep her sanity, she evaluated what she knew to be true of their ships and her brother and father. They would not have waited more than a day or two beyond her sixteenth day to seek her. Torren would certainly have gone to Dornwold knowing he had no support in Castleton. Or, he could have been able to move easily alone to Claremont.

She huffed, "He would have found nothing at my father's home. The daughter he seeks is not there.

"Oh Torren, what have you done and where have you gone? The storms will not allow passage even if you find your way to a ship belonging to the Ice-landers. Lukah, however, would never let anything stop him from coming to me."

How very wrong she was. Days had passed, and soon weeks would be eaten by time as well. Galeena's fate was in her own hands. She could hold on and consume what was offered, or she could deny all, including the comforting tea, and release her spirit and that of her child to God.

Jaegar did not wish for her demise. He still felt she had to be of some value. He had faith that Torren sent her for a reason. With no other task, but to wait, the regent decided he would pursue more information about the prisoner.

Cinad was summoned. Upon his arrival to King Boersen's work chamber, he was asked, "Have there been any signs of her age?"

"I know not what you mean, Sir. Could you be more specific about signs?"

"Cinad, you have spent three weeks in her presence. Two upon the seas and one here in our village. What say you of her age?"

“She is sixteen. That was disclosed the morning we took her from Northanglia. What motivates your inquiry about her age, Sir?”

“I simply want to know with whom I am dealing. That Galeena could very well have been a child. Or, she could have been older than we think. I am not sure she is even a commander to a Northanglian king. They do not permit women to hold such positions. Tis forbidden there. Perhaps she is a very well trained and overly zealous foreigner of another land. Ponder her skin tone and dark hair.”

“Sir, tis not unusual for there to be a variety of countenances emerging from the Anglians. Greeks, Romans, Franks, Germaines, they all have made their way to those villages.”

Ignoring Cinad’s rationalization, Jaegar commanded, “Bring me the woman who cares for her. I wish to know if the prisoner has made any secret confessions, or if she has made any attempts to persuade others to empathize with or support her.”

Cinad attempted to reassure Jaegar. “Sir, Galeena has made no effort to beguile anyone. She tells no lies. We followed your son’s orders. He instructed us to retrieve King Wilhelm’s commander from a very particular beach. All in the western lands know that Wilhelm has two commanders of equal trust and power. All know that one is a woman. She has proven her might. She speaks with great wisdom. We have retrieved the correct person. No err has occurred. Galeena even said to me at first sight, ‘You are here for me aren’t you?’ She has owned

Torren's betrayal many times. We have the one he wanted removed from King Wilhelm's grasp."

"Very well. You need not seek the attending maid. I do still wish to see her though, so I shall retrieve her myself when I am ready."

Jaegar could not shed the layer of skin that bound him. He was uncomfortable and he hated not knowing his son's plan. A note should have been delivered with her. Why was Torren too hurried to even scribe a message?

Thinking on that, Jaegar recalled Adelia's parchments. He pulled them from his drawer and commenced his study yet again.

We rested unable to withdraw our souls from the other. Jaegar intentionally released breath after warm breath upon my flesh. I knew he was absorbing me through all of his senses. He inhaled the fragrance I had painted on neck and the musk of the dampness of my skin. Though we were secluded with a canopy draped over us, the faintest glow from the fire and the waxing moon allowed just enough light for us to capture images of one another. What we beheld told the entire story of our time together. Our love was not consensual; it was absolutely necessary to our continued survival.

Beneath him, not yet exchanging words, I wondered how he survived day to day without me in his life. I had a part of him, but he had nothing of me. Pondering the ache he must hide from the world, I remembered the band Styrke wears that is woven of my mother's hair. I decided I would make one for Jaegar before I returned to our farm. A smile crept to my lips imagining his antler amulet hung about his neck by locks of my woven hair.

"What doth you ponder Lillia?"

I told him of my intention and he kissed me to show his gratitude and acceptance of the unique gift.

Jaegar then said, "You know it shall be a treasure. Having you with me is all I've ever desired. I am not so ignorant nor childish to ask you to leave with me. You have chosen your life. There is no need to alter it now. I do dream of a day when you will choose to walk with me. For now, whilst I live in Danemour, there is no place for you by my side. There is work I have yet to complete."

Jaegar's prophesy would never come to fruition, but there was no reason to argue nor instill despair on his dream of ruling all lands. I avoided the thought and asked, "What is it that you continue to pursue Jaegar? Why is your obsession ceaseless?"

"Tis not an obsession, Adelia. As long as there are threats against Gudsfelt, my position in the Danemour court shall continue. I'll not have my father's and my mother's birthright stolen. Grandfather Boersen and

Styrke depend on me to keep the Danes at a distance. Someday though, someday, all will be settled. I earn more and more compensation with every miserable day that passes. I have mapped my destiny. Time leads all down their chosen roads."

Thinking of my own deeply held secrets, I replied to his declaration, "Yes, but sometimes there are mysterious roads that are chosen for us."

"No more talk of battles or possessions or paths, I wish only to dwell on what I know to be true in this moment. And that is, a child now grows between us."

I tried to move him, but he would not permit my distress. I shuttered to think of his claim. I begged, "Jaegar, please do not curse me with such a declaration. There will be no way for me to hide the identity of your babe. Please, I beg you, place not that burden, that torment upon me."

A rage was stirred within him. "Never call my child a curse, a burden, or a torment. Those are the words your God would find punishable."

"Stop! Stop convicting me! You have no way of understanding what such a fortune would mean for me."

His anger did not cease. Jaegar coldly stated, "When the time comes for my son to be born, return to me. I'll take him from you and keep him to myself. I'll die before

I allow another man to raise my child. The 'burden', the 'curse', you now carry belongs to me!"

I knew a child with Jaegar would never be a curse or a burden. But he needed to hear how I felt. Gently, I caressed his face and eased him to my side. I remained fixated as I reminded him, "I am married. A breach of my husband's trust and our physical bond is a mortal sin. Being here with you is punishable by death."

"You married me first, Adelia."

"But I married Wilhelm in the church."

"I do not believe that God has a preference of location when two people commit to loving forever."

"Jaegar, I did not make vows to you. I made sacred vows to Wilhelm before witnesses with my hand placed on the Holy words. The price of succumbing to your advances is my life."

"No one shall place a death sentence upon you so long as I live."

"God has that right and that power."

"No god I serve would sentence you for continuing to love the one who was placed at your side from infancy. God established our connection. And now, do you not believe that your God brought us together again? Speak only the truth, did you pray for a moment such as this?"

No words could be uttered. I simply nodded, squeezed my eyes closed, then covered my face. A heavy load of guilt was pressing upon my chest. Deep breaths were impossible.

Regardless of my woes, I knew pure thrill was Jaegar's. I did still belong to him. Though I truly love another, I was his just as I always had been. Jaegar took possession of me before we could even walk or talk. He held to me in every circumstance. He held to me in that moment. The love he has for me makes all I've kept from him nearly impossible to bear. The guilt I felt was too much, and I desperately wanted to tell him about his son,

"What?" He growled, then reread.

I desperately wanted to tell him about his son,

"His son? My son? Torren?" He continued reading.

I desperately wanted to tell him about his son, but I knew that Lukah was only safe if he did not exist. Jaegar would take him from me, or Lukah would insist on living with his father just as I had insisted on living with Alexar. I could not bear that separation from my precious boy. Lukah was my special secret, a secret I had kept even from my own mother.

Jaegar's lungs filled and he did not release the air they held. He read her words again and again and again. "Lukah?

I have a son named Lukah?" He sat up and was so distraught he could not read to the end of that scroll. Nothing else she had written held any interest for him. His eyes returned to the parchment. He has a son. No, he and Adelia have a son.

Frantically Jaegar flipped back to the first page. "How did I miss that? She said, 'I waved, confident my own children would be cared for in my absence.' How did I not see those words? I saw my child. I held my own son, and she never told me."

The morning they all were to set sail for Northanglia, a small boy ran from Adelia's party. Jaegar could not comprehend why the boy clutched his leg. He thought the child to have mistaken him for another. He spoke kindly to him and knelt to comfort him with a hug. Adelia and Wilhelm both rushed to their ward. Wilhelm removed the boy at once not giving Jaegar any opportunity for chatter.

"He was mine and he knew me. They feared he would choose me. They stole my son!" Jaegar yelled slamming his fists on the table top.

The parchments were locked in a drawer. He stood. Unsure if he should smile or kill something, Jaegar stormed to the cell of the young woman who may be able to help him. If she chose not to, or if he suspected she was lying to him, he would make sure she regretted it.

Chapter 41

News that Galeena was refusing all food had reached Jaegar. He had not been concerned about the woman's choices to live or die until he needed her. En route to her shed, Jaegar called for a hearty plate of meats, roots, bread, and boiled herbs to be delivered to the prisoner.

Cinad unlocked the door and opened it for his ruler.

The conditions repulsed Jaegar. "Get her cleaned and bring her to me well presented."

Ladies were summoned to escort Galeena to a suite within the great home.

Slowly she walked. Her mind conjured images of running and playing with her great-grandmother and great-grandfather. Galeena was certain she saw Adelia glide past her and kiss her fingers. She heard a voice behind her say, "This is yours my love. Tis all yours. Do not give up."

A tub of hot water awaited its occupant. Galeena allowed the women to help her remove the clothing she had been wearing for nearly a month.

"These shall go to the fire," one said in Norse.

"You'll receive no argument from me," Galeena replied in their native tongue.

Knowing they could communicate with her, they began asking questions. Their main focus was on her lack of a will to live. "Just appease Jaegar, girl. He tortures you by leaving you in that horrible shelter to get what he wants, and that is information."

"I've shared all there is. I've no more to say."

The women helped Galeena into the tub. Unaware, just resting in the silence, as she lowered and submerged, glances were exchanged amongst the maids.

"You are frightfully thin, Miss."

"That surprises you?" she asked in response.

"You're with child. You should have more flesh than what you've got. Jaegar doesn't harm you. You harm yourself by refusing all that is presented. Give your babe a chance."

Galeena gaped at the woman as she spoke. She then pleaded, "Please, tell no one of my condition."

"No one to tell. No one has asked."

"Even if you are asked, please feign ignorance."

"Won't be a lie. I am ignorant. I've no way of knowing why you don't want you or your babe to live."

"I don't want to be a prisoner. That's what I don't want."

"Shhh... Just soak."

Jaegar paced in his private study. The platter he had ordered for Galeena had been delivered to his chamber and it sat untouched.

More than an hour after her removal from the frigid outbuilding, Galeena walked as proudly as she was able into his midst. One of Annika's dresses had been placed on her. It made sense because Annika was of a thin stature. Typically, Galeena had much more substance to her, but the situation had chiseled away at her build. The women had brushed and plaited the long dark tresses, then pulled wisps to frame her gaunt and emaciated face. She was quite striking even in her fragile state.

"Sit. Eat."

"I've told you. Death is preferable."

"You will eat or I will hold you down and shove this meat down your throat."

"If you feed me, you best be ready to also fight me."

"Ready I am. I'll not even bind you. Your blades will be returned. Nothing about you scares me, child."

Cinad intervened, "Sir—"

"Leave us or you die first."

Galeena looked to Cinad and offered a strained smile. She needed him to know that he need not worry about her any longer. Cinad reluctantly backed out of the room and closed the door.

"I do not aim to scare you, Jaegar. I aim to see you removed."

"Do you believe you have that power?"

She silenced, so he spoke again. "Will troops be sent for you?"

Galeena did not know if or how she should answer him.

"Eat! Perhaps you'll have clearer thoughts with nourishment. That way you'll be able to formulate your lies with much more speed. It will be easier to convince me if you are astute."

Shall we live? Her heart asked her babe.

We shall, for now, was the response.

Galeena sat and began pulling pieces of bread. She dipped them first in the broth to soften them, then others she dipped into her tea. The meat was eaten with great delicacy as well. Not having had solid foods for a while, she did not want to upset her ailing system.

Jaegar watched in silence, intrigued by her gentility. When she appeared to be more lively, he asked, "You were to marry the Prince of Solsworth?"

A cloth accompanied her plate so she dabbed it to her lips while she chewed and swallowed the bits that were in her mouth. "Um, yes. Prince Henry is his name."

"That I believe. Next, why are you betrothed to a prince?"

"Henry is trained and grows in wisdom. I am trained in warfare, strategy and protection. The kings felt I am the most beneficial option for a wife. It seems that having married two Viking women has brought to their minds that a strong female can be of value as a queen. Although, tis a ludicrous notion for any other woman of our land."

"Will they come for you?"

Galeena knew they would. However, the food had sharpened her wits. "Tis difficult to say with certainty. Tis simple to find a mate for a future king. Henry and I have only been introduced once. He has no attachment to me. As I said, he is intelligent, he may not see any reason to risk ships for my retrieval."

"And your king? If he believes you have enough value to sign for your marriage to a future king, he must hold you to some higher level of esteem. What did he have to gain from releasing you to another nation? Won't he want to fulfill that plan?"

"I cannot speak for King Wilhelm. Perhaps you can though. You've met him." She then asked, "May I stand for a moment? I've not had any opportunities for movement. I'd like to work my limbs, reach, stretch."

An extended hand toward his room invited her to move at will.

Galeena twisted and extended. She looked at ornaments that were placed about the room on shelves. She studied the portraits that hung on the walls. "This?" she pointed. "I presume this is you and Adelia?"

He nodded.

"Your ages?"

"We were both ten. Adelia and I celebrated our births only days apart."

"You appear so much older than her?"

"That was always a curse."

Though it was difficult to pull her eyes from her mother, it was necessary. Galeena sauntered back to her plate and took a few more bites from a standing position.

"You seem to be feeling much better, Galeena. Your color has even returned. Your blood must be flowing once again."

"Yes. Thank you. At this moment, I believe a few more meals will point me in the direction of my former self."

Galeena then asked, "What do you want with me, Jaegar? Why have you decided I am interesting in your world?" After the questions left her lips, she immediately thought, *He read my mother's scrolls. What did she reveal to him? If he knows who I am, why is he not hiding me. These people could revolt if they learn he has treated their named queen in such a way. Perhaps he has an offer. Perhaps I should call for an audience and announce my identity. I am here, they will have to accept me.*

"I see the concern in your eyes. You worry about what I truly do want with you. Rest. I'm not someone who takes women against their will. I have no need."

That thought had never entered her mind. She held steady. "Then tell me, why do you want me here?"

"Tis not you I want, tis my son."

"I told you, Jaegar, Torren could be in any one of three places. The ground, Dornwold, or Solsworth. He was going to sleep when I last saw him."

"Tis not Torren I speak of, tis a man named Lukah."

"Lukah?"

"Do not play with me like I am a child. Where is Lukah?"

"Lukah is in Northanglia," she said with defiance and snobbery.

"He belongs to me!"

Galeena laughed. "He belongs to no one."

"Tell me of him."

"He has probably killed Torren by now."

Jaegar dreaded the image he was fed by her. He thought of Adelia's prophetic words that their sons would battle. He yelled, "You'll not tease me about my sons! You'll not treat this as a game!"

"I speak the truth," she offered with a soft yet cruel tone.

"You do have a calloused soul."

"I do not. I have a guarded soul."

"So you do not deny that Lukah is my son?"

Galeena thought about her brother. For the first time she was able to compare him to Torren. Living between the two, they had nothing in common. But separated from the both, she could see what others saw. She replied, "I do not deny that Lukah is Norse. I've no right to reveal his parentage to anyone."

"So he is my son. I know he's my son. Adelia named him. I have met him."

"Then why do you need me here? You do not need my statement if you have Queen Adelia's."

"I needed your confirmation. Tell me of him."

"As my equal in guard, his loyalties lie only with King Wilhelm. That is all you need to know of him."

"Stop. If you generate another stab at me with your words, you will regret it. Tell me what I want to know."

She glared.

"Speak!"

"Lukah bears the exact image of Torren. He has white hair with curled ends. He is smaller but equal in every way. I've witnessed their sparring. I intervened. One would have died and I could lose neither."

"You could lose neither? What does that mean?"

She had revealed too much. A cover was urgent. "I told you, Torren befriended me."

Jaegar laughed. "He convinced you he loved you didn't he? That is why you preferred death. That is why you said you would kill him."

Galeena could say nothing.

Jaegar added, "Now, what am I to do with you?"

To that she could respond. "What would you do with any enemy soldier? What would you do with the last daughter you so eagerly seek? What would you do with someone who will seek your death if given the chance?"

"The answer is death to all," he fell into thought for a moment, then said, "unless you can convince me that you have some value. You've repeated that you have none. Do you wish to change your statement? Is there anything about you that I will find interesting?"

"I've yet to answer if King Wilhelm will come for me. Are you interested in that?"

"Torren had you taken because he knew their king would send for you. That would reduce the numbers and increase his chances of finding Adelia's daughter. There is no way they would bring her here. Does my son, Lukah, protect his sister?"

"We all do," she replied. "Helene will not be found until she is ready to be found."

"That is why she is useless. This nation awaits her. They have faith in her yet she ignores her people. Nothing irritates me more than being at the whim of a weak and fickle child."

"What will you do with her, Jaegar? You want the truth from me. I deserve the truth from you? Disclose your plan."

Jaegar stood from his seat across from Galeena's plate. She watched him carefully. She was feeling stronger, but not yet strong enough to fight. He knew about Lukah. The decision now had to be made about her own identity. She would reason with him, then reveal herself. Jaegar walked slowly toward her and stopped at an arms reach before her. He remained deep in thought.

"What troubles you?" Galeena asked.

"The child is now the sister of my son. For years she has been a girl who would come here to rule this land as a part of Northanglia. We are Norse. We have no desire to be one with the western nations. I have hated her for so long, that I don't know how to recover from that. I also don't know if I *want* to recover from such an emotion. I may still wish for her elimination if she will not release her claim. Lukah now has the rights as a male heir."

"Lukah is of Styrke. He is not a Boersen."

Jaegar turned to her, "He is marked?"

"He is, though he'll have no relation with you if you harm Helene."

"The girl needs to renounce her claim, just as Adelia and Olivia did, or she may never be safe."

"Jaegar, no amount of contemplation makes Gudsfelt yours. You have no rights to decide what will become of it. You are the one who will be in danger if you don't step away and return to Danemour."

"I am the only one who has brought peace by uniting these lands. You have no idea what I have sacrificed to ensure everyone is safe. War will begin again if I am forced to leave here. This is my home!"

"You have done much to secure all, but you have sought only your own advancement. And you seek it at another's expense. Jaegar, we get but one life. You, nor any other human, has the right to take what God has created. If one is a dangerous adversary and seeks your harm, then defense is necessary. However, seeking to kill someone because they have what you desire is wrong. Your true enemy is desire, greed. Gudsfelt is not yours. You are merely a trusted steward."

"What of my possession of Danemour? Was it wrong for me to take control there?"

"That is a matter for God to decide. However, if those people meant only harm to your family, then perhaps it is your right to protect by any force. Danemour is not Gudsfelt. Keep your Dane lands. You need not steal from the Boersen's."

"I wish to rule *here*. This is equally my home, my land, my family. I want Gudsfelt because I am a Boersen."

"Others, who love you, have disagreed. For years they have disagreed."

Galeena angered him. By saying that all the people he loved and worked for never found him worthy infuriated him to a point of no return. The enemy had said the wrong thing.

She made all worse by adding, "You are far too connected to Danemour, Jaegar. The landholders here will not fully trust you. They also will never follow anyone not descended from

King Boersen. Gudsfelt is not like other Norse lands where battles and kills decide kings. This is a nation of wise merchants, skilled farmers, and fierce fighters. They demand adherence to laws, traditions and earnings."

He was being called a foreigner in his own home. How dare she exhibit such pride as an outsider. Her insolence enraged him, and though he immediately regretted it, he turned and as he did, he struck her across her face with the back of his hand.

Though her disposition had been improving, the unexpected attack caught her off guard, and it nearly eliminated her ability to speak. The ground she had gained was now lost again. All was gone. There was no more strength left in her. Galeena fell to her knees, sat back on her heels, looked hard to the floor, and she released silent tears. Her mother loved this cruel man. What did she see in him? Some tears were for the loss of the one woman who would have collected the strike for her. Some tears were because for some reason, she still loved the man who fathered the babe she carried. Some tears were because she no longer thought she wanted to be Queen of Gudsfelt. And some fell simply because she was in pain; she ached.

"You will sit in judgement before our counsel until all are in agreement of what shall be your fate. I am done with you. You no longer serve any purpose in my life or in my nation."

A sniffle preceded a weak lift of her eyes to his. "What does that mean?" she asked. Her hand rose to wipe the blood from the fresh gash he had opened on her cheekbone.

"It means you will hold this kneeling position in our Great Hall for as many days as it takes for every governor to be heard."

"Even those who are not born of Gudsfelt? Even those who are traitors, invaders, like you?" Galeena chided.

The guilt of hitting her suddenly left him. He no longer held any remorse. His hand was raised to her once more, but it lowered. Jaegar leaned downward to her. Gritting his teeth he said, "If I were you, I would not anticipate being sent back to Northanglia, nor would I anticipate seeing Solsworth."

Humiliation was the course she chose for him. Galeena decided she would wait until she had an audience before claiming *her* throne.

Chapter 42

King Wilhelm's ships departed on the tail of a great storm. Another followed in the distance, but they prayed they could stay in between the two. The cargo was precious. All rulers and descendants, of five nations were on board the ships. The kings, a queen, and Jaegar's children represented the heirs of Northanglia, Dornwold, Solsworth, Danemour, and Gudsfelt.

They embarked on their travels nearly two weeks after Galeena had been taken. Twas expected that their progression would be slower than that of the Vikings, but they had faith they would arrive safely.

In Gudsfelt, messengers were immediately dispatched to the landlords throughout the small nation. All were being called for a gathering.

Galeena had been ordered to retake her seat at the table while Jaegar met with his advisors who represented both Norse nations. She settled and even though the food was cold, she chose to eat more as she watched and listened to the activity within the chamber.

The last aid left the suite and Galeena still sat. Jaegar had her undivided attention. "I've sent for Cinad to return. You'll be taken back to the outbuilding. Someone will come for you. Prior to supper, the first of our governors will have arrived. Their decisions on your fate will be heard by you and every other citizen who wishes to attend."

Nothing he said mattered save the banishment to the vile shelter.

A tap upon the door was acknowledged with a welcome into his work room. Cinad entered to a distraught and speechless woman.

"What transpires, Sir? May I be of some assistance?"

"Return her to the holding shed."

Though disputing Jaegar's orders could be detrimental, Cinad stood firm and refused to fulfill the command. "Keep her strong, Jaegar. Although you have her on trial, they will be watching you as well."

"Yes, Jaegar," a voice supported Cinad.

Jaegar knew the voice too well. He leaned to peer around the man before him, and responded, "Fredric, your presence is welcome as always." The men approached one another and exchanged an embrace.

Galeena finally exhaled and relaxed her shoulders.

Fredric spoke again, "Word reached my farm that you hold an Anglian girl, and as I was riding to meet the woman I also received a notice that the governors are being called forth for a unified decision about her."

An explanation began, "Torren sent her. She has killed many—"

"In the line of duty?" Fredric inquired.

"She's an enemy soldier. I've passed no judgement on her. I've broken no laws. The gathering of the lords is by my command. My grandfather would have done the same."

"I presume this is the girl? I'd like a private meeting with her, Jaegar."

"Shall I step out, Sir?" Cinad offered.

"I've nothing to hide. You may question her yourself. You are a land owner." Jaegar turned to Cinad, "We shall both give them privacy."

The ruggedly handsome man watched the two leave and listened for the door to latch. He then turned to Galeena. She did not rise.

"Join me please," Fredric extended his hand the direction of the velvet settee that was positioned across the room before the fireplace. "I feel a meeting with you should be held in a locale specifically arranged for a social gathering."

Galeena nodded and his right hand reached to escort her.

His seat was taken only after he was certain she was comfortable. The woman in his presence was refined. She sat with her hands on her lap, her spine straight and her shoulders back.

Fredric did not desire idle chatter. "Tell me who you are because you are not simply an enemy soldier."

"I can trust you?" Galeena asked.

"Beyond a level you allow yourself."

A slight tilt of her head was followed by, "I am the last Daughter of Boersen."

If he was surprised, Fredric showed no signs of the emotion. He tucked his lips in and pressed them, then asked, "Is there a reason you are still hiding your status? Do you not want the title King Boersen has handed down to you?"

"I revealed myself to the troops that invaded Northanglia and they did not believe me. The strung me between two trees and commenced to pursuing their vindictive punishments. Torren released me, though I knew Lukah was nearby."

"Lukah?"

"My brother."

"Adelia has a son?"

"Adelia and *Jaegar* have a son?"

"Is Olivia aware?" Fredric was calm yet withholding his shock.

"Aye. She is."

As he pondered the new information, Galeena continued her explanation. "I held my peace on the ship because I was curious to meet Jaegar as an enemy. The days that have passed, I decided my death would be a harsher punishment for him. Then, today, since learning that he has summoned all of the governors throughout Gudsfelt, I decided I much prefer a complete audience when I share my title.

"My mother has always told me to wait for the perfect time to arrive before revealing myself. She and my father both assured me that I would know. I would have no doubts. Fredric, I finally know after all of these years what they meant and why I was concealed."

"What did you have to gain by accepting your own death instead of your title?"

His eyes lowered with hers. Galeena held her belly.

"You carry a babe?" Fredric was nearly incensed.

"I carry *Torren's* babe."

With that specification announced, Fredric knew that there was no denying Jaegar would have certainly suffered beyond comprehension had he killed his son's child. He asked, "What of Torren? Is there affection between you?"

She shrugged, "There was or I'd not be sitting here in this condition. However, there is no more because... I am sitting here in this condition."

"Torren will return. Give him opportunity to explain before you decide hatred is where you shall reside."

"Cinad told me Torren sent the Norse ships for me, me!"

"Pass no judgement. You have experienced a lifetime of waiting for the right time, this situation is no different. I feel you must wait. I've known Torren his entire life. It would be most difficult to convince me that he meant harm to you and his child."

"He knew nothing of the babe when he dispatched the ships."

"Of that you are certain?"

"I am certain."

Fredric thought for a moment, then said, "I'll be taking you into my custody. Jaegar will trust me and he will trust that you will not flee by presence. Tis obvious I have no doubts of the same."

"Thank you Fredric. Jaegar was ordering my return to that wretched holding cell. As you can imagine, death was preferable to that place."

A smile and a squeeze of her hands was given as he said, "Perhaps as queen, you can repair it, or destroy it."

"Destruction would be my choice."

"For now, I'll allow you to decide your near future. Do know though, you will not be permitted to refuse meals, nor will you be allowed to provoke a physical reparation from Jaegar. You know more than him and you need not cause any unnecessary misery to him. He is the son of your grandmother. He is the man your mother chose first. And, he is the grandfather of your unborn child. Desist from agitating his soul."

"He has been cruel and has planned a regicide. Despite his endearing qualities, Jaegar has committed crimes."

"He has not yet. Olivia appointed him regent. He is the King of Danemour and Dornwold. And, he has called for a trial for an enemy as opposed to an execution. Do not provoke him.

Clearly you have wounds that need to heal from previous challenges."

"I'll comply."

Chapter 43

Three days of trials had passed. With her face toward the crowd, Galeena held her kneeling position with reverence. She spoke not a word of defense on her own behalf. Every voice was heard.

In the Great Hall of the Boersen stave manor, Jaegar sat on the raised throne. Galeena was a distance before him on the wooden floor. Fredric and Cinad kept silent observations from their placements to the left of the accused.

Into the evening, men and women gave advisement on how to handle the deceptively unassuming woman. Most found her to be interesting and they admired the hidden strength she possessed. Others felt she was of no use and to try to force her into service would undoubtedly mean the death of some of their own men. She was unpredictable and therefore unanimous sentencing was difficult.

Hours past the noon of the day, darkness was soon to encroach. All who held power in the Boersen Assembly had spoken, though no resolution had been reached. Jaegar stood and placed himself in a looming position over Galeena. She did not acknowledge him. He opened his mouth to speak but a disturbance stole his attention.

Through the gathering, even from her lowly position, Galeena smiled at the man who approached.

"Lukah," she whispered as she released a puff of air through her nose.

Jaegar heard her desperate call and looked down to her. "Tis Torren," he corrected.

"No Jaegar, that is Lukah."

Voices muttered, gasps commenced. Galeena knew Torren must be behind her brother.

Alas, yes. There they both were, walking toward her and their father. Lukah stopped and took a stance of solidity. He looked at her but once. His desperation to defend her was being suppressed. For he knew twas his father he'd have to face, and Jaegar's presence was far too fascinating. Torren never glanced at his father, he rushed directly to his wife.

The cuts and bruises were scrutinized. The sores about her bound wrists were studied. Her hair, her lips, her placement below Jaegar, every image crushed him. Torren raised Galeena to her feet. She was still not certain how to react to his attentions. He cupped her face and kissed her with the utmost delicacy. He then lowered and kissed the home of their babe.

"Is all well?" Torren asked in reference to his unborn child.

A cold nod of affirmation was all he received in response.

Jaegar was keenly interested in all of Torren's actions, but he also did not want to miss a moment of capturing the son who had been withheld from him. Back and forth he looked between the two. They truly were nearly identical, other than their heights.

"Who did this to you, Galeena? Who injured you? Who dared strike my wife and cause harm to her and my child?" Torren's grip was tight, but not painful.

She said, "You and your father."

"What? Why would you accuse me?"

"You ordered all of this," her tone was turning to one of disgust as her anger increased.

Every person, including Fredric and Cinad, watched and listened with great interest.

Torren pleaded his defense, "I never meant harm to you. The message I sent to Dornwold gave specific instructions of when to come for me. I would not have left you alone had I any suspicions the ships would have parted for our lands ahead of the scheduled time."

Galeena wasn't sure if she should believe him.

"He did nothing, Galeena," Lukah spoke on his brother's behalf. He then said, "I allowed him to believe the messenger he dispatched had reached Dornwold. The truth is, I went to Dornwold and told them where and when to arrive. They were to collect me, not you. I planned to come to Gudsfelt alone to face Jaegar. The ships did arrive prematurely by several hours.

You were to be on your way to Claremont or Solsworth. I did not know Torren lived, and I surely did not know that you and Torren were at our cottage in the Applewoods."

Galeena stared into her brother's eyes as he released his confession.

"Forgive me?" Lukah asked.

"Always, my dear brother," she whispered. All she could feel was gratitude that the man she married and loved did not betray her.

Torren turned his attention to Jaegar, "Father, she carries my child. She is my wife. You beat her?"

Jaegar defended himself, "She told me nothing, and she chose spite over silence on more than one occasion." With a pinched brow, he looked at Lukah, "She called you brother." His eyes were then opened, "She's the Daughter, isn't she?"

Torren and Lukah both nodded.

The audience was silent. Two men had arrived of Jaegar's blood. They quickly deduced that Adelia had a bore a son and a daughter.

"Jaegar,"

The Viking searched for the man who addressed him.

Wilhelm stood at the frontline of the governors. Jaegar still did not move from his spot. Lukah stepped aside to give Wilhelm a clear view of the man he had always despised.

"You've come to retrieve your daughter, Stephan?" Jaegar asked.

"No. I've come to deliver yours."

The Viking was perplexed, unsure if he understood the words spoken to him.

Wilhelm led from behind him a very little girl: the most beautiful child many had ever set their eyes upon. She held to her guardian's hand with both of hers. She gripped his first and last fingers in her fists while pressing her nose and forehead to the back of his hand. Wilhelm knelt beside her and hugged her as a father would who was comforting his apprehensive young one. Once her arms were about his neck, twas obvious she did not want to let go. He squeezed her, "I love you my sweet girl." He kissed her cheek.

Galeena looked to Lukah and Torren with fury. "You brought her? How could you?"

Lukah stood strong, "This is where she belongs. This is where mother wanted her, Galeena. Do not fight this."

Torren remained silent, but she knew he shared Lukah's claim.

Very slowly Jaegar stepped toward the little cherub. He bent and extended his hand as he approached. Clearly, he was terrified of frightening her.

"You've always known, tis to him you belong. You've always known. Lukah has prepared you. He is here for you. Galeena is here as well." Wilhelm pointed at Torren and smiled, "Look my dearest, your new brother watches over you now too." She wiped the tears that crept from his eyes with her soft little fingers.

The little girl smiled and waved at all of her siblings. Galeena forced an endearing sentiment even though she was in disagreement. All her little sister had ever known was Claremont. Removing her from her only home was too risky. The little girl could run away or be scarred from the loss of her father. Decisions were being made that could not be undone.

Jaegar knelt, then sat on the floor. "Stefan, she's truly mine?"

"She is Jaegar. But, you are never to abandon her. Adelia required that she never be in line for rule of any nation. And, you are to never leave her in the care of any other being. I have raised her as my own. Adelia confessed her dealings with you before our ship left Danemour more than six years ago. I did not have her banished. I accepted her, just no longer as a wife. The day of her birth, I begged Adelia to be strong. I promised my full acceptance of her and your daughter if she would stay with me. Adelia said, 'Just love her. I am sorry. Do not force her to pay for the pain I have caused. I do love you Stefan. I do.' And she left us. Their mother died just after giving birth. My children, Lukah and Galeena, always knew of their little sister. I would not have kept this child from her siblings. Driesel left Galeena and moved into Claremont to care for her."

"What is your name, my sweet?"

The softest little voice replied, "I am Nossa Helene Styrkes, daughter of Jaegar."

He coughed and tears fell. Through a strained attempt to breathe and speak, Jaegar said, "I am Jaegar, my love. I am yours, forever. May I hold you?" He held out both hands while he continued crying. "May I please hold you, Nossa?"

She nodded, smiled and climbed onto his lap. Her tiny feet stepped right on his calf and his thigh. Her little hands braced on each of his shoulders. From where she stood, she looked down on him. "You're my father?" Nossa asked.

"I am."

"Is that my mother's hair?" She picked at the amulet and stroked the band that was tied about his neck.

"This is your mummy's hair."

"I have one too!" Nossa squeaked and pulled her necklace from beneath her rosy, silk frock. "Mummy made me one, and Lukah!" She pointed to her brother. The daughter of Jaegar was suddenly relaxed and happy that she had found where she belonged.

Jaegar buried his nose at her neck. He held her as he cried the same tears he shed alone in the woods the day Adelia sailed away from White Crested Cove with Alexar.

Nothing would ever bring his wife back to him, but nothing would ever take his child away from him either.

The crowd slowly dispersed. Wilhelm sat on the floor with Jaegar and Nossa. They filled Jaegar with stories of her first six years. He stared and listened while he stroked her soft, sunshine colored, curly tresses and marveled at how they reached the entire length of her back. The strands had not been tamed nor styled, but they had been cleaned, fragranced, and brushed to perfection. Her eyes were green and blue like the sea on a bright, clear day. Her skin was as smooth as an untouched shoreline. She was a natural beauty.

Olivia and Alexar appeared as the governors parted the room. They had witnessed all.

Jaegar asked, “Did you know of her, Mother?”

“No Jaegar. I did not. Alexar told me about her after Fredric left Solsworth. He wanted no one to know. Adelia lived life very afraid. Though she was so very capable and strong, she feared always for her children. She had been taken twice, and she never wanted that for Lukah, Galeena or Nossa.”

“What now, Mother?”

“Galeena shall take her place as Queen of Gudsfelt. Her husband will be at her side. Lukah’s birth will be validated with the Northanglian church. He will be acknowledged as Adelia’s first born by marriage to Jaegar of Styrkeson and Stenbjerg. The marriage document will be annulled due to abandonment, and her current certificate of marriage with Wilhelm will resume precedence. Lukah is thus the sole male heir to Northanglia. We would all like for you to declare him ruler over Dornwold as well.”

“Tis done,” Jaegar agreed still holding his child with great protection and love.

“I shall return to the west with my husband.” Olivia had never released Alexar’s arm throughout her speech.

Jaegar was at peace with his mother's joy.

Wilhelm informed him, "We rest for three days, then return to Northanglia. I plan to spend this time with *all* of my children."

"We shall have three days and nights of feasts then. Galeena will be crowned while you are still here."

Looking to Lukah, Jaegar asked, "And you, what are your plans for the future?"

"I shall be here until the late spring if that suits you. Dornwold will be dormant for the winter. Northanglia has a strong king of good health and discernment. When my time comes, I'll take my place as king of two nations. I've no desire to expedite my future. All will happen in God's time."

"Thank you for staying. Shall you travel to my farm with me and my daughter?"

"I'd very much like that. My sister and I are looking forward to living on a farm. You'll find I am quite experienced at laboring with my hands." Lukah then asked, "What of Danemour?"

"Eventually, it shall be for Torren to decide. For now, I've earned that crown and will be maintaining my hold upon it. Fredric will be assisting me with all regulating and governing. The Styrke farm is the ideal location for me to live. It rests just on the border of both nations."

"I remember," Lukah concluded.

All attention was finally turned to Galeena and Torren. He held to her with great care. One arm was behind her and the other covered their babe.

"You nearly died, Princess Helene," Jaegar informed her.

She nodded and said, "Aye, *you* nearly died as well."

He chuckled at her humor.

"Did you have a plan from the start?" Jaegar then inquired.

"No. I only kept waiting for my mother to lead me in the right direction. She is always with me."

"I believe you."

Galeena and Torren left the gathering. He led her to his private chamber and opened the door for her to enter. The room was grand; it was regal. "Such fine furnishings you have," she remarked.

He replied, "Yes, my father is a king. See how simple it is to speak such words?"

She laughed. "All I can say is that I had to wait until my heart told me to reveal myself. I wanted you to love me, not view me as an obligation. If I would have revealed who I am too soon, I would have never known your true feelings for me. As your wife, your loyalties needed to transfer to me."

Galeena then asked, "Did you ever jump from the ship in your dream?"

"I did. The seas were angry and without knowing it, I had left you onboard at my father's mercy. Tis apparent now that your hope is correct. I did need to remove myself from Jaegar's commands. And though I loved you from the first moment I saw you, I understand you needed to know my true loyalties. Galeena, you have me, all of me."

Torren led his wife across the room. He pulled the dress from her shoulders and did not stop until it was piled on the floor. She was beginning to grow. The sight of her lifted him. Galeena released the ties that bound him. Together, they took to their bed and stayed there until they hungered for something other than each other.

* * *

The coronation was planned for Galeena. A public ceremony and presentation were announced and the courtyard of White Crested Cove was filled. As reigning queen, Olivia performed the traditional speeches and declarations. Jaegar had no interest in participating. He stood as part of their present and past with Nossa in his arms.

The Boersen dagger had been returned to Olivia, and she held it to pass on to Galeena.

Before the dagger was placed upon her open palms, Galeena had Torren extend his hands as well. "You are not my shadow, we are equals."

She looked to their grandmother and said, "We shall both be named today."

Olivia placed the dagger across four hands and said, "King Torren of Jaegar and Styrke. Queen Galeena Helene Stefania Styrkes, Daughter of King Boersen."

All was official. A king and queen of Gudsfelt had been declared.

* * *

During the days before she was named queen, at rare moments of silence, Galeena read Adelia's scrolls so they could be returned to their safe haven in Northanglia.

When the time came, Galeena gave life to a son. Later, she gifted Torren with a son and daughter. Then, her third and final term of carrying, she delivered another daughter.

For the remainder of her years, Galeena began and completed her own histories. She did so not because life was dull, but because she grew to learn the value of having knowledge and sharing knowledge.

We know of these stories now because Nossa also became highly educated and a great leader in their part of the world. She was not a queen nor the wife of a king. She was a woman who traveled to as many nations as she could reach with one purpose: teaching men, women and children how to read, write, and barter.

Nossa carried Galeena's pages to Northanglia, and there she translated all of the scrolls of her sister, mother and grandmother. She then packed them safely in a chest and called them the most valuable of all treasures.

Thus, I, a descendant of these women, have been able to share their stories with you.

www.ingramcontent.com/pod-product-compliance
Lightning Source LLC
LaVergne TN
LVHW050918080826
845145LV00001B/118

* 9 7 8 1 7 3 2 5 4 4 3 9 0 *